"Thank you f[...] to my sister," Joseph told her softly. "I have never seen her so happy."

Nugget broke free and skipped ahead. Annabelle didn't have the heart to stop her.

"I'm glad to have given her something to be happy about." She smiled. Joseph wasn't too bad. Cleaned up the way he was, it was almost easy to pretend he was just a normal man.

Annabelle stumbled slightly. Joseph wasn't a normal man. And it wouldn't do for her to entertain feelings when she knew she couldn't count on a miner to stick around. Not that she had any intention of entertaining feelings about any man.

At least not here in Leadville. The town was full of shiftless drifters, and the one time she'd let her guard down to trust in someone, he'd betrayed her. Something she'd do well to remember in the presence of this man.

Especially the way Joseph's sparkling smile made her tingle all the way down to her toes.

DANICA FAVORITE

has spent her life in love with good books. Her job doing online promotion for a major publisher has given her the opportunity to meet many of the authors who inspired her growing up. Never did she imagine that the people who took her to faraway places would someday be the same folks she called friends. She'd say that work isn't really work for her, but in case her boss ever reads this, she works very hard.

Danica graduated with a B.A. in history and political science from Regis University. While her degree doesn't qualify her for anything resembling a real job, it gave her imagination room to soar and more fodder for her writing.

Having spent most of her life in Colorado, she loves the mountains. She lives in the Denver area with her husband, Randy, who inspires her to chase after her dreams. Together they have four children and a dog who thinks he's also one of the kids.

Put it all together and you find an adventurous writer who likes to explore what it means to be human and follow people on the journey to happily ever after. Though the journey is often bumpy, those bumps are what refine imperfect characters as they live the life God created them for.

Rocky Mountain Dreams

DANICA FAVORITE

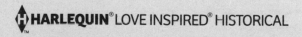

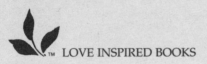

LOVE INSPIRED BOOKS

ISBN-13: 978-0-373-28289-0

Rocky Mountain Dreams

Copyright © 2014 by Danica Favorite

www.Harlequin.com

Printed in U.S.A.

You intended to harm me, but God intended it
for good to accomplish what is now being done,
the saving of many lives.
—*Genesis* 50:20

An author's first book often comes from years of support from friends and family. This book is no different. It would take an entire book to thank all those who've supported me through the years, so here is my general thank-you to all those who deserve it. You know who you are. Thank you.

For those who didn't get to see this dream come true before their passing—Theresa and Pat, you guys get the first nod. Your love and support meant a lot, and I wish you could have seen this come true.

Randy, Army Girl, Accountant, Cowgirl and Princess, thanks for putting up with crazy writer mommy.

Chip, I guess you told me so. Thanks.

Everyone else, I'll catch you on future books.

Much love to all,
Danica

Chapter One

1881

The soft breeze floating off the Mosquito Range made the air feel more like midsummer than early June in Leadville. Which meant Annabelle Lassiter could almost declare mud season officially over. Though today's walk to the post office hadn't resulted in a letter from her aunt Celeste, surely she could escape this town and its painful reminders soon.

She paused as the parsonage came into view. A man waited on the porch. Annabelle sighed. Her father's mission to care for the miners in Leadville was wonderful, but these days, they had more hungry people showing up on their doorstep than she knew what to do with. They had food aplenty, but Annabelle's heart didn't have the strength to keep working when it seemed like every day held a new heartbreak.

Annabelle pasted a smile on her face as she walked up the steps of the parsonage to greet the man so covered in grime she couldn't make out his features. Probably a younger man, considering his hair was still dark.

This place had a way of aging a person so that appearances could be deceiving. Two white eyes blinked at her.

"Supper's not 'til seven." She'd learned not to be too friendly, too welcoming, lest her words be misconstrued. Besides, her face was too weighed down by her heart to find it in her to give this stranger a smile.

Those eyes continued staring at her. She'd seen dozens of men just like him. Miners willing to spend everything they owned to strike the big one, and when they ran out of options, they arrived on the Lassiters' doorstep.

As she got closer, she noticed a small child huddled next to him. So he was one of those. Bad enough to waste your life on a fool's errand, but to take a child with you...

"Of course, if you'll come around back, I'm sure I can find something for your little...girl." At least she hoped that's what the child was. Underneath all that filth, it was hard to tell. Whatever kindness Annabelle had left in her remained reserved for the children. Innocent victims of their parents' selfish dreams for riches that most who came to Leadville never found. Or when they did, they squandered their money in the many saloons in town. The Colorado mountains were tough on anybody, but especially on the little ones.

"I need to see the preacher." The man's voice came out raspy, like he'd spent too many days underground working the mines.

Annabelle tried not to sigh. Her father held more grubstakes and pieces of paper promising repayment when the mine finally paid out than she could count. If they had a penny for every paper they held, they'd be richer than these miners ever thought they could be. But, if she turned this one away, and her father got wind of it, he'd be upset.

"Come around back, then." Maddie would have her hide if she brought them through the front parlor. The last thing she needed was to be at the other end of Maddie's tongue for more bootprints on the carpets.

The man stood, and the little girl buried her head further into his side. At this angle, Annabelle could see sloppy braids cascading down the girl's back. Poor child.

"It's all right, sweetheart." Annabelle knelt in front of her. "My name's Annabelle, and my father is the preacher. We'll help with whatever you need."

Round eyes with dark centers blinked at her. The little girl let loose of her hold on the man's filthy pants enough for them to walk down the steps and around the path to the backyard. Knowing her father, he was puttering in the garden, hoping to coax their spindly plants into doing something they were never designed to do at this elevation and these temperatures.

But he had faith that if Jesus could feed the masses with His loaves and His fish, then their tiny plants could keep their community fed. Annabelle shook her head. Too bad that faith hadn't yet panned out.

"Father?" Annabelle spied him plucking at a half-dead tomato plant.

His straw hat bobbed as he looked up at her. "Who've you got there?"

He didn't wait for an answer but stood and started toward them, brushing his hands on his pants.

"Joseph Stone, sir. I need a moment of your time." The man glanced at Annabelle like whatever he had to say wasn't meant for a female's delicate ears. There wasn't much Annabelle's delicate ears hadn't heard. Such was the life of a preacher's daughter in a mining town. Her family had come here to make the miners' lives better, and that meant dwelling in the deepest muck found in the human heart.

But just as working in the mines had a way of prematurely aging a man, helping the miners had a way of tearing at a person's heart. She wanted to love and care for people like this man and his little girl, but her heart felt like it had been wrung out so completely that there was nothing left to give. Surely if she left this place, her heart would finally have room to heal.

"I'll go put on some tea." She glanced at the man. "Or would you prefer coffee?"

He stared at her. "Nothing, thank you."

No, he probably just wanted Father's money. Some might say it was wrong of her to judge so quickly, but enough miners had come to their home that she no longer had to guess what they wanted.

Annabelle smiled at the girl, pulling on her heart's last reserves. "Want to come help me in the kitchen? I baked a whole mess of cookies earlier, and if you don't help me eat them, my father and I are going to have to do it ourselves. You don't want us to get bellyaches, do you?"

The little girl smiled, which would have been a pretty sight if those baby teeth of hers weren't almost all rotten. How could a man be so selfish in his pursuit of riches that he'd let this sweet thing have such a rough life? Not her business. As sweet as this little girl was, Annabelle couldn't let her heart get too involved.

"Can I?" She looked up at her father with such hopeful eyes.

"Annabelle will take good care of her. She has a way with youngsters," her father said quietly. He, too, had a heart for the children.

The man, Joseph, nodded. Annabelle held out her hand. "Come along now. We'll get you washed up at the pump, then go inside for some treats."

The little girl looked at Annabelle's hand, then took it. "Nugget."

"I beg your pardon?" Annabelle looked at her.

"My name is Nugget," the girl said softly.

Annabelle suppressed a sigh. Her father was one of those. So enraptured with the idea of getting rich, he even named his child after the evil silver.

"That's a nice name." It wasn't the girl's fault. From the way her face lit up at Annabelle's compliment, she'd probably gotten more than her share of teasing for such a ridiculous name.

Once she helped Nugget wash up, they went into the house.

The little girl looked around, then ran her hands along the lace tablecloth adorning their kitchen table. "This is pretty, like at Miss Betty's place."

What had they gotten themselves into? Miss Betty was one of the town's notorious madams. Her father had helped plenty of women escape that profession. Still, Annabelle had never been inside one of those places, and for a child to know…was simply unfathomable.

How unfair that someone so young had seen the inside of a brothel. Worse, that if something wasn't done to help her, the little girl probably would end up working there someday. One of the harsh realities Annabelle faced daily.

Which was why Annabelle had to get out of Leadville. Though her father would tell her she should not grow weary of doing good, she was weary. Weary of helping people like this little girl and her father only to have it end badly. Perhaps they helped some people, but these days, all Annabelle could recall were the great losses.

Annabelle put a kettle on the stove for tea, then got out a plate of cookies. "Do you like snickerdoodles? They were my late mother's favorite recipe."

"You don't got no mama, neither?"

Annabelle closed her eyes, trying to push the memories away before looking at Nugget. "She died of a fever last winter."

Her father's faith hadn't done them much good then, either. Their prayers hadn't worked for her mother, or Susannah, or her brothers Peter, Mark and John, or anyone else for that matter. Half of their congregation had died from the same fever that had killed Catherine Lassiter. Even the two miners she'd worked so hard to nurse back to health. Though the fever hadn't taken them. No, they'd lived only to find death in a drunken brawl in one of the saloons.

No wonder her heart was so weary.

But bitterness wouldn't help this child, and she at least could offer the little girl kindness.

Annabelle gave Nugget a small squeeze. "I'm sorry for your loss."

"My mama had the pox."

Ears burning, Annabelle forced herself to focus on being compassionate rather than frustrated at a world that would let a little girl like Nugget know about the pox. Times like this, it was difficult to understand why her father chose this life. No matter how many people they helped, they continued to encounter more tragic situations every day.

"You poor thing." Annabelle wrapped her arms around the girl, knowing that one hug wouldn't make up for anything. But her heart ached for this child, and she couldn't help but give what little she had to comfort the girl.

The back door banged open, and Nugget jerked away. Annabelle looked up to see their housekeeper returning from her errands.

"We have a visitor," Annabelle said.

Maddie looked the little girl up and down, then gave Annabelle a knowing glance. She liked the invasion of her household even less, but the tenderness in her eyes reminded Annabelle that she wasn't the only one with a soft spot for children.

"How about some tea to go with those cookies?" Annabelle gave Nugget a little pat, then busied herself with fixing the tea. She stole a glance at Nugget, who nibbled at a cookie.

Well, she wasn't starving. The hungry ones wolfed down the whole plate at once, and Annabelle always felt compelled to send them away with sandwiches. But this little girl...

At least her father kept her fed. Maybe she shouldn't have judged him when she'd first encountered them. She knew nothing of their story. Once upon a time, Annabelle would have wanted to hear that story and see what she could to do to help. But it seemed like too many of the stories Annabelle participated in only ended in heartache.

The only thing Annabelle could let herself help with was making sure this family didn't go hungry. Still, there were hungers that went deeper than the need for food. Of those, Annabelle knew. She might not have ever gone to bed wondering where the next meal was coming from, but she always went to bed wanting. Someday, she would have a life outside of a hopeless ministry that only broke her heart more and more each day.

Surely her aunt Celeste would send for her soon. Then Annabelle could move back East, where people's lives weren't filled with empty dreams of riches. Maybe there, she could meet a man who wasn't blinded by tales of the mother lode. The search for silver brought too much heartache to a body, and Annabelle was ready to leave this life behind.

The little girl tugged at Annabelle's skirts, reminding her of the steaming kettle, and that as easy as it was to dream of a new life, there was still so much work to be done here.

Joseph Stone followed the preacher into the church, watching as Annabelle escorted his sister into the house. Though she hadn't seemed very warm toward him, Annabelle had treated his sister with more kindness than the other ladies they'd encountered in town.

Most of the pretty girls he knew wouldn't have taken the time to be nice to a young child, let alone someone as ill-kept as Nugget. Not that he had much experience with pretty girls. The only woman who'd paid him any notice, Margaret Anderson, had thrown him over for Walter Blankenship because, in her words, "Walter didn't have any brats to care for." Probably for the best. If Margaret hadn't been able to stomach the idea of helping him care for the siblings he had back home, how could he have expected her to have anything to do with a child of Nugget's background?

Not that he'd put Miss Annabelle Lassiter in the same category. Sure, they were both pretty, but Annabelle's blue eyes were more like the sky on a cloudless day, unlike Margaret's—

He had no business thinking about any girl's eyes, especially not a preacher's daughter's. And especially not when he had a family to provide for and a father to find.

The preacher didn't speak until they were seated at a desk in his office. Joseph respected that. The other miners had told him that Preacher Lassiter was a good man who treated all with respect.

"What can I do for you, son?"

Son. Not in a condescending way, but in a way that sounded like he actually cared. In a way that made him wish his own father was more…fatherly. And not a low-down snake who'd put him in this predicament.

Joseph swallowed the lump in his throat. "I need help. My father, William Earl Stone, came here several years ago in search of silver. I need to find him."

His chest burned with the humiliation of what he'd encountered searching for his pa. "When I made inquiries about him, I was directed to Miss Betty's." Hopefully his face wasn't too red at the mention of the place, especially in front of a man of the cloth. But Preacher Lassiter didn't look like the mention of a house of ill repute bothered him.

"When I got there, they gave me Nugget. Said she was my pa's, and to give her to him because her ma was dead."

It still rankled to know his pa had reduced himself to visiting those women. At least his ma wasn't around to witness his pa's betrayal. Joseph swallowed the bile that rose up every time he thought about his poor ma, waiting for news of a man who had to have betrayed her the minute he arrived in town. Oh, he didn't doubt that Nugget was his sister. She had the look of his sister Mary, waiting back at home for a pa not worthy of her regard.

Preacher Lassiter leaned forward on his desk. "What do you want me to do? Find a home for the little girl?"

"No!" The word burst out of his mouth. Much as he hated to admit it, Nugget was kin, and she was an innocent child who didn't deserve the life she had.

Joseph leaned back against the chair. "I don't know what to do. Ma died nearly four months ago. Pa stopped sending money shortly before her death, and I just know Ma died of a broken heart because the bank told her they were going to take the farm."

No expression crossed the preacher's face; at least none Joseph could discern. "I've got five sisters and a brother staying with an aunt in Ohio. We've got no place to go. Aunt Ina is threatening to send them all to an orphanage. I've been working hard to make up for what Pa used to send, but it's not enough. When Ma got sick, the doctor was so expensive. I couldn't afford it all and we lost the farm."

Joseph's gut ached at having to share so much of his personal business with this man.

He looked the preacher in the eye, straightening in his chair. "I'm not asking for me. I know how to make it on my own. I've been doing it since I was a boy. But I've got to do better for my brother and sisters. I need to find my pa and get the money he's been denying us so I can keep them out of an orphanage."

The last word squeaked out of him—a painful reality he didn't want to face. Especially now that he had another sister to consider. How could he be responsible for sending seven kids to an orphanage?

"The boardinghouse wouldn't let me keep Nugget there with me. Called it improper. I can't afford the hotel. We've been staying in a tent outside of camp, but it's no place for a little girl. I've been working in the mines to send money to my aunt so she'll keep the others a little longer."

And, from the letter he'd just received, probably not much longer if Daniel didn't stop his antics. It wasn't Daniel's fault, not really. But living with all those girls, and not having a man's guidance...

Joseph let out a deep breath. "Sir, I know you get all sorts of people on your doorstep, but I need to find my father. You're my last hope of finding him. People say there isn't a miner in these parts you don't know."

The preacher rubbed his stubbled jaw. "What'd you say his name was?"

"William Earl Stone." He exhaled, then said, "The lady at Miss Betty's called him Bad Billy." He wasn't sure he wanted to know the reason for his pa's moniker, not with the way the woman had winked when she'd called him that. One more reason to hate the man.

The preacher closed his eyes for a moment, then sighed. "I didn't recognize the full name, but at mention of Bad Billy, I know who you're talking about."

What kind of man had his pa become, that even the preacher had that disgusted look in his eyes?

Joseph swallowed. "Can you tell me where to find him?"

"I'm sorry, son. Your father died nearly six months ago."

Dead. So Joseph had spent everything he had on a fool's errand. He should be comforted to know that the reason the money had stopped was that his pa had died. But comfort wouldn't feed his family or keep them out of the orphanage.

Chapter Two

Joseph stood and extended his hand. "Thank you, sir, for your time. I appreciate your assistance."

The preacher didn't take it. He looked up at him with cornflower-blue eyes that inappropriately reminded Joseph of Annabelle.

"Sit back down, young man. You have a problem, and informing you of the sad news of your father's passing doesn't solve it. I can't in good conscience let you leave until we've got a better solution for your family."

A man who'd spent years caring for a family in place of an absent father didn't weep. But in the face of the past few weeks, combined with the news that it had all been for nothing, this man's kindness made him want to do so.

Preacher Lassiter stood. "It seems to me that as your father's son, you'd be next of kin. Therefore, I think it fitting that I give you some papers your father entrusted me with. I recognize you from a picture he showed me."

Hopefully those papers would lead to the source of the money his pa had been sending. It hadn't been much, but maybe, just maybe, it would be a start. One of the men he'd sat next to on the train had talked about places out West that still needed settling. He could take advantage of the Homestead Act. Sure, it wouldn't be the farm they'd lost, but it would be enough. Farming was good, honest work, and certainly more rewarding than all the time Joseph had spent in the mines.

For the first time since coming out here, Joseph felt hopeful that maybe things would finally be all right.

"I appreciate that, Preacher. Anything you can do is a blessing."

The preacher smiled at him. "Call me Frank." He pulled a key out of his pocket and walked past him. "I've got his things in a safe I keep in the other room, so I'll be right back."

It had to be a good sign that his pa's papers were important enough to be kept in a safe. Maybe his snake of a father had done right by his family after all.

Joseph looked up to see a portrait of Jesus staring him down. He gave a long sigh. It had been wrong of him to be so disrespectful of his pa. Someday, he'd be able to ask forgiveness for it. Right now, though, he couldn't be sorry. Not with all the mouths he had to provide for. And the fact that his pa was the very reason they were in this predicament.

Was it wrong to reserve his forgiveness and apologies until after he knew his family was safe?

Probably so. But it had been a long time since Joseph had been to church. Not since his pa left and one of the women in their old church had said something to his ma about her husband never coming back. After that, Ma hadn't wanted to be around the mean, spiteful women, and Joseph had too much work to do to argue.

The door opened again, and Frank returned, carrying a stack of papers. "Your father had interests in a number of mines. I grubstaked him on a few of his projects."

It didn't seem very pastorly for a man of God to give out money for prospecting. "Why?"

He smiled, again reminding Joseph of Annabelle. "Because a man has a certain level of pride. It's easier to ask for money if you think you're giving someone something in return. So I give the miners what they need, and they give me a ten percent ownership in their mines. It eases their pride knowing that they're not taking a handout."

Frank's grin turned a bit mischievous. "I've never had a single mine pan out, but boy, wouldn't that be something."

"It sounds like gambling." On one hand, it was nice that the preacher was willing to give money to miners in need, but how was he helping those men? How many of the men taking money from the preacher had families back home who could've used that money?

"Now you sound like my daughter." Frank sat back in his chair. "I see it as an investment in these men's dreams. When I was a boy, I wanted nothing more than to be a preacher. But my family came from money, and such things weren't done. So I followed their plan and found myself rich and miserable. When I told my wife I was leaving the family firm to become a preacher, she asked me what had taken so long."

The peace flitting across Frank's face stirred envy unlike any Joseph had ever experienced. What would it be like to give everything up to follow your dreams? Of course, it had been so long since Joseph had dared dream anything, he wasn't sure what that would be.

"So here I am, spreading God's word in an ungodly town. And if I find a man whose dreams I can encourage, I do. I call it an investment. I suppose the difference between my investments and gambling is that I don't expect a return. At least not here on earth."

So nonchalant about being able to give it all away. "Doesn't the church object to you spending their money on such a foolish endeavor?"

Another grin. "I don't use the church's money. The money I invest comes straight out of my personal income. It irks poor Annabelle to no end that I help the miners, but they've got to have someone who believes in them."

Maybe. But he'd have to agree with Annabelle that he'd be better off not funding such schemes. "How much was Pa in to you for?"

Frank chuckled. "Again, it was not a loan. I gave him money freely. But that's not the right question. The question is, how much will you be able to get from his mines?"

With that, Frank sorted through the papers. "I have here papers for five different mining claims. As far as I know, not one has panned out." He looked up at Joseph. "However, about a week before he died, your father was anxious about the Mary May. He came to me and asked if I could keep his papers safe."

"Did someone kill him?"

Frank shrugged. "Hard to tell. He fell down a ravine. Did he fall or was he pushed? No one knows. And no one really cared enough to find out."

Joseph supposed he should care, but honestly, if his pa wasn't already dead, he might have to kill him himself. "Why would someone kill him for holdings that aren't very valuable?"

Frank looked around, slowly. "Every now and again, I'd find bits of silver in the offering. I never knew where they came from. I figured it was a miner's way of giving back but not wanting to call attention to himself. One day, I noticed your father slipping silver into the offering when he thought no one was looking."

He leaned forward and lowered his voice. "Now I ask you. Why would a man hide having so much silver?"

With what Joseph was learning about his pa, he had a pretty good idea. "So he wouldn't have to give your share to you? Only he felt guilty about not giving something to the church, so he put in a portion?"

Frank leaned back and gave another shrug. "Or maybe he'd found the big one and was trying to go about securing it before making the big announcement. Like I said, he'd been talking about the Mary May last time I saw him."

At least his pa had some loyalty, naming the mine after one of the daughters he'd abandoned back home. Not that it would give her any comfort at all.

Joseph riffled through the crumbled, dirty papers. Each of his sisters had a mine named after them. Maybe he'd give each of his siblings the papers to their mines. Probably worthless, but at least something to remember their pa.

"You think I should check out the Mary May?"

"Wouldn't hurt. He had a cabin up that way. Maybe you'll find some of his personal belongings or something that can help your quest."

Joseph sighed. The preacher was right. It wouldn't hurt. Maybe this cabin would be a safer place to keep Nugget. "I'll check it out. See if the cabin is livable."

Frank pointed at the shadows in the window. "Not tonight, you won't. It's going to be too dark to head up there now, and having been to the cabin once, I can tell you that Billy did a real nice job of making it hard to find."

Somehow, his pa's cleverness at making a hidden

cabin didn't bring the same kind of twinkle to his mind as it did to the preacher's eyes. Maybe he'd once had that kind of fondness for his pa, but after cleaning up so much of his pa's mess, he wasn't so kindly inclined.

"Thank you, Preacher. Would you happen to know of a place willing to rent a room to us tonight? I've tried just about everywhere, but being where Nugget came from and all, no one wants us."

Maybe the preacher could put in a good word for them. It was only one night. Then they could go to his pa's cabin and make it a temporary home for Nugget. What his siblings would do when they found out...well, it'd be like losing their parents all over again. Especially for the girls, who'd been sheltered from such things.

"You'll stay with us, of course. It's a shame to have all those bedrooms sit empty when there are heads needing a place to rest. And I told you, it's Frank." The preacher's smile appeared benign, but Joseph saw the underlying power behind it. There'd be no arguing with this man.

And really, it would be foolish. He was running out of money, and with an extra mouth to feed, he had to think beyond his pride. But someday...he'd keep an account of all the preacher had done for him and his family and he'd pay him back.

"Again, my thanks. Your generosity is—"

"None of that." Frank held up his hand. "The Lord has been generous to me, so it's only right that I am generous in return."

Frank reached into his desk and pulled out a coin. "Take this. Go on down to the bathhouse on West Seventh. It's run by a couple of nice widows who will take good care of you."

Joseph didn't need a man of the cloth to tell him he reeked. But every penny he wasted on a bath was a penny less for his family. "Thank you, but—"

"No buts. Maddie, that's my housekeeper, is one of the most particular women you'll ever meet. If you don't go to the bathhouse and take care of it, she's liable to haul you out back and scrub you down herself."

Joseph took the coin and stared at it. Still, it seemed a shame to spend it when he'd just received a letter from Aunt Ina asking for more money.

"Thank you," he finally managed to force himself to say. "What about Nugget?"

"Don't worry about her. Like I told you, Annabelle loves children. Once I tell her what's going on, she'll have Nugget cleaned up, and if I know my daughter, she'll probably have found her a pretty new dress and done her hair all up. You won't find a better person to leave Nugget with than my Annabelle."

Joseph remembered the looks of disgust the other women in town had given them as they'd walked in search of the church. Annabelle was different. She'd taken Nugget's hand and treated his little sister with respect.

All these warm feelings did nothing to dispel his wariness. In fact, it only made them worse. Liking a golden-haired girl such as Annabelle couldn't be on his mind. He'd come to Leadville to solve the problem of how to care for his siblings, and so far, all he'd come up with was another mouth to feed and a few probably worthless pieces of paper.

Thinking thoughts he had no business thinking about a girl was just borrowing trouble. And Joseph already had more than his share.

Annabelle reached to knock on the door to her father's office just as the door opened, causing her to nearly run into the miner's chest.

"Where's Nugget?" Joseph peered around her, invading her personal space.

"She's fine," Annabelle said, stepping out of the man's way. "Maddie's got her taking a bath in the kitchen, so if you could give her a little privacy..."

She entered the office, looking around to see any sign that her father had yet again funded some foolish endeavor. "Maddie also wanted me to tell you that supper's going to be ready at seven. We'll be serving outside so if you could get some men to put out the tables, she sure would appreciate it."

No sign that anything was missing, so at least this man wasn't a thief. One time, a miner stole the gold crucifix from her great-grandfather right off the church's wall. And her father, with his forgiving soul, had let him.

"What'd I tell you," her father said, putting his arm around her. "You don't have to worry a bit about Nugget. Go take your bath so you can be back in time for supper. Maybe some of the miners your father knew will be there."

Joseph cleared his throat. "Are you expecting many?" This time, his voice sounded less raspy, more husky, and less like he'd spent too much time in the mines. She briefly wondered what he'd sound like singing in the church, but then shoved that thought out of her mind.

Her father gave her a squeeze. "Only the Lord knows. But He always provides enough. My dear, sweet Catherine, before she passed, had a heart for making sure those boys had a home-cooked meal. Every Wednesday night, and also after services on Sunday, we invite anyone who wants to eat over for supper. I don't know what I'd do without Annabelle to carry on the tradition."

Annabelle's heart sank at his words. How was she

supposed to leave Leadville and move on with her life when her father needed her so desperately?

"Your kindness is much appreciated," the miner said gruffly. So unlike most of the miners who'd grown to expect the handouts. This one was different.

Not that she'd allow herself to see him as different, she told herself as sternly as she could. Seeing miners as individuals and caring for them as people was dangerous stuff. Getting attached had gotten her heart broken more times than she could count. Which was why, after all the tragedies of the winter, Annabelle absolutely was not going to find herself caring about this miner or his child.

She'd do her duty, feed them, give them what they needed, then send them on their way. Just like she did with everyone else. And when the letter from Aunt Celeste came, giving her the means to escape, she was going to do it, and pray that somehow her father would find a way to get on without her.

Because if her heart was forced to take on any more burdens, it would certainly crumble under the weight.

Chapter Three

One would think that by now, Annabelle's back wouldn't ache so much after feeding a hungry crowd. But every muscle in her body hurt. Not to mention her head from the din of all the voices in the backyard. She returned the last plate to the cupboard, looking around the kitchen to make sure her share of the chores were finished.

Despite their best efforts, the floor looked like a herd of cattle had tromped through the kitchen. Maddie wouldn't be pleased. She went to grab the broom when Maddie's voice interrupted her.

"I'll finish in here. The poor lamb is all tuckered out. I've got her on your bed, but I imagine you'd rather her on Susannah's. Why don't you get that fixed up? I've already done Peter's room for the miner."

The miner. Her father had never allowed a miner to stay in the house before. Of course, none had brought a child with him, either. She supposed she should give him a little credit; after all, he'd taken responsibility for a child borne to him by a woman of questionable morals, and certainly in her line of work, he couldn't really be sure that the child was his.

Nugget lay sprawled across Annabelle's bed, her feet tangled in the quilt Annabelle's mother had made. Rosy cheeks had replaced the grubby face, and in the dim candlelight, Nugget looked almost like a porcelain doll. Hard to believe the tiny girl was six years old. Just two years younger than Susannah had been when she died. Such innocence almost made Annabelle want to believe she was making a difference helping with her father's work.

Annabelle pulled out the linens and made up Susannah's bed, trying not to remember the way her sister had traced the pattern of the quilt at night to fall asleep. She forced herself to push aside the memory of Susannah's sweet voice asking Annabelle to tell her one last story. She wasn't ready to confront the loss of her sister.

Every day. Every day her father asked her to do one more hard thing for the sake of his ministry. And every day, she had to shove one more piece of her hurting heart into the abyss.

But as she lifted the sleeping girl off her bed and into the newly made bed, she told herself that maybe somehow it would be worth it. And maybe someday, it wouldn't hurt so much. Though she suspected it wouldn't happen until she could finally leave this place and all its painful memories.

Maybe now that her father had some time to grieve, he wouldn't mind so much letting her go to Aunt Celeste. Maybe there, she could build a life for herself. A life that didn't include putting her heart out to be broken on a daily basis.

"I was going to have her stay in my room." The miner's voice came from her doorway.

Annabelle jumped at the interruption, then took a breath as she smoothed the covers around Nugget. "I've already gotten her settled. Besides, it's not seemly for her to share your room."

"She's my sister. We can share." He stepped into the room as if he was going to snatch Nugget away.

Annabelle stood. Sister? She hadn't expected that. What sort of man took on the care of a sister when he barely seemed capable of taking care of himself? Yet again, she realized that this man was different. And she didn't like it.

Ignoring the desire to know more about his situation, she looked at him with the same detachment she gave everyone else. "You're a grown man. You deserve your privacy. Besides, just look at her."

As if to prove her point, Nugget snuggled deeper into the covers, giving a small sigh.

"I haven't ever seen her look so…"

Clean? Content? This man didn't seem to know anything about raising a child. But for the first time, she could understand his protectiveness. And she had to give him credit for trying.

Annabelle sighed. There was no escaping the compassion leaking into her heart.

"Nugget's so peaceful, isn't she? It'd be a shame to disturb her." Annabelle gave the miner a smile. "Why don't I show you to your room? It was my brother Peter's."

She swallowed the inevitable lump at the mention of his name. This stranger wouldn't understand how much she'd lost. Hopefully, they wouldn't stay long. She refused to get attached to one more person who was just going to leave anyway.

"I'm not putting him out, am I?" The gruff tone to his voice made Annabelle pause. He seemed uncomfortable with the hospitality. Unlike so many of the people she encountered, this miner wasn't a taker. Her conscience told her she shouldn't judge, but her heart reminded her that it could no longer afford to be open.

"Peter died seven months ago." As many times as she stated that fact, it didn't get any easier to accept.

"I'm sorry for your loss." Words she heard often enough, but the sadness in his voice made Annabelle's heart constrict. He'd lost someone recently, too.

"It gets easier every day." A lie, but since that's what everyone told her, she supposed it must be true for some people. It was the answer she'd learned to give to quiet the well-intentioned words of sympathy that never seemed to do any good.

The miner stepped into her space as she pushed the door open. "Does it?"

His dark eyes searched hers, making her feel exposed, vulnerable. People weren't supposed to ask those questions. They were supposed to move on and leave her to dwell in her private pain.

She turned her head away. "Of course it does."

Doing what she did best, Annabelle pressed on, ignoring the tickle at the back of her throat as she surveyed the room she'd barely dared enter since Peter's death. She'd liked to have said it looked exactly the same, but it didn't. The lamp that had sat on the table beside his bed was gone. Her father had given it to a needy parishioner. The same with the blanket that had always lay across the foot of the bed. Her grandmother had made it, but that hadn't stopped her father from giving it to someone in the mining camp. And if she looked in Peter's closet, it would be empty.

Yes, it was selfish to cling to them; after all, they were only things. If her father knew these thoughts, he would tell her about storing up her treasures in heaven instead of on earth, and that these things would be far more useful to the people here than they were to Peter's memory.

Those emotions, like everything else, were quickly pushed away. Her father expected her to be a part of his ministry, and that meant making this man feel comfortable in their home.

"Maddie filled the pitcher with some clean water for your use." Annabelle gestured to the dresser. "If there's any other need I can attend to, please let me know."

She turned to leave, but he stopped her. "Wait."

"Is there something else you need?"

His features were cast in shadows, but she could still see the hard catch in his jaw. "I'm sorry if my question offended you. I didn't mean to put you out."

He might as well have taken that pitcher and dumped it on her. Annabelle glanced at the open door. Her father would be up soon, and he would know that she hadn't been very welcoming. She sighed. She was trying, she really was. But her father was so focused on providing for the miners' needs that he never seemed to consider hers.

More selfishness. And none of it helped the man in front of her. The man who looked like he was staring down into the depths of her soul. A place no one, not even God, was allowed to look.

"I'm sorry." Annabelle looked at the floor. Swept clean, of course. If only Maddie had left one stray dust bunny that could swallow her whole.

Annabelle took a deep breath. She'd hurt this man's feelings, and she hadn't meant to. But with all the miners, she had to keep her heart locked up. She'd let one slip past her guard. One to whom she'd given her heart.

And he'd deemed his search for riches more valuable than their love.

The miner standing in front of her? Now that he'd had a bath, she could tell that his hair truly was the color of soot, and it curled around the top of this collar ever so slightly. His eyes, too, were dark, and the light caught them just enough that she knew he meant business. This wasn't some miner. Not anymore.

Bad enough that he had to sleep in Peter's room, worse that by closing herself off to him, she now had to admit the truth.

"I lied. I don't know if missing someone gets easier. I wake up every day wishing I could hear my brothers or my sister, and especially my mother, walking through the door. But they don't. And I guess having you here makes it more real that they never will."

Everyone expressed sympathy over her losses. But what she saw shining in Joseph's eyes was deeper, more personal. She couldn't afford to get personal, not again. They were both supposed to say the proper things, like that Annabelle was getting over the loss of her mother and brothers and sister, and that Joseph was sorry to hear about it, and every other pithy comment that everyone said because it was what you were supposed to say.

Because she'd already said all of those deeply personal things to another man, another miner, and despite her offering up everything her heart had, he'd left, chasing after rumors of gold in the Yukon.

Getting personal was no longer an option.

"Annabelle?" Her father's voice boomed through the room as he pushed open the door. "You've made sure Joseph is comfortable?"

Annabelle let out a long sigh, exhaling all of the

thoughts she shouldn't have been thinking. "Of course I have." She turned to the miner. "You have everything you need, don't you?"

He glanced at her, the sympathy still shining in his eyes. "Yes." He turned to her father. "Your daughter is most gracious."

At least he brought it back to what people were supposed to say.

Her father came into the room and kissed the top of her head. "I don't know what I'd do without her."

She smiled up at him, trying not to let the guilt over all of her wrong thoughts drag her down. As much as she hated this position, her father was all she had left of her immediate family.

"I think that's all then." She leaned up on tiptoes and gave her father a kiss on the cheek. "Good night." Then turned and gave the miner as much of a smile as she could muster. "And good night to you, too, Joseph."

Before either man could say anything else, she turned and left the room, retreating to the once-safe haven of her bedroom. There, Nugget slept, her tiny body reminding her that even the slightest bit of sweetness still had a bitter taste. Because as much as she wanted to take this little girl into her arms and give her the love she deserved, Annabelle absolutely was not going to get attached. Not when, like every other child she encountered in her work, Nugget would soon be gone.

Because that was the reality of life in a mining town. People either went broke and left, struck it rich and left, left in search of a better prospect, or left the earth completely. Regardless of the reason, they all left.

There wasn't enough of Annabelle's heart remaining to let anyone take any more.

* * *

Joseph watched Annabelle's retreating figure, her skirts swishing behind her. She moved with the grace of any of the fine ladies he'd encountered, but there was a humility to her that he'd never known.

Back in Ohio, he'd encountered plenty of girls who turned up their noses at the Stones' poverty. Only Margaret had openly accepted him and promised to love him no matter what. She'd been filled with grand dreams of the farm they'd build together and how everything would work out. But when his ma died and he'd made it clear that his siblings were part of the package, Margaret had a change of heart and married another.

He once thought Margaret was made of the cloth he believed he saw in Annabelle, but appearances were deceiving. As much as he'd like to admire Annabelle, he had to remind himself that he had too many other responsibilities to put any energy in that direction.

He forced his attention to Frank. "Thank you again for your hospitality. Your daughter went above and beyond in preparing rooms for us."

Frank gave that wistful look Joseph was beginning to see as the Annabelle look. "It'll be good for her to have another little girl in the house. She used to share her room with her sister Susannah. She likes to pretend that she's fine, but don't let her fool you. Annabelle misses her terribly."

Joseph's gut churned. He'd liked to have credited it to a filling supper after going so long without, but he knew better. Not after her hard-won admission of grief. He'd thought about offering her comfort for her loss, but at Frank's expression, Joseph was glad they'd been interrupted. His thoughts and questions were better left for the man of the house, not a woman he found himself inappropriately attracted to.

"She mentioned this room belonged to her departed brother. I didn't realize that she'd lost another sibling, as well."

Sorrow filled Frank's eyes as he looked around the room. "Yes. This was Peter's room. Sickness hit Leadville hard this past winter. We lost my wife and four of my children. Annabelle is all I have left."

Maddie's biscuits thudded in the pit of Joseph's stomach. Having spent the better part of a month trying to track down his father to save his own siblings, he couldn't imagine what it must have been like to watch them all die.

"I'm so sorry for your loss." Joseph spoke softly, realizing that the other man had retreated into his own grief. "It's good of you to let us use their rooms."

Frank's head snapped up. "What else would we do with them? The good Lord provided, and it seems wrong to not share what He has given us. Just…" He looked around the room, then his gaze settled back on Joseph.

"Go easy on Annabelle. She gets awful mad when I give away any of the family's possessions, and even though she's playing the part of the gracious hostess, I know she's upset."

He gave another wry smile, and Joseph realized that Frank was trying as hard as Annabelle seemed to be in dealing with his heavy losses.

"Then why do this? If it pains her, then perhaps I— "

"I can't allow her to wallow in her grief. Her mother, brothers and sister are with the Lord. There's no reason to be sorrowful."

Except the preacher's face spoke of his own great sorrow. "Having you and Nugget here will be good for her. Already I see a light in her eyes I haven't seen since…"

His shoulders rose and fell. "I know you feel guilty at accepting my charity, but you're doing me the favor. It was good to hear laughter in this house again."

Frank turned to leave, but his final words burned through Joseph's heart.

A house without laughter. Without noise. Even Joseph would admit that this month without the cacophony of his siblings' voices had made for some lonely nights. He'd gotten through by telling himself it was temporary. But for Annabelle and her father, the silence was permanent.

Lord, forgive me for judging.

The biscuits collided angrily against each other, reminding him that he had a lot to beg the Lord's forgiveness for. He'd been angry and resentful over his situation, but as he looked at what the Lassiters were going through, he realized that he had no call to complain.

"Sir?"

Frank turned. "I told you to call me Frank."

Joseph nodded slowly. "Yes. Frank. I…I was wondering if you had a spare Bible in the house."

Silence echoed briefly against the walls. Joseph's heart thudded. It shouldn't have been that difficult a question to ask a preacher.

"Annabelle still hasn't forgiven me for giving away Peter's. Barely nineteen years old, and my boy had his heart set on becoming a preacher. He would have wanted me to share God's word, but Annabelle…she was furious."

The older man's voice cracked. "I'm sorry, I shouldn't have burdened you. I…"

"Forget it." He'd already made Annabelle uncomfortable enough. "I'm sure I can find one in town tomorrow. It's just I— Well, you reminded me of how much I've lost track of my faith."

Some of the tiredness left Frank's face. "I'm glad. As for the Bible, I'll let you read my own tonight. When a man's got a yearning for God's word, it's best to fill it immediately so nothing else sneaks in."

He was about to tell Frank it wasn't necessary, but Frank had already left the room. It humbled Joseph to see how freely the man shared all that he had. A lesson Aunt Ina would benefit to learn. Her last letter had complained of all the money she'd spent on his siblings and that she fully expected to be repaid for her sacrifice.

If he'd tried to pay Frank back, the man would be insulted. Joseph looked around the room that had once been occupied by a beloved son and brother. No wonder Annabelle had seemed so tense earlier. He sat on the bed and ran his hands along the fine quilt covering the bed.

Joseph didn't know much about women's handiwork, and had taken the blankets and quilts in their home for granted. But to Annabelle, who'd been upset over a Bible, this was probably yet another memory of her brother.

"That was the first quilt my wife ever made." Frank's voice came from the doorway. "Her family was horrified that she was wasting her womanly talents on making quilts instead of embroidering fancy linens. It has some mistakes, but that's why I love it. She wasn't afraid of the mistakes that come with learning."

Frank had crossed over while speaking, then handed him a well-worn Bible. "I hope it gives you the same peace tonight."

The lump that Joseph had been successfully swallowing all evening wouldn't go away this time. Everything had meaning to the Lassiters, yet they were both able to share. Frank more willingly than Annabelle, but even her, he couldn't fault for being stingy.

"Thank you, Frank. Your generosity means the world to me."

Frank gave a small nod. "I hope someday you pass on that generosity to someone else."

The floorboards creaked as Frank once again retreated, leaving Joseph in the cozy room bathed with soft candlelight. He glanced at the Bible, which smelled of the hope and promise of things yet to come. So far, he hadn't found any of the answers he'd been seeking in Leadville. But Frank Lassiter had given him the hope that he'd finally come to a place where he could.

Chapter Four

Annabelle walked into Jessup's Mercantile, Nugget's hand clutched tightly in hers.

"I ain't allowed in here," Nugget whispered.

"You're with me, so it'll be fine. Be a good girl, and I'll let you choose a peppermint when we're done."

She gave the little girl an encouraging squeeze and a smile.

"I don't like peppermints. The men who visited Mama always gave 'em to me, and then I'd have to go away."

After a day with Nugget, none of her experiences should shock Annabelle. But each one put an anger in her heart that wasn't going to be easily erased. How many other children endured what poor Nugget had? Despite her anger, Annabelle felt powerless to do anything.

"I'm not going to make you go away." She gave Nugget another squeeze. "But I will let you pick out whatever treat you'd like."

Nugget's grip loosened in her hand.

"Who is this young lady you have with you today,

Annabelle?" Mrs. Jessup greeted her with a smile as Nugget shied into Annabelle's skirts.

"Good morning, Mrs. Jessup." Annabelle returned the greeting. "We have a very special guest staying with us, so I've brought her with me to pick up a few things for Maddie. Nugget, please give Mrs. Jessup your most polite how-do-you-do."

Mrs. Jessup blanched. "Nugget? That isn't the child from…" She glanced over Annabelle's shoulder in the direction of State Street.

Annabelle straightened her shoulders as Nugget let go of her hand and clung to the back of Annabelle's skirt. She reached behind and gave Nugget a pat on the head. "Why, yes, she is. And she's currently our guest, so please treat her with the respect accorded all of our important guests."

"But that child is filthy and full of bugs."

"Am not!" Nugget burst out of Annabelle's skirts. "Mama made sure I didn't get no bugs."

Annabelle put her arms around Nugget and pulled her close. "Maddie scrubbed her clean herself. Didn't find one bug on the sweet little girl." She did her best to keep her voice modulated and calm. Nugget was just a child, after all, and didn't deserve Mrs. Jessup's scorn.

"Is that the dress I ordered from New York City for poor Susannah?"

The horror on Mrs. Jessup's face brought a pang to Annabelle's heart. After all, it wasn't Mrs. Jessup's sister who'd died.

"Why, yes, it is." Annabelle gave a smile in spite of the sick feeling in her stomach. "And I'm sure she'd be pleased that it wasn't getting eaten by moths in some closet. All Nugget needs are a few ribbons for her hair to make her the picture of sweetness."

Wasn't that the very thing Maddie had said this morning? And Annabelle had politely agreed, all the while resenting having to give up Susannah's dress. But now, in the face of such meanness, she'd parade Nugget around with Susannah's beloved china doll to show the world that she didn't give a whit where Nugget came from.

"Your mother would be horrified that you're associating with such people."

Her mother would have been ashamed it had taken Annabelle so long to take up Nugget's cause.

"What people? Nugget has done nothing wrong. She's a good girl who hasn't given me a bit of trouble."

Mrs. Jessup's face turned as red as the bolts of flannel she kept for the miners. "She was raised in that…place!"

"And she's now a guest in my home." Annabelle didn't mean to raise her voice, but when she did, a group of women looking through the buttons stopped and looked up at her.

"I understand that your mother is gone and I'm sure your father has no idea how to explain such delicate matters to a young lady, but let me assure you that no good can come of—"

"What? Taking in a child who needs a home?" Annabelle gathered Nugget closer to her. "My mother and father both instructed me on such matters, and when a sinful woman was brought before Jesus, he asked those without sin to cast the first stone. I am certain that none of us can lay claim to leading such a blameless life."

Mrs. Jessup couldn't have exploded any more brilliantly than the time the old cookstove's pipe had been blocked by a nesting raccoon.

"You…get…out…" she thundered, pointing at the door.

Annabelle smiled sweetly. "With pleasure. I'll be

talking to my father about taking our business to Taylor's. Come along, Nugget."

She grabbed Nugget's hand and ushered her out the door. Once they arrived on the sidewalk, Annabelle tried taking a deep breath, but Maddie had laced her too tight. What a bad day to be fashionable.

Nugget tugged at her hand. "I told you I weren't allowed to go in there."

Annabelle straightened. "That's right. You're not allowed to go in there. You're too good for the likes of Mrs. Jessup."

She scanned the street and looked toward Taylor's Mercantile. Her boast in leaving Mrs. Jessup's had been just that—a boast. Her father was very strict about which stores she shopped in, with all the riffraff that came to Leadville. She wasn't supposed to go anyplace else alone.

But even her father wouldn't be able to fault her disobedience in light of Mrs. Jessup's meanness.

"Come on, Nugget. You might not like peppermints, but I could use a sweet right now."

She grasped Nugget's hand and strode across the street to Taylor's.

Joseph had just stepped through the back storeroom into the main store with Frank and Mr. Jessup when he heard Annabelle's raised voice.

"And now she's a guest in my home!"

Joseph stepped forward to come to Annabelle's aid, but Frank held his arm out. "Let her fight her own battles."

"But that's my sister they're arguing about."

"Annabelle is doing fine. Listen to her."

The pride in Frank's voice was obvious. Joseph had

to admit that he hadn't seen this side of Annabelle. She might not think much of him, but she'd protect his sister with everything she had.

Mr. Jessup shifted nervously. "I should probably go out there and…"

"You should," Frank told him quietly. "But first, you need to know that while I respect you as a friend, I'm going to stand by my daughter's decision unless your wife apologizes to her."

"Apologizes?" Mr. Jessup's face turned redder than a hot coal. "After your daughter insulted her and practically accused her of not being a Christian?"

Joseph couldn't help but grin. Annabelle had done just that, and beautifully so.

"No hard feelings, Bill." Frank held out his hand for Mr. Jessup to shake, but he didn't take it.

"Joseph, I know we've spent a lot of time picking out the gear you'll need for your father's cabin, but I believe we'll be taking our purchases elsewhere. Go ahead and set the things down. We need to go make sure the girls are all right."

Joseph did as he was bade and followed Frank toward the door. Mrs. Jessup stopped them.

"Did you hear what that daughter of yours said to me? Without a mother, she's going positively wild."

Frank nodded. "And I couldn't be more proud. Good day, Mrs. Jessup."

As they strode out the door, much to the shocked faces staring after them, Joseph was proud to know her, as well. Annabelle Lassiter was one of the finest women he knew.

He watched as Annabelle crossed the street, firmly clutching his sister's hand in hers.

"Annabelle!" Frank called his daughter's name, and she paused to stop and wave.

The two men rushed over to Annabelle and Nugget.

"Good," Annabelle said with forced cheer. "I'm glad you're here. I've decided that we need to start shopping at Taylor's. My friends assure me that Taylor's is perfectly respectable, but I'm sure you'll want to see for yourself."

Frank laughed. "Annabelle, my dear, Joseph and I were in the back during your argument with Mrs. Jessup. We heard the whole thing."

Annabelle's face fell, and for a moment, without the false cheer or guarded expression Joseph was used to, she looked almost pretty. "Oh," she finally said. She looked down at Nugget, then back up at her father.

"Well, if you think I'm going to apologize, then—"

Her father held a hand up. "I'd be disappointed if you did. I told Bill that unless Mrs. Jessup apologizes to you, we won't be patronizing their store anymore."

Annabelle's cheeks tinged pink, and a smile lit her eyes, the blue even more striking in the sunlight.

All right, Joseph would admit it. Annabelle Lassiter was downright pretty. But that momentary admiration was all it could be.

"But that does leave me in a bind." Frank put his hands in his pockets and rocked back on his heels. "I now need to make arrangements with another store to get supplies for our ministry. As members of our church, the Jessups gave us a good discount."

"Oh." This time, when her face fell, Joseph immediately felt guilty. He hadn't meant to bring grief to them or their ministry.

The false cheer Joseph was used to seeing on Annabelle's face filled Frank's. "It's all right. The Lord will provide. And since I haven't had the pleasure of getting to know Mr. Taylor, perhaps it's about time I did so. He belongs to the new church across town, but God's children are all God's children, right?"

Annabelle nodded slowly.

Frank turned to Joseph. "While I'm conducting business with Mr. Taylor, I hope I can trust you to stay close to Annabelle and Nugget. Though I've also heard good things about Taylor's, I'd feel better knowing they had some protection until we've experienced it for ourselves."

Annabelle gave a small but ladylike grunt, and Frank shot her a look. Joseph couldn't help but grin as he watched the tiny rebellion cross her face. The independent woman didn't like it one bit, but she'd obey.

Joseph held up an arm. "Ladies?"

Though Annabelle took it, he could feel the glower come all the way from her face down through her gloved hand to his arm. Some might call it unladylike, but he appreciated the feisty woman who very clearly knew her own mind.

They walked into the store, and Joseph noticed how Nugget still clung to Annabelle's skirts.

"Are you all right?" He ruffled his sister's hair with his free hand.

She looked up at him, wide-eyed. "Uh-huh. That lady was mean, but Annabelle showed her." Then she looked at Annabelle, like she believed more in Annabelle than she did in him.

"What if they're mean to us here?"

The already proper woman straightened even more. "Then we'll find another store. And we'll keep trying until we find someone who will treat us with respect."

Annabelle's conviction shamed Joseph. With all the

places that had turned them away, he'd taken Nugget and slinked away with his tail between his legs. If they had refused Annabelle, she probably would have given them the what-for.

"Thank you." He turned and looked at Annabelle.

She looked confused. "For what?"

Joseph nodded his head toward his sister. "You treat her with dignity."

Her face colored, and she reached for Nugget's hand. "Come on, Nugget. Let's go look at some ribbons."

So far, no one had noticed their presence in the store. Frank appeared to have already engaged in serious conversation with the proprietor.

As they walked toward the ribbons, a woman approached them. "Hello. I'm Mrs. Taylor. Your father said you needed help with your shopping."

Joseph examined her face for any sign of the judgment he'd come to expect with Nugget. But she appeared pleasant and willing to do business with them.

"Thank you, yes." Annabelle gave the woman the kind of smile Joseph wished she'd direct at him. "Our housekeeper, Maddie, provided me with a list of items. But I'd also like to look at some ribbons for Nugget."

Annabelle pulled the little girl off her skirts and in front of her. "Nugget is my friend, and I hope you'll be kind to her."

"Of course." Mrs. Taylor bent in front of Nugget. "Why don't you go select a peppermint for yourself?"

"Thank you all the same, Mrs. Taylor, but my friend doesn't care for peppermint."

How did Annabelle know that Nugget didn't like peppermints? He'd shoved dozens of them at the poor child before she'd finally told him that she didn't like them.

The genuine affection in her face as she looked at

Nugget tore at Joseph's heart. And the smile Nugget gave her back was enough to make him melt.

"Well then, come along." Mrs. Taylor's voice was pleasant, accepting.

They wound their way through stacks of goods, neatly displayed. All the while, Mrs. Taylor spoke of the weather and treated them as she would any other customer.

With each step, Joseph felt more of the worry fall off his shoulders. By the time they arrived at the ribbon display, he felt as light as any other man shopping in a mercantile.

"Here are the ribbons. Are you looking for something to match that pretty dress of yours?"

Mrs. Taylor bent to Nugget, giving her a smile that spoke of understanding and kindness.

"Annabelle?" Frank's voice called from the other side of the store. "Can you come here for a moment?"

She immediately looked at Nugget.

"It's all right," both Joseph and Mrs. Taylor said at once. He stopped himself, then looked at Mrs. Taylor.

"She'll be fine, truly," Mrs. Taylor said. "I have a little one myself, and I miss her dreadfully. She's visiting my mother, and I can't wait until she gets back next week."

"I…" Annabelle looked at Joseph.

"We'll be fine."

She nodded slowly, then went to her father's side.

"I promise I'm not like that awful Mrs. Jessup," Mrs. Taylor told him. "Pastor Lassiter told us what happened in her store. I can't say I'm surprised. She's been spreading rumors about us ever since we opened."

Mrs. Taylor put her hand over her mouth. "I'm sorry. I shouldn't have shared gossip about her. I'm sure she means well. It just burns me sometimes…" She shook her head.

"Anyway, on to more pleasant things." She held up a ribbon. "What do you think of this ribbon, Nugget? It would bring out the pink flowers in your dress nicely."

Nugget looked at the floor.

"It's all right. You can look at the ribbon," Joseph told her.

As he watched the emotions play across his sister's face, he realized how hard it must be to have grown up the way Nugget had. How many rejections had she faced because of who her mother was?

Nugget looked, but didn't touch. She just stared at it, wide-eyed. "Sometimes the men would bring me ribbons."

Mrs. Taylor knelt in front of her. "I'm not like those men. I'm your friend."

Nugget looked up at him, and Joseph nodded. He was quickly learning how precious friendship was in this place, especially with a child like Nugget. She reached for the ribbon.

"May I put it in your hair? Annabelle is going to think you look so pretty."

With deft fingers, Mrs. Taylor put the ribbon in Nugget's hair. The shy little girl preened as Mrs. Taylor held up the mirror.

"See? You look very pretty. Why don't you go show Annabelle?"

Nugget skipped all the way to Annabelle. Joseph watched her with a lightened heart. He'd been worried about his family accepting her, but surely with the acceptance she was finding here, his family would eventually warm to her.

"I knew her mother," Mrs. Taylor said over his shoulder. "Lily was a kind woman. She came to town with a worthless husband. When he died, she didn't have anyplace else to go. So she took up the life she did. She wasn't a bad person."

Her words were meant as a kindness, but they hurt. "Did she know my pa was married?"

"They're always married, sugar. Sometimes, though, we're fortunate, and we find someone who will take us away."

He turned and looked at her. "You?"

Mrs. Taylor shrugged. "Things aren't always what they seem. I didn't know your father, but I'm sure that his relationship with Lily had nothing to do with your mother. Mining is lonely business."

Hard to imagine this genteel lady in the place where he'd gotten Nugget. Also hard not to blame his father, despite Mrs. Taylor's words.

"How do you know all of this?"

She smiled. "Because I've been there. And if you ever need anything for Nugget…"

He watched as Nugget giggled at something Annabelle said to her. "Thank you. It's good to know that she's got so many people who care about her."

Something he hadn't expected. But the longer he spent in Leadville, the more he was learning to expect the unexpected. Just then, Annabelle turned and looked at him, the smile in her eyes blinding.

He couldn't help himself. Joseph smiled back. His growing affection for Annabelle was perhaps the most unexpected of all. And it was something he needed to avoid giving in to at all costs. With all he had to focus on, he couldn't afford to divert his attentions.

Chapter Five

Annabelle headed home with a little girl on one arm
and a sedate man on the other. She glanced over at Joseph, who seemed to be focused on the girl who proudly
showed off her new ribbons.

"Thank you for your kindness to my sister," he told
her softly. "I have never seen her so happy."

Nugget broke free and skipped ahead. Annabelle
didn't have the heart to stop her.

"I'm glad to have given her something to be happy
about." She smiled. Joseph wasn't too bad. Cleaned up
the way he was, it was almost easy to pretend he was
just a normal man.

Annabelle stumbled slightly. Joseph wasn't a normal
man. And it wouldn't do for her to entertain feelings
when she knew she couldn't count on a miner to stick
around. Not that she had any intention of entertaining
feelings about any man.

At least not here in Leadville. The town was full of
shiftless drifters, and the one time she'd let her guard
down to trust in someone, he'd betrayed her. Something
she'd do well to remember in the presence of this man.

Especially the way Joseph's sparkling smile made

her tingle all the way down to her toes. Despite the chilly breeze coming off the mountains, she suddenly felt warm. The lace at the top of her collar itched.

Annabelle quickened her pace. The faster she got home, the faster she could take off her gloves and adjust her collar. Surely the sudden warmth was due more to the clouds moving off the sun than the fact that Joseph had moved closer to her.

"Joseph! Annabelle! Watch!" Nugget spun around and around in a circle, nearly running into a group of ladies.

Joseph dashed forward to catch her before she fell. "Whoa, there, Nugget. This street's too crowded for your antics."

She fell into his arms, giggling. "I was being a dancer like Mama's friends."

Though Annabelle was briefly scandalized by the reference to Nugget's mama's friends, the thought stopped in her brain as she watched Joseph swing Nugget. He tickled her, then placed the still-giggling girl on his shoulders.

There weren't many men in Annabelle's acquaintance—well, there weren't any, actually—who would be so loving toward a little girl. Especially one with Nugget's background. Joseph's gentility reminded her a lot of her father.

Something to keep in mind. Both men were impossible dreamers. Her father because he believed that his work with the miners would somehow make a difference. Joseph because as a miner, he was after the impossible dream of striking it rich. The difference was, Joseph's dream would take him away as soon as he realized chasing after silver was a worthless dream.

No, entertaining thoughts of Joseph was out of the

question. Just because he exhibited fine qualities of character didn't mean he was of good character. Henry had taught her that.

They approached the Tabor Opera House. Its elegance stood out among the dust of Harrison Avenue, reminding Annabelle that profit could come out of the mountains. Maybe some, like the Tabors and a few other fortunate people, made a big strike. But too many ended up on her porch, dead broke, hungry, and willing to risk it all for another chance that never came.

In the end, no matter how many of the dazzling grins he gave Annabelle, Joseph was one of them. A miner whose dreams were bigger than his common sense. Otherwise, he'd never have ended up on her doorstep with a little girl who deserved a better life.

"Annabelle!" Lucy Simms, one of the girls she'd gone to school with, waved her over. "I have news."

"I can spare only a moment," Annabelle told her. "I need to get home."

The other girl's conspiratorial grin did not bode well for a quick conversation. "Papa has given permission for me to take a trip East so I can see the world before I settle down. He's going to ask your father if you can accompany us. I heard him tell Mama that your father has been looking for a proper escort to take you to visit your aunt."

Annabelle's heart leaped at the thought of her father looking for someone to escort her to finally visit Aunt Celeste. Her father hadn't been ignoring her. Why hadn't he said anything?

"Annabelle, watch this!" Nugget's voice stopped her from questioning the situation further as she watched the little girl spin, nearly falling into the street as she did so.

Fortunately, Joseph was there to grab her, then knelt

before Nugget, probably to give her a more stern warning about being careful.

"That sounds lovely," Annabelle told Lucy. "I would love to hear more about it, but—"

Nugget had broken free of her brother and was hurtling toward her. "Annabelle!"

"Another one of your father's projects?" Lucy's disdainful look at Nugget was hard to miss.

Annabelle's back stiffened. Coming from Lucy, the thoughts that had consumed Annabelle sounded completely selfish. Was it so wrong to want to leave the ministry for a life of her own?

But as Nugget raced into her arms, tears streaming down her cheeks, Annabelle couldn't bring herself to think of Nugget as a mere project.

"Nothing like that." Annabelle gathered Nugget close. "They're friends. I'm sorry, Lucy, but I really must go."

The look Lucy gave her told her that she didn't believe Annabelle one bit.

What should have been victory at knowing her father had finally relented in letting her visit her aunt now felt like failure.

Which was fine. Annabelle wasn't sure what to believe herself. She took Nugget by the hand and started toward home.

"She's got to learn to be careful near the street." Joseph caught up to them, apparently thinking she'd taken Nugget's side.

"I know," she told him, continuing forward. "We've been gone too long. Maddie will be concerned."

Lucy stepped in with them. "I thought your father was expecting you."

"Yes, yes, he is." Annabelle didn't break stride. "I

need to do some work for him, but Maddie is expecting me. I have to be home for them both."

Her words seemed like falsehoods even to her. But she couldn't stay and play mediator, not with her warring heart, or Lucy, or between Joseph and Nugget.

Spots danced in front of Annabelle's eyes. The sun. It was too bright. The air. Too warm.

Somehow, though, the ground didn't seem all that hard when she woke. She hadn't realized she'd fallen—

"Annabelle? Are you all right?" Joseph's voice jarred her.

She nodded slowly and started to sit up.

"Careful." He knelt beside her and offered his arm. "Let me help you."

"I'll fetch Dr. Owens," Lucy said, her voice full of concern.

Joseph helped her to her feet. "I'm all right. I just got a little dizzy. And the boards in the sidewalk were a bit uneven."

She couldn't help releasing Joseph's protective arm as quickly as possible.

Annabelle turned and gave Lucy a smile. "I'll be fine. Thank you for your concern."

Joseph's eyes were on her the entire walk home, making her feel more exposed than when she'd lain on the sidewalk.

What was she supposed to say that wouldn't make her sound like a complete ninny? *I'm trying hard to keep it all together for my father's sake, but everyone keeps pushing in places I'd just as soon keep hidden?*

Even in her own mind, it sounded ridiculous.

Fortunately, they were close to the house, and soon she'd be able to fix herself a cup of tea, then she could rest, and all would be well.

When the house was in sight, Nugget raced ahead. "I'm going to show Maddie my new ribbon!"

Annabelle couldn't help the smile that crept across her face. Nugget was a delightful girl. In spite of everything she had experienced and witnessed, she still maintained the childlike innocence that anyone would be hard-pressed to resist.

"Ah, there it is." Joseph touched her cheek briefly. "I was beginning to think we should send for the doctor after all."

She wasn't sure if the sensation left by his momentary touch was a good thing or a bad one. Certainly the way it made her stomach turn inside and out wasn't a comfortable sensation. Nor was there any comfort in the way his eyes seemed to be searching deep within her.

"I just need a cup of tea."

Annabelle tried to keep her voice steady. The last thing she needed was for everyone to get concerned for her health. Then her father might never let her leave.

"Are you sure?" Though Joseph's touch was gentle, it burned, like getting too close to a fire. She should have taken a step back, but having his hand on her arm was just as—

A team of horses galloped by. She turned her gaze to watch the matched set in the beautiful carriage. Trimmed out in the finest gold, it had to belong to one of the mining barons.

Annabelle's heart sank as she pulled her arm away. Men like Joseph came to town believing they'd leave in a carriage like that. Few did.

She straightened. "I'm perfectly fine. But the longer we dally, the more likely it is to worry my father."

"He knows you're safe with me."

Except she wasn't. Every kindness from Joseph only

punctuated the fact that she couldn't allow herself to enjoy it. Henry had been all politeness and kindness—until she'd truly needed him. And he was gone.

The ache didn't leave until after she was seated in the kitchen, Maddie fussing over her.

"I can't believe you fainted and didn't let anyone call for the doctor. You should have at least had someone get you a carriage." Maddie placed a cup of tea in front of her.

"I got too warm, that's all." As Annabelle sipped her tea, she watched Joseph slip in the back door.

Annabelle looked up at him. "Would you care for some tea?"

"Thank you, no." He turned his gaze to Maddie. "I want to visit my pa's cabin. Frank gave me the information, but I'll admit the directions don't make much sense."

Maddie stirred the pot of soup. "I never venture out of town. Don't want to get mixed up with the riffraff. Annabelle used to go up to the camps with her father. She might know."

Annabelle slumped in her seat. She had purposely avoided going to any of the mining camps since the illness that had taken her family. It hurt too much to see the work they'd done together, and realize that for the ones who'd died, it had been all in vain.

"Of course I'll help." She tried to sound cheerful, but the look on Joseph's face told her that he didn't believe her.

Joseph held up a hand. "Don't put yourself out on account of me."

"I want to," Annabelle said quietly. She wanted to add that she was sorry for not being more welcoming, but that would only serve to get a scolding from Maddie.

Surely he would be able to accept her peace offering after explaining her feelings last night. This was as much as she could give, and he had to be gentlemanly enough to know that.

The door opened, and her father walked in. "The soup smells delicious, Maddie."

Maddie beamed. "I'll get you a bowl, and for everyone else. Joseph is going to look at his father's cabin, and Annabelle fainted dead away on Harrison Avenue. A bit of soup will perk everyone up."

"I did not faint dead away." Annabelle met her father's look. "I got too warm, that's all."

"She did, too!" Nugget piped up. "Fell on the ground and everything."

The worry on her father's face nearly killed her. After having so much illness in the family, the last thing he needed was to be concerned about Annabelle's health. Especially if what Lucy had said was true. He'd never let her leave if he thought she was taking ill.

"I'm fine. It was just warm, and my dress was a bit… tight." She whispered the word, knowing that ladies of her acquaintance often said that they sometimes got a little dizzy if their corsets were too tight. She would have easily said such a thing to her mother, or Maddie, if they were alone. But her father, being a man… still, if it eased his worry, a little diminished modesty would be worth it.

"Well, land's sakes, child!" Maddie set the bowl in front of her with a thud. "Why didn't you just say your corset was too tight? No sense in suffering misery for the sake of fashion. I told you I thought that dress was too much. I don't care what the other girls are wearing. We're getting you upstairs and changing out of that monstrosity and into that nice calico where you don't have to be laced so tight."

Annabelle's face heated. She'd at least been discreet in her words. But for Maddie to be so free in front of… She stole a glance at Joseph, who winked at her.

Annabelle looked down at her bowl. Of all the…

"It's all right, Annabelle. I have sisters. I never did see the point in those contraptions making a woman miserable."

She opened her mouth to say something, anything, to make this man know that such talk was completely inappropriate. But Maddie was tugging her out of her chair.

"Let's get you changed."

If only a change of clothes was enough to fix the woes in Annabelle's life.

Chapter Six

Joseph watched Annabelle leave with a smile. She was like a wet cat when she got all riled up. And even though he assumed he was supposed to take her seriously, it only made him want to laugh. Someday, she'd figure out that she didn't have to pretend with him.

Wait. What was he talking about, someday? As soon as he finalized his pa's estate, he'd be taking what he could and going back to his family in Ohio. There he wouldn't need to worry about getting closer to Annabelle Lassiter.

Frank coughed, and Joseph looked up. He probably shouldn't have said all that about corsets. At home, that's all his sisters ever talked about. But in polite company, it was highly inappropriate.

"I'm sorry. I should have been less frank with your daughter."

Frank smiled. "No need for apologies. When her mother was alive, she had a woman to tell her these things. Poor Maddie isn't equipped for the society Annabelle runs with."

"It must be hard on her, losing her mother."

Joseph took a mouthful of soup, pleased that the flavor was every bit as good as the aroma that had been tantalizing him since this morning.

"I'm sure it's just as hard for you and your sisters," Frank said in a pastorly tone.

Joseph looked around the large table. "We at least have each other."

He continued eating his soup, remembering Annabelle's confession from the previous night. Yes, he'd lost his parents, but he had his siblings left. People to care for, people who counted on him, people who cared about him.

Who did Annabelle have other than Maddie and her pa?

"You must miss them." The knowing smile warmed him even more than the soup. How could Annabelle be devoid of the same warmth?

"I do. But I'll wrap up things with my pa's estate, then return home." Hopefully with enough money to get by until he could support them all. As his ma's sister, Aunt Ina would surely refuse to help their pa's out-of-wedlock child.

"I hope you find what you're looking for," Frank said, then continued eating his soup.

It was too bad there weren't more men like Frank Lassiter in Ohio. He would never forget Frank's kindness. Someday, he'd take Frank's challenge and help someone else in need.

Annabelle returned, wearing a faded dress and an equally faded expression on her face. The wet cat look had been replaced by the look the cat would have after being dried off—slightly more comfortable, but still resentful.

"There you are, Annabelle. And looking just as

pretty." Her father's flattery did nothing to erase the scowl on her face.

"You'll feel much better once you get some soup in you. Since Joseph is going to need help finding his father's cabin, you could go with him. It's near Greenhorn Gulch. You know where that is."

"Of course, Father."

She sat down and ate the soup placed in front of her, her face expressionless and her gaze completely on the bowl.

Joseph should learn to accept Annabelle being distant, but she was like a burr under his saddle. He wasn't going to be satisfied until he fixed it and fixed it good. His sister Mary would tell him it was his failing. Having to get to the bottom of things and solve the problem. They'd always thought he'd become a lawman for that very reason. But the pay wasn't enough to support the family and run the farm.

So instead, he was here, chasing down his deadbeat father's estate, and trying not to be attracted to the lovely woman sitting before him. He'd admit it, even in the dress she looked none too happy about wearing, Annabelle Lassiter was still a beautiful woman. And when she forgot herself for a moment, she brought so much light into the room.

But those were thoughts he needed to do his best to temper. Though Margaret's defection had hurt, she'd been right. Joseph could barely provide for the family he had. He needed to focus his attentions on caring for his siblings, not courting a lady.

After lunch, Annabelle took him and Nugget to the livery. They saddled up her family's horses, then rode out of town toward a place her father had called Greenhorn Gulch.

Rocks jutted out around them, and stumps showed where trees once stood. The sure-footed paint Joseph rode had no trouble keeping up with Annabelle's blue roan. The mare was perfectly suited to Annabelle, who seemed completely out of place in this desolate land stripped of what had probably once been a beautiful forest.

"What happened to all the trees?"

"Cut down to make support beams for the mines and places for the miners to live." Her voice had a coldness to it.

"You don't approve?"

She led her horse across a shallow creek. "It's not my place to approve, but I think it's a fool's errand. People are willing to risk everything to get rich, and most of the folk who come out here never do. They abandon their families, leaving behind perfectly good lives in the vain hope that they'll strike silver. When they get here, they're willing to lie, cheat, steal and do anything else to gain an advantage that doesn't exist."

She could have been talking about his pa. He'd come out here with the goal of finding silver to provide what the farm could not. But the little girl sitting in front of him on the saddle was proof of how his pa had discarded his principles.

But he refused to accept Annabelle's evaluation that it happened to everyone.

"Some people get rich."

Annabelle looked over her shoulder at him. "Don't even entertain that line of thinking. Before you know it, you'll be living in the filth, blinded by the tiny flecks you think mean something but turn out to be nothing."

"My papa found a treasure." Nugget, seated in front of him on the ample saddle, piped up. "He was going to build me and my mama a bigger house than anyone else in Leadville."

The glance Annabelle gave him was enough to melt the rocks around them. "So you are one of them."

She turned her gaze to Nugget, and he could tell it immediately softened. "You should just take her back to wherever you came from. Now, before you wind up losing whatever else you have left."

Annabelle probably saw a lot of hardship in her line of work. It was natural that she'd want to be protective, especially of Nugget. But she didn't understand. He had nothing to go back to. Only a family to send for, and he already knew there wasn't a place here for them. His only hope was finding something of enough value in his pa's possessions that he could use it to move the family west.

"All I want is what my pa found. Nothing more. Just enough to get home to my family and make sure they're taken care of."

"That's what they all say." Annabelle clicked her tongue and set her horse to a faster pace. The rocky path had widened until a large mining operation came into view. He'd spent some time working in a similar place when he'd first arrived in Leadville, bringing the ore to the smelter. Tents and ramshackle cabins dotted the area, but Annabelle made no motion to slow her pace.

He glanced behind him, noting that from this elevation above town, the view was so majestic, it was easy to forget the abysmal conditions of the mining camp they'd passed through. On the hardest days, it was this picture of being above the clouds covering the valley below that had kept him sane.

Once they passed through the camp, Annabelle followed the creek back into more rocky terrain. Joseph had to give her credit for her adept handling of the horse. His sisters probably wouldn't have been able to do the same. They came around a rise and into a smaller clearing.

"Hey! This is where my papa lives," Nugget cried out as she tried to scramble down from the saddle.

Joseph held her tight. "Wait. I want to be sure it's safe."

Annabelle slowed her pace, then pointed to an outcropping of rocks. "Based on the map, that's where the cabin is."

"How did you get to know the area?"

She shrugged, and said in a dull voice, "My father's ministry is helping the people in the mining camps. Many of them don't venture into town because they're so afraid that if they leave, they'll miss out on the big strike. So we go to them."

"How often do you come out?"

"I haven't in a while." The familiar look of sadness crossed her face. "Not since everyone got sick."

They dismounted, and she led them to the other side of the rocks, Nugget skipping on ahead into the cabin.

"She's still here!" The little girl ran out of the cabin, carrying a worn rag doll. "I forgot her last time we came to visit Papa, and I've been missing her terribly."

Nugget hugged the doll as Joseph stared at the place his pa had been calling home for the past five years. Sandwiched between outcroppings of rocks, the cabin was little more than a one-room shack built mostly of rocks, twigs and mud.

"I guess we found it," Annabelle said, looking resigned.

"Thank you. I would have never found it otherwise." Even though Nugget had recognized the area, it was clear she wouldn't have found it, either. When she'd tried to get off the horse, she was looking in the opposite direction.

He walked into the dark building, grateful when Annabelle handed him the lantern. She obviously knew what she was doing. Looking at this place, Joseph could see why she sounded so disillusioned.

As he held up the lamp to illuminate the room, Annabelle walked around, lighting the lamps she found.

It was a simple room, with a small stove, a bed, a trunk and a few boxes. His pa had given it a touch of home, the bed covered with a quilt Joseph recognized as the one his ma had tearfully pressed into his arms when he'd left.

One of the crates was turned on its end, like a makeshift chest of drawers, with a picture of his family, as well as a picture of a bawdily dressed woman—Nugget's mother, he assumed.

He walked over to the pictures and picked up the one of his family. If only Annabelle's judgment of the situation hadn't been so true. His pa had abandoned them to give them what he'd claimed was a better life. Only it hadn't panned out, and now Joseph was looking for something, anything, to pick up the pieces.

"That your family?" Annabelle stood behind him, her voice thick.

"Yes."

Nugget entered the room and noticed him holding the picture. "Papa said that someday I'd meet the rest of my brothers and sisters. That's how I knowed you when you comed for me." She pointed at the people in the picture.

"That's Mary, and Bess, and Evelyn, and Helen, and Rose, and Daniel and there's you." She frowned as she pointed at Ma. "And that's the other lady. Mama said she was the reason why I couldn't meet you yet."

Joseph swallowed the unexpected grief and tried to ignore the anger burning his insides. Pa had never planned on coming home. At least not to his ma. Ma had been a good woman. She hadn't deserved this. Once again, he wished his pa was alive just so he could kill him himself.

"She was my ma. She was a good woman."

Nugget's eyes widened. "Papa told Mama she was a shrew."

It was wrong to disrespect your father, but if his pa was here now, Joseph would have no problem punching him. And yet, he could stand here and do nothing—not contradict an innocent child who hardly knew what she was saying, and try to avoid the knowing look in Annabelle's eyes. Not that the girl looking around the cabin knew anything at all.

Annabelle had moved on and was looking at a stack of books beside the bed.

"Your father was a reader?"

"No." Joseph coughed and took the book from her hands. "My sister Mary and I are. Mary thought that if we sent him with our favorite books, he'd have something of us so that he wasn't so lonely."

He glanced over at the little girl now rummaging through the trunk. His pa had obviously had no problem with loneliness. After having done the math in his head more times than he cared to count, Joseph figured his pa had met Nugget's mother shortly after coming here the first time. Which meant his pa had gone home to Ma after being with Nugget's mother. And then left his ma to return to a woman who— If it weren't for the women present, Joseph would have wanted to smash the pictures representing his pa's lies.

"I'm sure the books gave him some comfort. It looks like he jotted notes in the margins." Annabelle gave him a small smile, as if she was trying to be sympathetic.

Her words made him pause as he looked at the book. Why would anyone jot notes in the margins of *Ivanhoe*? Joseph flipped through the pages and noticed that random words had been circled, and sure enough, when you looked at some of the margins, his pa had made notes.

Only none of them made any sense. One page would have *Mary May* scribbled on the side, then some words would be circled. Why would he write Mary's name on the pages of Joseph's book?

He noticed that Annabelle had begun looking at his pa's other books, sitting on the bed, and Nugget had joined her. He couldn't deny that her treatment of his sister was genuine. One light and one dark head were pressed together, whispering over the books Annabelle was looking at.

"Do you like to read?" He moved back toward them, and Annabelle looked up, a real smile filling her face.

"It's my favorite pastime. I love reading about the far-off places and countries. There are so many wonderful things in this world, and I would love..." She gave a soft sigh, then closed the book she'd been looking at. "Well, my place is here. The only way I get to see the world is through one of these."

A wistful look crossed Annabelle's face, and Joseph realized that there was far more to her dream of travel than she was saying. If conditions were different, he'd want to know more, but how could he give her any indication of his interest and raise false hope in her? Maybe Annabelle's reticence was for the best.

Annabelle ruffled Nugget's hair and stood. "Enough of that talk. Did you find what you were looking for?"

Back to the old Annabelle. Fully on task and avoiding anything personal. Clearly she had more sense than he. Nugget remained on the bed, looking at one of his pa's books.

"I need a pencil," she announced, unaware of the tension in the room.

"Oh, you're much too little for that." Annabelle held out her hand to Nugget. "We'll go pick some wildflowers while your brother finishes what he needs."

Nugget gave her a glare that made Joseph want to laugh.

"Papa lets me draw in his book." Nugget stood, and proudly stomped over to one of the chests, leaving one of the books open on the bed to show a childish drawing scribbled over the pages of one of Mary's beloved books.

Joseph's gut clenched. His sister's favorite book had been reduced to worthless garbage by a pa who had left his first family in need for a new life.

Annabelle caught his eye, and again he saw genuine emotion. Pity this time, and he wanted none of it.

"Such a shame," she said in a quiet voice. "She loves stories, though, so perhaps I can help her learn to respect books. I can remember when Mother was giving us lessons, and Susannah, who was just a baby, got her hands on an inkwell and one of Father's books. I thought poor Mother was going to die of apoplexy. But Susannah learned, just like Nugget will."

"I'll teach her," he said gruffly, and went to the trunk where Nugget was still rummaging for something to write with.

"What are you looking for?" He knelt beside her and put his hands over hers.

"I want to make a picture for Papa," she told him, those big green eyes reminding him so much of his sister Mary. Mary, who had the most loving heart in the world, but was going to be so hurt when she finally learned of the horrible sins their pa had committed.

How do you tell your siblings that their beloved pa was an unfaithful liar and cheat?

"You know your papa is gone, right?"

Nugget nodded, big eyes staring at him. "But someday when I meet Jesus, I'll see him again. And he'll want to see all of my pictures. He loved it when I made him pictures. He'd hand me a book and tell me to make him something pretty."

Joseph's stomach turned over again. How could his pa have been so careless with the things he and his sister held so dearly?

A stack of envelopes caught his eye. He'd recognize that writing anywhere. Ma's. With childish scribbles drawn over it. Even his ma's letters weren't sacred. But why would they be? His pa hadn't kept his marriage vows sacred, either.

Joseph's heart twisted inside him as those letters beckoned at him. His ma hadn't been perfect, and in most recent years, with their pa gone, she'd been unbearable at times. But he couldn't help himself when he took that stack of letters and put them in his pocket. Tonight he would read them and grieve, both for parents lost, a marriage broken, and the realization that everything promised them had been a lie.

Annabelle watched Joseph talk to the little girl by the trunk. It had been difficult for Annabelle, going through her mother's belongings, and even more difficult for her to watch her father give them all away. But it couldn't possibly compare to the difficulty of going through a parent's belongings with the evidence of that parent's sin right there.

"Nugget? Are you ready to collect wildflowers? I'm sure Joseph would like some time alone, and I know Maddie would be pleased to have a bouquet for the table."

Nugget didn't move from her position. "Papa always has me make a picture for him when I come so that he has something to remember me by."

For the first time, Annabelle realized that as much as she had been focused on her own grief, and tried to understand Joseph's, she hadn't looked too deeply into the grief of a little girl who had lost not only a mother, but a beloved father. Being in this cabin made Annabelle realize that poor little Nugget had been just as close to her father as Annabelle was to hers.

Well, as close as they'd been before the family had gotten sick.

But now…as much as Annabelle tried to embrace her family's mission, she couldn't. And how could she remain close to a man who would eventually see through her attempts to pretend everything was all right when it wasn't?

The backs of Annabelle's eyes prickled with the tears she couldn't allow herself to release. Because if she let herself cry, she'd be too focused on her own pain to be of any use to Nugget or Joseph.

Which was the cruelest trick of all. She'd been fine, just fine, until they'd come into her life, forcing her to acknowledge all she'd lost.

The worst part was that as much as she tried to harden her heart and not let herself love again, she only found it softening toward the sweet little girl and her brother who would soon be gone, just like all the others.

The sunlight nearly blinded her as she exited the cabin. Though she had lit every lamp in the place, she hadn't realized how dark it had been until coming out into the open. Birds trilled in the meadow, singing beautiful but shallow songs of hope. They could afford hope. But for Annabelle, hope was nothing more than a fairy tale. She had to keep herself from believing the myth that caring for Joseph and Nugget would end well.

Joseph would return to wherever he came from, defeated by the dream of his father's riches, taking Nugget with him.

Somehow, she had to find a way to convince her father to let her go East with Lucy and her family. There, she could stay with her aunt and finally have the space to let her heart heal. Until then, she'd endure the best she could, hoping against hope that she'd have some of her heart remaining in the end.

Chapter Seven

Nugget skipped out of the cabin, placing her hand inside Annabelle's with such love and trust, it was hard to remain detached, especially when the skies were so clear and blue. She'd even take away her resentment of the birds, who meant no harm with their innocent songs.

"Are you ready to find some flowers for Maddie?"

Nugget smiled, the grin stretching from ear to ear. "I'm going to press them in one of my books."

They'd passed some young cow parsnip at the entry to the meadow. There, they could not only find some pretty flowers, but maybe even some greens to bring home for dinner. After a long winter with few fresh vegetables, it would be a welcome addition to their supper. Her mother used to say that anytime they had a chance to experience God's bounty, they should. Annabelle's heart gave a pang.

Why did the things that occurred to Annabelle most naturally hurt so much? She should have been able to more easily erase the memories so that she could do a simple task like picking wild plants without that awful prick at the back of her throat.

Nugget seemed to sense where Annabelle was heading, because as they got close to where she'd spotted the wild greens, Nugget took off running.

"Flowers!" The gleeful shout rent a hole in Annabelle's heart. The joy should have made her happy, and she wanted to be happy, but mostly, Annabelle wanted to cry.

Surely her father would let her visit Aunt Celeste if she was traveling with Lucy's family. The sights, and the parties, and being a world away would lessen all the pain.

"Look how beautiful!" Tiny fingers thrust a crisp white flower in Annabelle's face, and even she couldn't deny the sweetness.

"Thank you." She made a show of smelling it. "Beautiful. Perhaps we can find enough to bring back to Maddie."

"What will we put them in?" Wide eyes stared back at Annabelle. Though Susannah had lighter hair and was slightly older than the small girl, Annabelle couldn't help but remember that same face staring at her last summer.

So not fair.

Annabelle turned away before the little girl could see the tears forming in her eyes. It wasn't right to inflict her grief and fear on an innocent child.

"I'll see what I can find in the cabin."

At least she had a viable excuse. And unlike Joseph, Nugget didn't dig deeper into Annabelle's heart or question her motives. Maybe for some, letting go was an easy task. But the harder Annabelle tried, the more it hung on, like the sticky ooze from the creek.

She left Nugget in the meadow, singing a song, and plucking flowers. A small smile cracked Annabelle's face, reminding her of the impossibility of resisting the sweet child.

When she returned to the cabin, Joseph sat on the bed, engrossed in a book.

"Good reading?"

He looked up. "My pa's journal. Not all of it makes sense, but I was hoping it would offer some clues as to where he might have found the silver."

Silver. Always silver. But maybe she could get him to see reason before it caught hold of him.

"They always claim to have found silver, but…" Annabelle shrugged. "There are a lot of charlatans out there who will seed an old mine with a few nuggets to trick people into thinking they've made it big."

She gestured around the cabin. "This is not the home of a man who found silver. You've seen the mansions in town. That's where the ones who strike it big live."

Joseph closed the book and looked up at her. "I know." He sighed, then set the book down. "But he sent money home. More money than our family had ever seen. I've gotten dozens of jobs, but nothing that brought in the kind of money he sent. It had to come from somewhere."

Even in the dim light, she could see the lines drawn across his face. Was he thinking the very thought that had occurred to her? A person didn't get the nickname "Bad Billy" for being an upstanding citizen.

"I don't think it was silver," she told him in the most gentle tone possible.

The look on his face made her wish she hadn't been the bearer of bad news. But he was fortunate to face the truth now. She looked around the room and spied a bucket on one of the crates.

"I'm going to finish picking flowers with Nugget. I found some greens that will be good to take home to

Maddie. We've only got a few minutes longer before we need to start heading back. Otherwise, it'll get too dark to find our way home."

Annabelle grabbed the bucket, wishing that the truth wasn't so harsh. But that was the trouble with dreams. Believing in tales, but not having the proof to back it up, meant that disappointment was inevitable.

At least Joseph was able to see the truth sooner rather than later.

Annabelle headed back outside. Once again the light nearly blinded her. But not so much that she didn't recognize another horse. And a man talking to Nugget.

"Hello!" Annabelle waved her hand and started in their direction. The man looked up but didn't return the wave. Instead, he took Nugget by the hand.

Annabelle quickened her pace toward Nugget and the man. "Nugget!"

The closer she got to them, the more her heart thudded. Nugget was tugging against the man's grasp.

"Let go of her!" Annabelle ran in their direction. "Joseph!"

Hopefully if the man heard that there was another man present, he would leave poor Nugget alone.

"Stop!" Annabelle's throat hurt from screaming so loud, but it distracted the man enough that Nugget was able to tear away from his grasp and run in her direction.

Annabelle gathered Nugget in her arms and started toward the cabin. The man took a step in their direction, then stopped. A quick glance over her shoulder revealed Joseph running toward them.

"What's going on?" His shout spurred her to turn and run to him, clutching Nugget tightly.

"The man...he was trying to take Nugget."

Nugget whimpered against her bodice. Joseph's face hardened.

"Get inside the cabin and bar the door. I'll handle this."

Annabelle didn't need to be told twice. This kind of lawlessness ran rampant in the mining camps and surrounding areas. Even being in town could be dangerous, but at least there, no one dared accost an innocent child.

It wasn't until they were safe inside the cabin, the door barred, that Annabelle dared breathe. Just one more reason to want to leave. These ruffians…

Nugget lifted her head, and Annabelle realized that the child's tears had soaked her bodice through.

"Oh, sweet girl…" She smoothed Nugget's hair and began humming a melody she remembered from her mother. Nugget rested her head back against Annabelle, and Annabelle continued humming and rocking the little girl as she tried peering out the cracks in the wall to see if the horrible man had left.

"Don't let him take me," Nugget whimpered. "He's a bad man."

Annabelle lifted the little girl's head and examined her face. "Do you know him?"

Nugget nodded, then peered around at the door as if to see whether the man was coming after them.

"Who is he?" For once, Annabelle wished she would see the miners as individuals, rather than just a whole group. Maybe she would have recognized him.

The child gave a shrug, those wide eyes still focused on the door. "Dunno. But he shouted at Papa a lot."

A man who shouted at the little girl's father a lot who just happened to be at the cabin to try to take her. No, Joseph's father wasn't a legitimate miner. He was something far worse and more scary. How had her own father been fooled into helping this man?

Someone pounded on the door. "Annabelle, it's me. Joseph. It's safe to come out now."

Still clutching Nugget to her, Annabelle opened the door, and Joseph gathered them in his arms. Warmth rushed all around her. She closed her eyes and breathed in deeply of a strong, earthy scent. His hard chest felt so good against her cheek, and his warm body cradled Nugget between the two of them. Safe.

"Are you all right?"

"I'm—" Before Annabelle could finish telling him they were fine, he'd taken Nugget from her grasp and was cradling her like a baby. Of course it was Nugget he was worried about, and the reason he'd gathered them in his arms. She'd been foolish to get wrapped up in a moment of fancy.

Fancy was what got everyone here in trouble.

"I'm sure she's fine," Annabelle told him, clearing her throat, and silently applauding herself for making it sound like she'd known who he was interested in all along. "I didn't see any injuries, so she's just a little scared, that's all."

He ignored her, keeping his gaze focused on Nugget. "What happened out there?"

"I was picking flowers, and Annabelle went to get a bucket. When she was gone, the man came from the trees and asked about Papa's treasure. I told him it was a secret and to go away. Then he grabbed me. But Annabelle saved me."

Dark, sparkling eyes stared up at her. "You won't let the bad man get me again, will you?"

"Of course not." Annabelle reached over and brushed

a hand across the little cheek. "We'll tell my father, and he'll make sure we all stay safe."

A bright smile lit up Nugget's face, and she pulled a hand away from Joseph's embrace. "I saved us some flowers."

Her little fingers were stained from the mush that she'd been keeping in her tiny fist. Annabelle couldn't help smile at the thought that in all of the danger they'd just faced, Nugget was determined to keep her flowers safe.

Joseph set Nugget down. "Why don't you go look at your books while I talk to Annabelle?"

Nugget let out a long groan. "You guys want to talk about the bad man. Mama and Papa never let me hear about the bad man, either."

"You know about the bad man?" The disbelief in Joseph's voice made Annabelle's heart sink. He probably had no idea what sort of skullduggery his father had been involved in. Annabelle didn't, either, but from the whispered conversations she wasn't supposed to hear when her father was talking with the sheriff, she knew enough.

Nugget nodded and looked at Annabelle.

Joseph whipped around. "You knew?"

"Once we were in the cabin, Nugget told me she recognized the bad man as someone she'd once seen arguing with her father. But that's all I was able to find out. Were you able to find anything?"

"No." A dark look crossed his face, and Annabelle could only imagine what poor Joseph must be feeling. "He got away."

Annabelle had gathered that much on her own. "Maybe my father knows something that can be helpful. He's good friends with the sheriff."

His shoulders relaxed, and he glanced in the direction of Nugget, who had turned her attention to the books. "Why would someone want to take a child?"

Because there was a lot of meanness in this world, particularly in a mining town, where the lowest of the low hung around, hoping to find riches.

Unfortunately, most of the people seeking riches weren't kindhearted souls wanting to do good for others. At least that had been Annabelle's experience. What that had to do with taking an innocent child, she didn't know, but she didn't question things like that anymore.

"Because Papa knew where the silver was," the little voice piped up.

Annabelle sighed. Especially when Joseph headed her way and asked, "And did he tell you where it was?"

She couldn't bear to look at him, or to hear the rest of the conversation. Annabelle went outside for a breath of fresh air in hopes that her churning stomach would calm down. The man's sister had nearly been kidnapped, and he wanted to ask about the silver. Maybe she and God weren't on the best of terms right now, but surely the fastest way to ruin was greed. The kind of greed that had men stealing children, and others too worried about the silver to consider their safety.

Please, God. Help me escape this horrible place. Let Joseph and Nugget leave here before anything worse happens.

The futility of her prayers was not lost on Annabelle. She looked around the clearing, realizing for the first time that the horses were gone. What a way for God to answer. She wasn't just stuck in Leadville, but in a ramshackle cabin so far from home that she wouldn't be tasting Maddie's cooking anytime soon.

She turned toward the cabin and saw Joseph standing in the doorway.

"The horses are gone," she said, gesturing toward the empty area where they'd grazed.

"Yeah." Joseph ran his fingers through his hair. "He took them."

Annabelle glanced over the hill toward the low sun. "It'll be dark soon. Too dangerous to leave the cabin now. We'll have to spend the night here, then set off first thing in the morning."

He nodded slowly. "You're taking this better than I thought you would."

"And what is it that you thought I'd do?" Annabelle's face heated. "Have a fit of vapors?"

At his slow nod, the heat in her cheeks moved to the back of her neck.

"I'll have you know that I have spent plenty of time in places worse than this, thanks to my father's ministry. Why, I could even catch us a couple of fish in the stream, clean them, and then cook them up for supper."

The look on his face screamed disbelief. Fine, then. She'd show him. Fortunately, she remembered seeing a fishing rod in the cabin. Without another word, she stomped past him, grabbed the fishing rod, then went back out the door.

"Annabelle! Wait."

She spun around and shot him her best glare. "What? Any other condescension you'd like to send my way?"

"No." He shoved his hands in his pockets. "I was just going to say thanks, that's all. And that I'm impressed. Back home, my sisters would have been horrified at spending the night in a place like this, and even more so at the thought of touching a worm, or cleaning a fish. There's a lot more to you than meets the eye,

Annabelle Lassiter. I see that once again, we've misjudged each other."

She supposed she should have been grateful for his compliment. But his words about misjudging each other grated on her conscience like the squealing wheels of the train pulling in to the station.

Joseph knew nothing of Annabelle's life, or her situation, least of all her capabilities. Yet here he was, admitting that. Trying to do what she supposed was the right thing. Which made her own thoughts on him even worse. She should be trying harder, but something in her fought it and wouldn't let her.

So she let his comment pass and walked toward the creek, where hopefully enough fish would be biting that they could have a decent supper. Walking back to town tomorrow would take considerable energy, and with a little girl to protect, things could get even more difficult.

"Annabelle!" Joseph called out to her again.

She stopped, but didn't turn in his direction. "I need to catch supper before it's too dark to see."

"I don't want you out there alone. That man could come back. We're safer if we stick together. Let me get Nugget, then we'll all go."

His logic made sense. And she shouldn't resent him taking charge. Her mother would tell her she shouldn't resent anything, but there was so much to resent these days.

"All right," Annabelle said, then sighed. At least with Nugget present, Joseph wouldn't be as likely to ask the kind of questions that made her brain whirl and her heart hurt.

Chapter Eight

They found another patch of flowers near the stream. This part of the mountains seemed relatively untouched by the mining operations. A few trees remained, and the stream wasn't clogged with the tailings from the mines. If you looked in just the right direction, you couldn't see the town or any of the mining operations. Beautiful.

It was a shame that the cabin wasn't bigger. Joseph could bring his family here to live. Unfortunately, the cabin was too small, too rough, and he couldn't ask his siblings to witness the evidence of their pa's foul deeds. Nugget would be hard enough to accept, but he was confident that once they got to know her, the rest of the family would love her just as much as he did.

Joseph smiled at his sister, who seemed to have completely recovered from nearly being kidnapped. If anything positive could come of such a disastrous day, it would have to be that surely this confirmed the existence of silver. Then, he could save his siblings from the clutches of his aunt Ina. *Please, God, let me find the silver soon.*

He wasn't asking for much, not really. Just for a place to live and a way to support everyone. He'd thought five sisters and a brother hard enough, but now that he had Nugget to think of, well, he supposed one more mouth wasn't too much more to consider.

Still, it'd sure be nice to buy Mary a pretty dress like the one he'd seen her admiring in the mercantile. He was closer to Mary than to anyone else, and when Ma had gotten sick, she'd taken over the mothering while he'd gone to work. Between the two of them, they'd kept things together, and he hoped to someday treat Mary to something nice for a change.

He glanced over at Annabelle, who'd taken off her shoes and stockings, then tied up her skirts funny so she could fish from the edge of the bank. It would probably offend her sensibilities for him to notice, but with the breeze blowing golden tendrils of her hair about her face, she looked almost peaceful. Back to the pretty girl he'd been admiring.

It was a shame he had nothing to offer her. Nugget was barely six years old, and though Mary was old enough to marry and start her own household, the others still needed his guidance. A woman wanted her own home, and her own family. Not a ragtag bunch of kids who'd lost their parents. Six. Hard enough to ask a woman to take on a child or two, but six, or even seven if you counted Mary, that was a lot. No, he didn't harbor any illusions of marrying and starting a family of his own.

But when Annabelle grinned and sent a splash of water in Nugget's direction, he was tempted.

The cool reception Nugget had been given by the women in town made Annabelle's kindness toward his sister all the more remarkable. She didn't see Nugget as being the child of a sinful woman, but as a child worthy of love.

"Got one!" Annabelle's clear voice interrupted his thoughts. "Joseph, help! It's a big one!"

He hurried over to the bank, where she struggled to reel in the fish. It was a big one, all right, and he wrapped his arms around her to help her pull it in.

Together, they reeled in the fish, water soaking them both as the fish fought for its life. Finally, they were able to get the fish on the bank, where it flipped and slipped, to the clapping of Nugget's little hands.

"Nice catch!" Joseph whirled Annabelle around, grinning.

She smiled, but released his hands. "You think you can do better?"

He glanced at the fish, still wiggling on the bank. "Probably not. But if you give me a chance, I just might."

She blushed when he winked at her, and he was reminded again of how charming she could be.

"I should tend to the fish," she said as she scurried past him.

Joseph grabbed the rod and started preparing it for another fish. Although Annabelle had caught a large fish, it wouldn't hurt to have more. They could take it with them on the walk home tomorrow.

"I'll do it," he said, holding the fishing pole in her direction. "Since you like fishing, I'll handle the messy work and leave you to the fun."

Her eyes flashed. "I can clean a fish."

"I don't doubt it." He smiled, hoping to disarm her once again. "But since you love fishing, I'd hate to spoil your fun."

Annabelle took the pole. "Oh. If you don't mind…"

"Not at all. I hate fishing. Too much standing around and waiting for the fish to bite. I prefer things that are more direct."

"If you're sure. Father and I loved going fishing together, but Mother said…" She turned her head away and started back for the water.

"Why do you do that?" he said to her back.

"What?" She looked at him, her brow furrowed like she was trying to decipher a puzzle.

"Hide." He bent down and grabbed the fish, but kept his eyes on her. "Just when you start to reveal a bit of the real Annabelle, you retreat into a place where no one can see you."

He couldn't read the expression on her face, but then, that was exactly what he was accusing her of doing. Hiding. Pretending. Who was the real Annabelle Lassiter?

"This is the real Annabelle. I like to fish. Some women would say that's not proper. So I only fish when I'm with my father."

A wistful tone filled her voice, and he wondered when she'd last gone fishing with her pa.

"You can fish with me."

Annabelle shook her head. "That really wouldn't be proper now, would it? I'm already going to have to be careful to avoid a scandal for being here, so the more we can avoid the appearance of impropriety, the better."

Annabelle was right. He hadn't thought of the consequences of them spending the night unchaperoned. They shouldn't have come at all. But he hadn't thought twice about it when her father had suggested the idea. Still…Annabelle was a lady, and…

If word got out about them spending the night alone in the cabin together, Annabelle would be unfit for decent company. She'd done nothing other than offer him and his sister her kindness—at the expense of her own grief. And now, because she'd agreed to bring them here, she'd suffer once more.

"I should marry you. To avoid scandal."

He'd never imagined himself saying those words, least of all to someone like Annabelle, but they slipped out. A man of honor, he'd spare Annabelle's reputation.

"But I won't marry you." Annabelle stalked the rest of the way to the water, fishing rod clenched in her hand, stating clearly that the conversation was over.

Nugget tugged at his hand. "That wasn't very romantical."

"Romantical?" He stared down at her. "What do you know of romantical?"

The little girl's face brightened. "When Papa got romantical for Mama, he went to the bathhouse and took a bath. Then he picked some pretty flowers and gave them to her. Mama said it was the most romantical thing ever, and she couldn't wait until he was free to marry her."

She stared at him with a knowing look. "If you're not romantical to Annabelle, she's never going to marry you."

Words from a child shouldn't sting. The comparison to his snake father was the lowest insult he could think of. Especially as they related to marrying a woman he had no business thinking he could marry. The honorable thing was to propose marriage. He had, and she'd said no. End of discussion.

Right?

Annabelle fought with the line that had somehow been tangled. Imagine! Telling her that he'd marry her, as if it were some kind of chore, like gutting a fish. Was she so unlovable that he wouldn't want to marry her?

Not that she wanted to marry him, of course.

But oh…the nerve of the man. Her finger slid along

the line, and the string cut into her skin. Blood oozed out, and she stuck her finger in her mouth.

She glanced over her shoulder. Joseph had squatted by Nugget and together, they were gutting the fish. Her heart wasn't supposed to melt at the sight. She should have been completely unaffected by the way he smiled at the little girl. So tender. Gentle. And Nugget's giggle…

There was so much to like about them. Annabelle recast her line, this time being careful of her injured finger. If only things were different. If she hadn't been abandoned by another miner whose lust for riches outweighed his feelings for her. Mining fever blinded people to what was right. Though Joseph was beginning his quest with what sounded like good intentions, they'd fade once he held that first glimmer of metal in his hand.

But even if Joseph were a blacksmith or a barber, or anything else, Annabelle's heart was too irrevocably damaged that she had nothing left to give anyone. And why should she? She'd lost too much to risk it again.

Another giggle rent the air. Another pang in Annabelle's heart. For all her attempts not to care for the little girl, she couldn't help but wish…

If Susannah had lived, she and Nugget could have been friends.

A tug at her line brought Annabelle's attention back to where it should have been. This fish wasn't as big as the other one, but it still took a good deal of strength to bring it in herself. But she wasn't afraid of the work. Work had never scared her. The strength required to perform such tasks was nothing in comparison to the strength of will it took to handle everything else in her life. If only the rest of her life was so simple as physical labor.

"I'm impressed," Joseph said over her shoulder as she finished bringing it in. "You should have asked for help."

"And spoil the fun?" Annabelle grabbed the fish and pulled it off the hook. "I told you that I love to fish."

The fish wiggled in her hands, and she tossed it in Joseph's direction. "Want to take care of this one?"

"I'd be happy to. It's the least I can do, since you've been so good as to provide dinner."

She watched as he brought the fish to Nugget for them to clean. One more thing she had to appreciate about him. He didn't coddle Nugget or treat her as less than capable because she was a girl.

"I'll head back to the cabin and get the stove ready so we can cook the fish."

Before she could turn back up the trail, Joseph stopped her. "We need to stick together, remember?"

Annabelle sighed. "You're right."

The look he gave her made her feel only marginally better. How, in all of this, had she forgotten that there was a man out there who wanted to harm Nugget? For a moment, she'd gotten lost in the joy of fishing and forgotten that they were all in very real danger.

A bird cried out, and Annabelle watched as it turned circles in the sky. As high up as they were, sheer cliffs still surrounded them from all directions. Trapped. And with night closing in, the only option they had was to remain united.

She gave another deep inhale before opening her eyes and looking back up at the cliffs.

Along the top of the ridge, something flashed. Like a light, only not so bright. Like a reflection. Was it the man who'd tried to take Nugget?

"Joseph?" She tried to keep her voice modulated,

not betraying the worry and fear that would frighten a little girl.

He must've sensed the edge in her voice, because he murmured something to Nugget, then stepped right beside Annabelle before quietly saying, "Is something the matter?"

"Look up at the cliff to the north. Just past my right shoulder. There's a flash of...something." She gazed at him, watching his face as he searched the spot.

"Is it silver?"

If he had been her brother, she'd have slugged him in the arm. Hard. Silver. Because that's all the people around here wanted to see. Joseph's sister was in danger, and all his mind could conjure was silver.

"If it were silver, dozens of miners would have found it by now. I'm worried that it might be someone watching us. Like the man who tried taking Nugget."

At her words, he stilled. Hopefully realizing that chasing after silver was foolishness in comparison to Nugget's life.

"I'm going to take a closer look. We'll return to the cabin. Once you two are safely inside, I'll see what I can find."

Annabelle's heart thudded against her chest. "I thought we were supposed to stay together. I can't protect Nugget by myself."

He stared at her. Long and hard. Like he thought her words were more foolish than the thought of an inexperienced man going after a child-stealing bandit.

"Don't go acting soft and feminine on me now. I know better. You are way more capable than you let on. I have no doubt that if someone came to the cabin, you could absolutely handle it on your own."

Annabelle swallowed. His stare bore into her as if

once again he saw deeper into her soul than even God. He was right. No one would harm Nugget. She'd already lost a precious child on her watch. Disease was something she couldn't see coming, and she couldn't stop once it came. But a man… Annabelle straightened her back.

"I could," she finally told him. "But I don't like it."

Then, because she couldn't let his foolishness pass without a remark, she looked him up and down. "You, on the other hand, I have serious doubts about. You don't know this land. And the type of men you're liable to come across…"

"You think I'm weak." The word came out as a slap in the face. No, no one could accuse this man of being weak.

"I think you're green, which is different from being weak. Out here, being green gets a man killed."

A sly smile slid across his face. "Does this mean Miss Annabelle Lassiter is worried about me?"

Oh! He was insufferable! "Fine, then. Take your chances." She spun and strode over to where Nugget was finishing with the fish.

Annabelle smiled at the little girl and pretended to inspect Nugget's handiwork while ignoring Joseph's soft chuckle. Had she said he was insufferable?

"You did a nice job, Nugget. We'll have a wonderful supper tonight." Annabelle picked up the fish. "Let's go back to the cabin and see what kind of feast we can prepare."

The little girl giggled. "My papa used to say that when we finally got our mine in production, we'd have a feast every night. I didn't know he was talking about fish."

More false silver dreams. Annabelle swallowed the

bitterness that rose up and smiled. "I'm sure he was talking about a different kind of feast, but I think this'll do just as good."

Nugget rewarded her with a heartbreakingly sweet smile. "You sound like my mama. Mama said we didn't need no feast, just each other."

Scary to be compared to a woman of ill-repute. Only, the more Nugget talked about her, the more Annabelle had to question that judgment, as well. Nugget's mother sounded almost nice, like the sort of person she might be friends with. Except, of course, for the sinful life she led. Which only made Annabelle wonder more. She'd always lumped sinners into a pile, where their badness made them almost intolerable. She'd never taken the time to consider that they might have good qualities, as well.

Her father would have probably given her a sermon on the topic—that all are sinners and fall short of the glory of God. But the ladies at church said that some sinners were worse than others. Only now she had to begin to wonder which sin truly was the worst—the way they treated a sweet girl like Nugget and her mother, who seemed like she was a nice person—or the life Nugget's mother led.

Annabelle tripped over a rock, stumbling, but managed to catch herself and save the fish.

"Are you all right?" Joseph grabbed her to steady her, then looked into her eyes.

How could he have known where her thoughts were going? "I'm fine," she said, then continued on the path.

If she wanted to condemn those who condemned Nugget's mother for being what she was, then she also had to look at her own judgments of people. Like Joseph. Like being upset at miners for vainly pursuing silver at the expense of all else.

Her father had once told her that he wanted to share real treasure with the miners, and that it was his duty to love them where they were at. That there was nothing wrong with pursuing a dream as long as you didn't forget the highest prize.

Annabelle sighed. It wasn't that she didn't like Joseph or even miners. But it was the only defense she had against the pain of what would be the inevitable loss.

Nugget giggled at something Joseph said to her. The little girl, and yes, even her brother, had already wormed their way into her heart. But if she could leave soon, surely the pain would be bearable. It would certainly be more tolerable than prolonging the acquaintance. The longer she was with them, the more the parting would tear at her.

Chapter Nine

Joseph stuffed the paper-wrapped fish in his pocket. True to her word, Annabelle had made their dinner a feast. He hated leaving so late, but Annabelle had refused to let him leave without food in his belly.

Annabelle handed him the shotgun they'd found buried under one of the floorboards. "I think you should take this."

"I've never been much of a shot." He stared at the gun, knowing that if he had to come up against the kidnapper, he wouldn't stand a chance.

Joseph closed his eyes and offered a silent prayer. He had to keep Annabelle and Nugget safe.

"What are you going to do when you meet up with whoever's out there? Invite them to church? Even my father doesn't venture out of town unarmed. When I agreed to the plan of you investigating, I assumed you at least knew how to protect yourself."

Which was the nice way of her saying he was the biggest fool ever. "What do we do about what we saw on the cliff?"

She inclined her head over to Nugget, who was bent over one of Pa's books. "We can't do much of anything.

We have Nugget to keep safe. At least, with the way the cabin is positioned, we'll know they're coming before they get here."

Annabelle held up the gun and said, "I'm pretty good with targets, but it's not as though I've ever shot a person before."

If only Mary could see him now. She'd probably love the fact that he had a whole list of things a girl could do better than he. No, not a girl. Annabelle.

"We do have the strength of the Lord. Why don't you pray for us?"

Except Annabelle didn't rise up to his challenge. Instead, her face fell, and she started to turn away. "Sorry, I can't."

He reached for her shoulder. "Please. Annabelle. Stop turning away from me, and just face it."

Her shoulders fell, and she slowly turned back to face him. A single tear ran down her cheek.

This Annabelle, this Annabelle he knew. It was the sad girl he'd seen try to hide at her father's house.

"Please don't tell anyone," she whispered.

"Tell anyone what?"

Another tear trickled down her cheek. He wanted to reach out to wipe it away, but feared that if he did, it would give her reason to run away again.

"I can't pray, Joseph. God doesn't hear my prayers." She closed her eyes, then her shoulders rose and fell again before she opened them and looked at him. "I'm a preacher's daughter, and God doesn't listen to my prayers. If anyone knew..."

The expression skittering across her face reminded him of one of the rabbits they caught in traps. She truly believed that people learning of her lack of faith would be the end of everything.

"Have you talked to your father about this?"

"No!" Annabelle took a step back. "And you can't tell him, either. It would kill him to know that after all he's done to save others, his own daughter doesn't believe."

His heart broke at the way her face twisted in pain. From his own faith journey, and how his family battled against Christian do-gooders, even if he did tell her father, it wouldn't make a difference in what Annabelle believed. She had to learn to believe on her own.

"Then I'll pray for us," he said quietly. "And I'll pray for you."

"Please don't waste your words on my account," she said, then turned to clean up the remains of dinner.

This time, he gave her the space she required. He'd seen farther into Annabelle's heart than she'd even allowed her father to see. With that, he had to believe that there was hope for Annabelle. Maybe even for him and Annabelle to be friends.

If there was silver, and the threat against them seemed to indicate there must be, then maybe he'd move his family out here. It would be good for Mary to have a woman friend her own age.

He smiled at the thought of Annabelle and Mary becoming friends. They both shared the same deep convictions and inner strength he so admired.

He glanced over at Nugget, engrossed in one of their pa's books. "What are you reading?"

"Papa's words." A sad look crossed Nugget's face. "I miss Papa. He would've made the bad men on the cliff go away."

So much for trying to keep Nugget out of this. "What do you know about the bad men on the cliff?"

Nugget shrugged, then hugged the book closer to her.

"They want Papa's silver."

He wished the little girl was old enough to tell him about more than just that their father had silver.

"Can you tell me anything about Papa's silver?" Joseph sat next to her on the bed, but she scooted away.

"No." Nugget hugged the book closer to her. "It's a secret."

Joseph sighed. She was just a child. She probably didn't know much anyway.

"It's all right. You don't have to tell your secret. Come here, and I'll read to you."

This time, Nugget rewarded him with a grin and fell into his arms. He breathed in her soft little-girl scent, cuddling her.

Since he wasn't going to be able to marry and have children himself, he had to enjoy these moments with his sister and cherish them as his own. Mary would call him daft, but she could someday have a family of her own. He would do that much for the sister he'd left behind to care for the others while he hunted for their pa. After the abuse she'd suffered at Aunt Ina's hands while protecting their siblings, well, he owed her. If only he'd known before he'd left just how bad it would be for them. One more reason to be angry at his father.

He caught Annabelle's soft humming as she cleaned up the remainder of their dinner. It was almost enough for him to be able to lose himself in the fantasy of having a real family. It'd be nice to have a woman who loved him to take care of them, and a sweet child of their own to love. But Annabelle wasn't his wife, and Nugget wasn't his daughter.

Margaret had been right about why he'd make a terrible husband. He was too busy with the family he already had to start one of his own. It was a good thing Annabelle had refused his proposal. He could rest with a clear conscience knowing he'd done the honorable thing, but also with the relief that he wasn't forcing a good woman like Annabelle to give up whatever it was she dreamed of.

"Read!" Nugget lifted her head and handed him the book she'd been looking at.

The Bible. Fitting, considering his prayers and Annabelle's confession. Maybe, as he shared the sacred words with his sister, Joseph would find some answers.

But as he opened the first pages, he realized the same thing he'd seen in his pa's other books. His pa had been using it to write his own notes.

Joseph started reading the opening lines to the book, but as the words swirled around in his brain, all he could think about was how they connected. His heart raced. The mines—his pa had secretly written the key to finding his treasure within the pages.

"Joseph!" Nugget tugged on his arm. "More!"

He patted the little girl's head and continued reading about Joseph in Egypt. Later, when Nugget went to sleep, he'd decode his pa's mystery.

Annabelle listened to the soft sound of Joseph reading to Nugget. It was peaceful, being in the cabin with Joseph and Nugget. For the first time since meeting them, her heart didn't hurt. Strange.

She put the last dish back in the crate. Maddie would tsk over her reddened hands when she got home tomorrow, but if that was the worst Maddie could find fault with, it would be worth it. Funny how as much as she'd been longing to go back east to visit Aunt Celeste, she couldn't think of a more contented moment than now.

It had grown dark, and the last remnants of light faded from the one tiny window the cabin had allowed. Their lamps would make them easy targets for intruders, but she couldn't bear to spoil the special time Nugget and Joseph were having. If only she had been given more similar moments with her own baby sister.

But she couldn't. All she could do was give that time to Joseph and Nugget.

Annabelle turned down the rest of the lamps, conserving oil, and making their presence as unobtrusive as possible.

"Everything all right?" Joseph paused in his reading.

"Fine," she said. "Everything's fine."

She stood at the corner of the window, looking at the dark landscape. The bandits could be anywhere, and she wouldn't see them. The door was already bolted, but would it be enough? She spied a large barrel in the corner. Against the door, it would be an additional barrier.

Annabelle started pushing the barrel.

"Let me help."

"I can do it. Nugget—"

"Is asleep." Joseph had come alongside her, and together they pushed the barrel in front of the door. Even in the darkness, she could see his smile. Sometimes she wished she could have his same calm attitude. With all that he lost, how was it that his burden would be so light?

Having Nugget must make it easier.

Annabelle leaned against the door. Wisdom said they should rest. But what if the men came during the night?

"Why don't you take the bed with Nugget, and I'll make a pallet on the floor? We should both get some rest."

She hated the way he could read her mind sometimes. It reminded her too much of how her father and mother had been together. Finishing each other's sentences, often so alike that…well, that didn't describe Annabelle and Joseph at all. Not only did they have no future together due to his mining ambition, but he wasn't the sort of man she could fall in love with. Why, she didn't even like Joseph.

Something tickled her on the back of the neck as a small voice reminded her that telling falsehoods was a sin. Fine, then. She mostly didn't like Joseph. Sometimes, like when he was caring for Nugget, he could almost be all right. Not that her admission made the tickle go away.

Annabelle looked around the cabin. No sense in thinking about Joseph, not now. Not with all the other things they had to worry about.

"I think we should be safe enough for the night. I thought I saw—" When she turned to point out the trunk she'd noticed containing a number of blankets, she saw that Joseph had already beaten her to it. Yet again, he'd known what she had been thinking.

She huffed out a breath. Coincidence, that's all. Joseph wasn't a stupid man. Of course he would remember that the trunk contained blankets. Obviously being in these close quarters was addling Annabelle's mind. She'd be thinking more clearly once she had a good night's sleep and was home safe.

"That's just what I was about to suggest," she finally said, almost forcing a smile, but stopping when she recalled how it usually served only to irritate Joseph rather than placate him as she intended.

Joseph shifted slightly, then looked at her in a way he hadn't looked at her before.

"I know you'd prefer to be anywhere but here, so um…" He shifted again, his shoulders rising and falling. "I appreciate everything you've done here with Nugget and me. I'm not sure what we would have done without you."

She'd been thanked countless times, but none of the thank-yous she'd ever received had made her so queasy. So... Annabelle closed her eyes. She'd done what was needed, nothing more. Which didn't explain why his thanks was so disconcerting.

"Of course I would help." She didn't look at him as she turned toward the bed she'd be sharing with Nugget.

But his silence didn't feel right to her at all.

Obviously she was overtired and overwrought after such a day. Once she'd had a good night's sleep, the jumble in her mind would make sense again. Then she could get them all back home and back to their normal lives.

Chapter Ten

Joseph tried making himself comfortable. He'd slept in far worse conditions, so he couldn't understand why he couldn't fall asleep. He'd need every bit of rest he could get for their trek in the morning.

He could hear Annabelle snoring softly. She'd be mortified if he said anything, but he wished he could tell her that her unladylike noises were actually somewhat cute.

Maybe if he took a look outside one last time to make sure everything was fine, he'd be more comfortable going to sleep. He stood, and in the faint light, could see Annabelle and Nugget curled up together. Absolutely beautiful.

A noise outside the cabin startled him. The men? Maybe his lack of sleep wasn't such a bad thing after all. Joseph tiptoed to the small crack that would allow him a view of the surrounding area. Two riders on horseback were in the distance, heading toward the cabin.

Hating to disturb Annabelle's peace, but knowing their safety depended on it, he crept to the bed, then shook her softly. As her eyes fluttered open, he put a finger to his lips, then pointed to the door.

She nodded, then scooted out of the bed. He couldn't help but notice how she tucked the quilts around Nugget as she left. Someday, Annabelle would make an excellent mother.

Which made Joseph want to smack himself for being so daft when they were clearly in danger.

They went to the crack, and Joseph pointed out where he'd seen the riders.

"Get the gun," Annabelle whispered.

He nodded slowly, wishing he didn't have to let Annabelle do a man's work. When they returned to town, the first thing he'd do was practice his shooting. If the place was so unsafe as for a man to teach a woman like Annabelle how to defend herself, then he'd need it, as well. Especially now that he had Nugget and her silver secret to protect.

As the riders drew closer, she set the gun down. "It's my father."

Though Joseph expected to have to face her father at some point, it somehow seemed more wrong for him to find them in the cabin together.

"Help me move this." She pushed at the barrel they'd only recently put in the way of the door.

There was nothing Miss Annabelle Lassiter couldn't do.

As the riders stopped just short of the cabin, Annabelle ran out, carrying a lantern.

"Father!" Her joyful cry made his gut ache. He supposed he wouldn't have had such a reunion with his own pa. Even more than before, he'd like to punch the man for messing up so many lives. Not only was there the obvious evidence of his pa's infidelity, but now, they had dangerous men after them.

What kind of man had his pa been, really?

Certainly not the kind of man who jumped from his horse and wrapped his arms around his daughter. He'd never seen such affection with his sisters.

Nugget made a small noise in her sleep as if to remind him he had another sister. A little girl who called their pa "Papa," with such fondness he had to wonder if he knew his pa at all. Could a man change? And if he'd changed, why hadn't he cared enough to make sure the rest of his family was provided for?

Annabelle, her father, and another man walked toward the cabin. He steeled himself for what would most likely be a confrontation ending in a marriage proposal. He knew how poorly that had gone over before. But with them being unchaperoned for so long, the preacher was bound to make him do right by his daughter.

Somehow, they'd make it work. And he'd make it up to Annabelle for ruining her life.

Joseph stepped out to meet them, but Annabelle shook her head. "We'll talk inside."

Once inside, neither Annabelle nor her father, nor the strange man made a move to add additional light.

"Annabelle tells me that you may be in danger." The preacher looked at him with a very unpreacherlike expression. "What did you see on the cliff?"

Joseph relayed the details as best as he could remember.

"I know the spot he's talking about," the strange man said. "I'll go check it out."

The preacher gave a nod, but kept his attention on Joseph. "Thank you for your quick thinking. I'm sure you saved both Annabelle and Nugget."

Annabelle gave a most unladylike snort, and despite the serious nature of the situation, Joseph wanted to smile.

"It was all Annabelle's doing. Her quick thinking and resourcefulness has been a real blessing."

This time, the preacher turned his attention to Annabelle, who appeared to back away from his examination. "Is that so?"

"I just did what I had to do." She looked away, then grabbed the pile of blankets Joseph had left on the floor. "I can make pallets for Nugget and I so you two can trade off with the bed."

"Annabelle—" Her father seemed to want to say something, but she cut him off with a glare.

"Not now. I did what I had to do, and that's that."

Even if he'd wanted to, Joseph couldn't ignore the bitterness that had returned to her voice. Somehow the carefree Annabelle had gotten misplaced with the arrival of her father.

Joseph reached out and took the blankets from her. "It doesn't make sense for you to disturb Nugget. You take the bed with her, and your pa and I will make do on the floor. I haven't been able to sleep anyway."

"That's because you've been on the floor while I've had the bed," she retorted, tugging at the blankets. "You need your rest."

"And so do you." He held them firm, glancing at her father for reinforcement.

"Joseph is right. Go to bed, Annabelle."

Finally. Someone with enough authority to get Annabelle to obey. Not without a fight, though. She practically stomped to the bed, then snuggled down into the covers.

Neither man said a word until Annabelle's soft snore sounded through the room.

"I'm sorry for my daughter's behavior. I realize this situation is difficult." Frank broke the silence first.

"You have nothing to be sorry for. Because of Annabelle, we had a fine dinner and were safe inside the cabin until you arrived."

He glanced over at the mounds on the bed before continuing. "Sir, I realize that my being alone with her is improper. I'd like to assure you that I took no liberties with your daughter's person. But if you feel it necessary for us to marry, I'll be glad to do so."

The words came out all in a rush, lest he lose the courage to utter them.

Frank, though, looked at him, then chuckled softly. "Son, you have a better chance of taking liberties with a mountain lion. Unless she feels it necessary, I won't be forcing you into a wedding."

Which should have left him feeling relieved, only it didn't. Worse, that traitorous part of him almost wished her father had insisted otherwise.

"There's something I don't understand." Joseph moved closer to the preacher so they could talk more. "In town, you acted like Annabelle was near perfect. Here, you seem to have a more realistic view of her."

Frank sighed. "I'm not blind to Annabelle's faults. Still, she's got a good heart. One that's been broken too many times by these mountains. I should never have sent her with you, but I'd hoped it'd bring some healing to her. All it's done is put her in danger."

For the first time, Frank sounded like a broken man instead of a man of God. "She wasn't always so bitter. But when her mother and brothers and sister died, she let the bitterness take over. If you'd been alone with her then, I'd have made you marry her. Because she'd have been impossible to resist."

It was almost on the tip of Joseph's tongue to tell

him that he'd gotten a glimpse of that Annabelle. But he wasn't sure that information would be helpful about now.

Maybe it was time to talk about more relevant information. "Who was that man you brought with you?"

"Slade Holmes. Best tracker I know. When Annabelle wasn't home in time for supper, I figured she might have run into trouble. So I found Slade and came up here."

"I'm sorry I didn't do more to protect them." He glanced over again at their sleeping forms. "I don't know what I'd have done if those men had—"

"Don't fret over what-might-have-beens. The girls are safe. That's all that matters." Frank grabbed a blanket and wrapped it around himself. "I'm going to get some shut-eye, and I suggest you do the same."

"What if the men come back?"

"Slade will give us plenty of warning."

With that, the older man turned and curled up on the floor, the conversation clearly over.

But it wasn't over, not in Joseph's mind. Not with the puzzling woman still snoring softly on the other side of the room. As much as Annabelle held the silver search in disdain, she had to realize that it was the only way he was going to save his family.

A small slant of sunlight roused Annabelle from her slumber. Nugget still lay curled beside her. She sat up slowly, looking around the strange room that had become familiar to her in less than a day. Joseph slept slouched in a chair, and her father was gone.

Slade must've found something.

Annabelle stretched, and careful not to disturb Nugget, slid out of bed.

She walked to the door, wondering if Slade and her

father were near. It figured he'd bring Slade along. One more reminder of all she'd lost.

"Morning." Slade's voice greeted her as she stepped out of the cabin.

She didn't look at him. "Morning."

"You can't hate me forever."

Oh, yes, she could. "I don't wish to discuss that particular topic. Where's my father?"

She scanned the area, noting that her father's horse was gone, but Peter's—now Slade's—grazed nearby.

"Maybe if you were a little nicer to me, I'd tell you."

Annabelle sighed. Staying angry did her no good, especially when she knew Slade was just trying to help. But forgiving him in theory was so much easier than in actuality. "What do you want from me?"

"How about a bit of civility? You lost a brother, but I lost my friend. Can't we call a truce?"

A truce. For the man who should have been getting the doctor for her brother but somehow ended up bringing home a pocket full of silver instead.

"What'd you do with the silver?" She hadn't meant to confront him with the question that had been plaguing her for months, but the words bubbled up of their own accord.

Slade's face darkened. "Your father went down to the camp at Greenhorn Gulch to see if he could get some food and borrow some horses."

"I'll start a fire." Annabelle turned toward the cabin.

She probably should have apologized for her rudeness, but it was hard enough being in his presence without having to also humble herself and admit where she'd been wrong.

Before she could enter the cabin, hoofbeats sounded in the distance. Her father. At least he hadn't witnessed her conversation with Slade. She'd have had to endure another sermon about forgiveness. Then, she'd have had to paste another smile on her face and pretend it was all right when it wasn't.

Nothing was all right. But if she didn't pretend, everything around her threatened to cave in. While she appreciated Joseph's attempts at wanting to do away with the falseness she surrounded herself with, he simply didn't understand it was the only way for her to survive the grief that tried to swallow her whole.

"Hello, Father," she said when he dismounted. "I was about to go inside and build a fire. I believe Joseph has some fish from last night." Hardly a feast, but at least it'd keep her hands occupied so she didn't go crazy.

"No need." He smiled and kissed the top of her head. "I ran into Gertie at the camp, and she's got breakfast for all."

"I wouldn't want to impose. I know how provisions are scarce for them." She gave a half smile in return.

"I told Gertie the same thing." The genuine smile her father gave made Annabelle's insides curl up. "But Collin's had a bit of good fortune lately, so there's plenty."

Yet not enough for them to leave the mining camp and live in a decent house. She'd never understand these miners. They settled for living in squalor and throwing their money back into a pit that might someday pay off.

Or, like Collin MacDonald, throw it all into a bottle that never did anyone, least of all his family, any good.

"That's very kind of her. We'll be sure to send a basket of Maddie's goodies to thank her when we're back home."

Her father sighed. As if he, too, was learning to see right through her. "I know it's going to be hard on you, seeing Gertie. Just remember that she was your mother's best friend, and that she loves you like her own."

"I'll try." It was the best she could do. She hadn't seen any of the MacDonalds since her family died. Her father had dutifully come from his visits to the family to let her know of how they were all doing, but she couldn't bring herself to visit. There were too many reminders of what she'd lost.

"I'll let Joseph and Nugget know." Annabelle went inside before the feelings got to be too much to bear. She knew it was wrong to shut out the remaining people who loved her. But what else was she supposed to do?

She'd tried so hard to build walls around all the things that hurt, and to keep out the people that reminded her of that pain. But now she was being forced to confront it, and that seemed like the worst injustice of all.

The mining camp was like so many of the places Joseph had visited looking for his pa. A sea of tents, rough-hewn cabins, and the stench of unwashed human flesh. However, instead of the wary stares he'd gotten on his trips, the people greeted them as they passed by.

"Howdy, Preacher."

"Morning, Miss Annabelle."

Friendly voices, friendly smiles, and if it wasn't for the tense way Annabelle sat on the horse in front of him, he'd think they were going to meet beloved friends. Children crowded around the horses, and several women looked up from the washing to give a cheerful wave.

The farther they went into the camp, the more Annabelle's back stiffened.

"Are you all right?" he asked in a low voice.

"I'll be fine."

He might as well have asked if she'd take arsenic in

her tea. They stopped near the center of the camp, and as everyone dismounted, he followed suit, then rushed over to lift Nugget down, then to assist Annabelle.

"I can do it," she said, her voice laced with sadness.

Her father smiled at him. "Now, Annabelle, you're a lady. Don't fault a gentleman for treating you as such."

When her shoulders fell in that resigned way of hers, Joseph felt half-bad for wanting to help her. Now that he'd gotten to know her, had heard about her pain, he wanted to give her space to deal with it.

"I'm sorry for troubling you," Joseph whispered as he finished helping her off her horse.

He leaned in with one final whisper. "Let me be a friend to you."

Crystal-blue eyes that could have matched the stream they'd been fishing in filled with water as she shook her head slowly. "Please. Let this be."

Frank was oblivious to the situation as he neared the campfire and had already begun chatting with the woman who tended it. Joseph watched as she led him into a cabin that appeared to be even rougher than his pa's.

"Is that where we're going?"

Annabelle shrugged and looked away.

"Annabelle!" A girl slightly older than Nugget came bounding toward them. "It's been ages since you've come to visit."

Joseph didn't have to watch to know Annabelle had stiffened beside him. He could feel it. As much as he wanted to give her some comfort, he had something else to worry about. Nugget had attached herself to his pant leg again. The sweet, cheerful girl had disappeared.

Whatever it was about this camp, he sure didn't like the effect it had on his womenfolk.

His womenfolk. Joseph shook his head. Annabelle wasn't his anything.

"I've been busy," Annabelle finally told the girl, her voice thick.

"We've missed you." The girl's sweet voice didn't waver. "I miss Susannah." The last sentence was spoken with such heartbreaking sadness.

"I miss her, too."

With the way Annabelle's voice cracked at that admission, Joseph wasn't sure she'd have the strength to say anything else.

All of this—everything from the time he'd spent with her in their home until now—it was all about the same thing. Annabelle's crushing grief.

"Annabelle," her father called, coming out of the cabin. "Bring Joseph and Nugget over so we can get washed up and eat."

The smell of frying bacon finally hit Joseph's nostrils. His stomach growled. Though Annabelle's meal had been wonderful, the meager leftovers they nibbled at this morning hadn't done enough to satisfy his hunger.

"Is Nugget the horse?" the girl asked, her voice filled with wonder. "We ain't never had a horse to breakfast."

"Nugget is my sister," Joseph answered for Annabelle. "And she's a little shy, so give her some time to get used to you."

He nudged Nugget to get her to move forward, but her hands dug farther into his pants. "I'm not hungry."

Annabelle was no help in the matter, as she just stood there, staring.

"Let's do as your father says."

With a soft sigh, Annabelle nodded. "Come on, Nugget." She held out a hand, as if that hand would somehow make whatever was wrong with Nugget suddenly all right.

Nugget loosened her hold on his pants, then took Annabelle's hand, still grasping him with the other.

They trudged toward the cabin with painful slowness. Annabelle because she seemed to be doing everything she could to avoid getting there, and Nugget because she wouldn't let go of Joseph or Annabelle.

"I declare, you are as slow as molasses, Annabelle." The older woman stepped toward them and wrapped her arms around Annabelle. And, by default, Nugget.

"I don't know what's kept you from us for so long, but you are a sight. All skin and bones, what is that Maddie feeding you? Or not feeding you, I should say. Well, never mind that, I just fixed a mess of fresh eggs, and we've got bacon and biscuits so flaky you'd think you were eating a cloud. Polly's becoming quite the cook, aren't you, Polly?"

The woman stopped her rambling speech to point out a girl stirring a pot over the fire.

"And you must be Joseph. Frank told me all about you. Says you've been looking into Bad Billy's estate. Now that's a sad state of affairs if I've ever heard one. Poor fellow got all mixed up with one of them dance hall girls and, well, she foisted someone's git on him. At least he died before he had to deal with the heartbreak of finding out she had the pox. Can you—"

"Don't talk about my mama and papa that way!" Nugget flew from the protection of Joseph and Annabelle, then kicked the woman squarely in the shin before running off.

"Nugget!" Annabelle and Joseph said the name in unison, but Annabelle propelled into action.

"I'll take care of it," she called over her shoulder, running after Nugget.

"And she will, you know," the woman said to Joseph. "Annabelle has a way with children. Such a terrible loss when she stopped coming here to work with the little ones. Come, let's get you a plate."

He looked at the woman, still full of cheer, and completely oblivious to Annabelle's misery.

"Thank you kindly, but I'd better help Annabelle." He looked her up and down. "And while I'm grateful for your hospitality, I would appreciate it in the future if you'd avoid making such comments about her mother or our father."

The woman flushed. "I meant no harm. I was only repeating what I—".

Joseph held up a hand. "I'm sure you didn't. But Nugget is my sister, and I take affronts to her honor seriously."

"Of course. I…" She looked at Joseph, then over at Frank, then back to Joseph. "I apologize."

"Thank you. I'd better see if Annabelle needs any help."

He left the woman standing there and headed in the direction he'd seen Nugget and Annabelle run. It didn't take long to find them, sitting beside a large rock at the edge of camp.

Annabelle held a sobbing Nugget in her arms, rubbing her back, whispering what he assumed to be soothing words into her hair.

"Is she all right?"

"Yes." Annabelle continued rubbing Nugget's back. "She's been so far removed from the gossip for a while that it's hard to have it come back at her. Especially with being reminded of their deaths. Poor little thing misses her mama and papa, and this just brought all the sadness back up."

She smoothed Nugget's hair. "But it's going to be all right. Everyone's entitled to be a bit sad from time to time when they miss someone they love."

The sweet kiss Annabelle pressed to Nugget's head tore at Joseph's heart. She wasn't just offering words of comfort to Nugget, she was telling it to herself.

Who rubbed Annabelle's back and whispered words of comfort to her?

The wind whipped down the hill, cold against their backs, reminding him that a warm fire and breakfast awaited them.

"We should get back."

His stomach concurred, grumbling its opinion.

"You go. We'll just be a little longer." The smile Annabelle gave him was mixed with sadness and unshed tears.

When did Annabelle get to cry over her losses?

Joseph looked around. Though people milled about the camp nearby, they were still out in the wild. "I don't—"

"We'll be fine." Annabelle pressed Nugget closer into her. "She's not all cried out yet. It's best if we let her get it all out."

More advice that he assumed had to have come from Annabelle's own life. Something she probably didn't allow anyone else to see, just like everything in her life. Had things been different for her when her siblings were alive? Back home, he told Mary just about everything. He sure could use her advice now. Of course, he'd never seen Mary cry. But surely she'd know what to do about the situation.

Though Annabelle seemed to have Nugget well in

hand, he couldn't help but wish for something to ease Annabelle's pain.

"You're sure you'll be all right?" He hoped the look of concern he gave her would be taken in friendship.

She nodded and gave the kind of Annabelle smile he lived for. Would that their lives were simpler. That he didn't have a family to provide for. Even then, what did he have to offer her, or any other woman?

"Thank you," he said instead.

"Of course." Annabelle snuggled Nugget closer in to her. "She just needs time."

The look she gave him made him wonder if maybe it wasn't just Nugget she was talking about.

But the impossibility of the situation and his rumbling belly pushed him in the direction of the camp. "I guess I'll get back then. Try to hurry. Nugget could also use some breakfast."

At the mention of food, Nugget's head popped up. "They don't want the likes of me at their table."

Then she burrowed back into Annabelle's shoulder.

Annabelle looked up at him. "I'll talk to her."

The memory of Annabelle facing down the woman in the mercantile flashed before him as he realized that his sister would have no greater champion than Annabelle.

"All right." He looked at her. Annabelle needed a champion, too. Unfortunately, it couldn't be him.

Joseph returned to the cabin, where Frank was eating outside with a crowd surrounding them.

"Did you find them?"

"Yes." He took the plate one of the young ladies offered him. "Nugget was hurt by the unkind references to her mother, and Annabelle was making her feel better. She's still grieving over the loss of her parents."

The word *parents* didn't come so hard as it usually

had. Not when he'd seen a little girl crying her eyes out over a mama who was gone. Nugget had woven herself into Joseph's heart, and for the sake of his sister, he had to let go of his discomfort with where she'd come from. But it didn't mean he had to forgive his father.

The older woman, Gertie, stood. "I should go to her and apologize. I'm sure Annabelle could use—"

"No." Joseph looked at Frank, hoping he'd give some assistance. "Annabelle is doing fine, and she…"

Was extremely uncomfortable around Gertie and her family. A person would have to be a fool or blind not to see it. But perhaps it would be indelicate of him to expose her in front of her pa.

Frank nodded. "She's still grieving, Gert."

"You know?" Joseph was grateful he hadn't yet taken a bite of the mouthwatering food in front of him. He'd have choked otherwise.

"Of course I know. I'd be a bad preacher, and an even worse father, if I didn't see how she tries to shut out everyone who loves her. I keep thinking that given enough time, and around the people she used to love, that she'd get over it, but…"

Frank stared down at his feet, and for the first time, Joseph saw him, not as the faith-filled preacher, but as a man who was trying his best for a daughter he couldn't reach.

"How is it that I can't reach my own daughter?"

Annabelle's shameful secret was shared by her father. She feared him knowing, yet he knew. Worse, he blamed himself.

"You can't blame yourself, Frank." Gertie sat beside him and put her arm around him. "She'll heal when the time is right. You just gotta keep praying."

Though Frank didn't seem heartened by Gertie's

words, Joseph realized that in all of this, he hadn't kept his promise to pray for Annabelle. True, it had only been a few hours since he'd decided that he needed to pray for healing in her relationship with God and her pa, but clearly, with Frank's pain so plainly displayed, he needed to be more diligent.

"Sir? If I may…" Joseph took a seat across from Frank. "Perhaps you should talk to her about this. When she held Nugget and let her cry, she said that sometimes a person needs to cry until it's all out. I couldn't help but wonder if Annabelle has had that opportunity."

"Annabelle never cries." Hard eyes stared back at him. Now he knew where Annabelle got it.

"Has anyone ever let her? Have you given her an opening to pour out her heart and share these things rather than let them fester?"

In his own words, he finally saw the truth in Annabelle's actions and words. She was trying so hard to shove down the grief and pain that she couldn't express that it was festering.

Joseph took a deep breath and met Frank's gaze. "Maybe if you talked to her as a father, instead of as a preacher, and just loved her for who she is, instead of her role in your ministry, maybe she could finally heal."

He expected an Annabelle-like outburst to tell him he'd overstepped his bounds. Instead, those eyes softened as Frank said, "Her mother was always so good at that. I'm just as lost as Annabelle without her."

"Then tell her that. I think it would help you both." With that, Joseph turned his attention to his cooling breakfast, knowing that he was dangerously close to interfering more than he ought.

Because as much as he was working toward the reconciliation between Annabelle and her father, he had a feeling that his own homecoming wouldn't be as smooth. Their pa's death would be hard enough to take, but the transition to accepting Nugget as their sister was going to be hard on the rest of his family.

One more thing he needed to be diligent about praying for. As selfish as it sounded, finding his pa's silver would make that acceptance a whole lot easier. But if they had to face poverty with another mouth to feed, he wasn't sure Mary, or anyone else, would be that generous with accepting Nugget.

Chapter Eleven

Annabelle felt stronger as she returned to Gertie's cabin. It wasn't so much that anything had changed, other than the fact that she knew if Nugget was going to be comfortable, she had to be brave. Which meant pretending that it didn't hurt to see Gertie and her children running and laughing like the world was just fine when Annabelle's had ended.

"There they are!" Gertie's cheerful voice rang out, and Annabelle forced herself not to cringe.

"Sorry it took so long." She avoided Joseph's gaze. Joseph, who knew her too well for their short acquaintance, would see right through her.

"You just sit right on down and eat." Gertie handed her a plate while Nugget clung to the back of Annabelle's skirts. But Gertie was wise to that trick. "And you, too, little one. You've got to come out so's I can give you a plate."

Annabelle relaxed slightly as Nugget peeked out. "You're not gonna say mean things to me?"

"No." To Gertie's credit, she squatted down to Nugget's level. "And I shouldn't have said those things about your parents, either. I'm sorry. You must've loved them very much, and I'm sure they must've loved you, too."

Her words brought Nugget out of hiding but didn't remove the suspicious look from her face. "I am mighty hungry."

"Then I have a mighty big helping of breakfast for you."

As Gertie handed Nugget a plate and they all got settled, Annabelle couldn't help but notice Gertie's kindness. Gertie had always been a kind woman. It truly wasn't fair that Annabelle couldn't bear to be around her mother's best friend. She didn't know why it hurt so much, but it did.

Loath to spend any more time here than they had to, Annabelle gobbled up her food as quickly as was polite. At least the first few bites. But she could feel the weight of Joseph's stare on her and she knew.

He knew exactly what she was doing and why. No matter that she hadn't told him the full story. He knew.

Why couldn't he be as oblivious as her father, who sat there, making a whistle out of a twig for the children? He accepted her excuses readily enough, and when she finished eating and suggested that they return home as quickly as possible because Maddie must be worried sick, he would agree.

But Joseph wouldn't.

Tears pricked the backs of her eyes and she tried forcing them away, but they wouldn't listen. She gave them a quick swipe with the back of her hand.

"Is everything all right?"

Of course Gertie would notice.

"The smoke is rather thick, that's all." To prove her point, Annabelle got up and moved to the other side of the fire. But as she passed Joseph, his eyes mocked her.

Stop hiding.

He could add it to the list of her sins.

At least Nugget felt better. She was attacking her breakfast with gusto, enjoying every bite, and completely unaware of everything else around her.

Annabelle didn't want to feel this way. She would've liked to have laughed with Polly at whatever joke Gertie was telling. But the rushing in her ears kept her from being able to even hear it.

Even her father was laughing.

She stabbed some of her eggs, knowing that if Gertie noticed her not eating, there would be questions to answer. If only it didn't taste like slag and there wasn't such a huge lump in her throat to make it difficult to swallow.

"What's your doll's name?" Caitlin had sat on the other side of Nugget and was staring at the tattered rag doll sticking out of the small bag Nugget carried.

"Surprise," Nugget said shyly, but a small smile crinkled her lips. It was good for Nugget to be able to relate to kids her own age. Annabelle knew that. Based on the reception the little girl had gotten in town, she was sure that Nugget probably had few playmates.

"I've got a doll, too. Want to see?"

As Nugget nodded, Caitlin pulled out the one thing sure to shatter the last shards of peace Annabelle had been clinging to.

Bethany. Susannah's favorite china doll.

The plate slipped from Annabelle's hands and crashed into the dirt. Among the remains of her breakfast, she saw spots unlike any she'd ever seen. She'd purposely put that doll in a special place, a place where her father wouldn't find it to give to one of his projects.

Caitlin sat opposite of Nugget, prattling on and on

about how it used to be her very bestest friend's doll, but now it was hers, so she named it Susannah.

A nice gesture that wouldn't bring her sister back.

"Are you all right?" Joseph slipped into the spot next to her and began cleaning up her mess. She could only sit there and stare at it all.

No, she wasn't all right. But she wasn't allowed to say so. She couldn't begrudge a poor child the joy of a precious doll. And yet, she also couldn't find it in her heart to share the child's joy.

What kind of monster was she?

No wonder God didn't listen to her prayers. There was absolutely no good in Annabelle Lassiter.

"Don't worry about it. Your pa and Gertie are over there talking."

His words were meant to reassure, but as she looked over, she noticed her father slipping money into Gertie's hands.

"He's really generous, isn't he?"

Annabelle could only nod. She supposed this generosity of spirit was something to be praised, something clear in the idol worship shining in Joseph's eyes. But what about her? Didn't she have the right to grieve and miss her family? Selfish, yes. But she'd spent so long putting her own needs aside, and just once, she wanted her needs, her prayers, her dreams, to matter.

"What's wrong?" He looked at her with such a caring expression she wasn't sure she could stand it.

"I just want to go home," she whispered.

Joseph nodded. He didn't try to make her stay and face whatever he thought was bothering her.

"I'll talk to your pa." Joseph got up and walked toward her father.

Nugget tugged on her sleeve. "I don't want to go. I

want to stay here with Caitlin. She's going to show me how to fix Susannah's hair."

Annabelle wanted to close her eyes and be transported to anywhere but here. But she was afraid that if she did, she'd see Susannah's smiling face telling her the exact same thing. So she swallowed the lump in her throat.

"I'm sure you'll see her again." Because she would face this irrational emotion. Not for her sake, but for the sake of a little girl who desperately needed a friend.

"When?" Two little girls stared at her, like they were used to promises adults made, but seldom kept. Something she had often been guilty of with Susannah. "Later," she'd tell her sister. Only later never came, and now Susannah was gone, and she'd never be able to do those things with her.

"We'll discuss it with my father."

Who was walking toward them with Joseph and Gertie in tow.

"Joseph says you want to leave. We just got here. Surely you don't want to refuse the MacDonalds' hospitality. You haven't even chatted with Polly yet."

Annabelle closed her eyes. They were supposed to be her family's dearest friends. And once upon a time, before Henry had left with Annabelle's heart, Annabelle and Polly would sit and giggle and admire some of the miners. What had Polly done with the shawl she'd been knitting for Annabelle's wedding trip?

It hardly mattered. There was no wedding, no wedding trip. Henry had gone without Annabelle, all because Annabelle had chosen to nurse her ailing family when the sickness hit. The worst part was, Henry hadn't even said goodbye. Polly had been the one to break the news of Henry's departure.

How could she face her friend now?

She opened her eyes and looked up at Joseph.

"I'm sorry. I didn't sleep well last night, so I'm tired. Of course we can stay."

"What happened to your breakfast?" Gertie pointed at the plate Joseph had cleaned up but hadn't found a way to dispose of yet.

Annabelle stared at the ground. "I'm sorry. I got distracted, and I was clumsy."

She was trying so hard not to offend anyone. To not wrap them up in what was obviously her grief alone. But nothing she did was right. This was why she'd stayed away. Why she couldn't come back. Everything in her hurt, but everyone else had moved on.

"Are you sure you're feeling all right?" Gertie knelt beside her and put a hand on her forehead. "You've looked awfully pale since you got here."

"Nothing a night in my own bed won't cure." She gave another half smile, then closed her eyes and took a deep breath. She would do this. She would make it through the rest of the day in the mining camp, and everything would be just fine.

Her father joined Gertie in front of Annabelle. "She did faint in the middle of Harrison Avenue yesterday. We all thought it was because her corset was too tight, but perhaps she is coming down with something."

The concern in her father's face undid her resolve. She couldn't let him think that his last remaining child was in danger, too. He'd lost so much, and even though she was trying to be brave for his sake, she couldn't have him thinking she was ill.

"Truly, I'm fine." She stood, and at the same time, all the tears she'd been trying to hold back came rushing out. "I just want to go home. I don't want to be here, where everything reminds me of everything I have lost."

The only good thing about crying like this was that she couldn't see anyone's faces to read their expressions. Especially Joseph's. Why his was the most important, she didn't know. But as much as she'd like to save face in front of him, the dam had been breached, and she couldn't stop any of it.

"I miss Susannah. I miss Peter. I miss Mark and John. I miss Mother. And I'm tired of pretending that it's fine. It's not fine."

Nugget wrapped her arms around Annabelle's legs. "It's all right, Miss Annabelle. You can cry just like I did when I was missing my mama. It's all right to miss your mama."

The little girl's kind words sent Annabelle to blubbering like a fool. She had said that very thing to Nugget. *It's all right to miss your mama.* But she had no idea just how powerful those words were until someone said them to her.

Gertie stepped forward and wrapped her arms around her. "Oh, dear heart, I should've thought about that. Of course a young lady would miss—"

Annabelle tried to shrug off the embrace. "Please, Gertie, I can't."

But Gertie only squeezed her tighter, and the tears kept rolling down Annabelle's cheeks faster and faster.

"You have to face this, my girl. You lost your mother, yes, but you have a lot of people who love you. You don't have to lose us, too."

Gertie's words throbbed in Annabelle's ears. Was that what she'd done? In shutting herself off from everything, could she have been making it worse?

Annabelle straightened, and moved out of Gertie's

embrace. This time, the older woman let her go. Annabelle turned and looked at her father, who held out a handkerchief.

"Thank you. I'm sorry, I didn't mean to go on like that." She blew her nose, an action that would horrify her mother, but she supposed her mother would be horrified by a lot of things she'd said and done lately.

Her father wrapped his arms around her. "No, don't be sorry for your tears. I suppose I haven't been very good at helping you grieve."

He kissed the top of her head, the way he did when she was little, and held her tight. "Your mother would have known how to talk to you, but I…I don't know what to say. I miss her more than you can imagine."

Annabelle looked up. Examined the lines in her father's face, noting for the first time that they'd deepened in recent months.

"You never told me."

"I was trying to be strong for you."

His words mirrored her own. Annabelle blinked away the tears. "And I was trying to be strong for you."

Her father pulled a letter from his pocket, the familiar script staring out at her. Aunt Celeste.

"Your aunt has been begging me to let you visit. The Simms family offered to escort you, but I…"

A long sigh shook his body. "I haven't been able to let you go. You're hurting so much, and I can't let you leave broken."

"I'm always going to be broken if I'm here." She looked around, noting that Joseph had taken the little girls closer to the fire, where they played with their dolls, and Joseph amiably chatted with Gertie and Polly.

She wanted to be able to interact with them. To talk

like they did in the old days. But those days were gone, and nothing would ever be the same.

"No," her father said softly. "You're always going to be broken if you leave without fixing this."

But he didn't understand. It wasn't hers to fix. Annabelle hadn't broken anything. She was the one who had been broken.

Annabelle pulled out of his embrace and smoothed her skirts. "So what now? You won't let me leave, and I can't stay."

Her father let out the exasperated sigh she'd grown too used to hearing. "Gertie has been asking us to come up for a while now. I've been making too many excuses. There are a number of parishioners I need to see and I haven't been able to spend nearly the time I'd like up here caring for them."

A familiar tightness closed around Annabelle's lungs. "Please don't ask me to—"

"I'm not asking, I'm telling." Her father stood immovable. "This shouldn't be a chore. You used to beg to spend more time here. No matter how many days you spent up here, you always wanted more. So for you to be so reluctant to stay up here—"

Her father looked her in the eyes, searching in a way that he hadn't done before. "Annabelle, if there is some reason, other than you being upset over the loss in our family, then tell me. Otherwise, we're staying. Long enough for me to finish my work, and, I pray, long enough for you to face the pain that has you so trapped."

And what if she suffocated in the process? Already her lungs felt like they'd been filled with the dreaded slag from the mines. Her eyes burned. And her heart might shrivel up and die completely. That, she supposed, would be a mercy. Maybe then, the pain would stop.

"What will I do while I'm here?" In the past, she'd visited parishioners, helped with Polly's chores, and then she and Polly would be on the lookout for—

Annabelle closed her eyes. Henry was gone, and who knew what had become of Polly's Tom? Regardless, there would be no giggling over weddings and babies.

"Joseph needs your help. If he's going to find his father's silver, he can't have a child underfoot. Mining is dangerous work as it is, and with the man who tried taking Nugget, he needs someone to take care of her."

Meaning Annabelle. And it didn't diminish the threat of the man who wanted to take Nugget.

"So we're still in danger?"

Her father shook his head. "Slade found some good tracks and he's confident that he'll be able to locate the culprit. You and Nugget will be safe enough with Gertie."

Leaving Joseph alone. "But what if the man comes after Joseph?"

"I'm glad to see you care about them. Now for you to start caring about the rest of the people in your life."

Annabelle drew in a breath. "Of course I care about the people in my life. I just…"

The look on her father's face told a different story. He didn't need to say it. She already knew that wallowing in her grief had been selfish. But remembering the sadness on Gertie's face as she reminded Annabelle of the people she'd been shutting out, Annabelle's excuses seemed rather thin.

"You're right. I should be more sociable toward Gertie and her family. I should talk to Polly."

It wouldn't be enough time to repair the breach, but she could make the effort. Maybe she'd even find the words to mend things with Polly. Of all things she regretted, it was that she'd said such harsh things the last time she'd spoken to the girl who'd once been her best friend.

It wasn't Polly's fault Henry had left. She'd merely been the bearer of bad news, and Annabelle had taken her heartbreak out on the other girl.

So many wrongs Annabelle had to make up for.

Her father followed her gaze to where Polly stood. "It would be a good start."

Annabelle swallowed. Her father didn't know the half of what had gone on. He'd been visiting a sick parishioner while Annabelle sobbed the whole story to her dying mother. None of them had realized how little time her mother had left, and sometime in the midst of Annabelle's pain, her mother had died.

She'd already been grieving the losses of Susannah and Peter. But that day, Annabelle had lost the man she'd thought she was going to marry, her best friend, and her mother.

Maybe Gertie was right. Maybe Annabelle hadn't had to lose everything. But as Nugget's laughter rang out across the camp, Annabelle wasn't sure she could risk opening her heart up again. What if she did everything right, and she still lost everything?

Chapter Twelve

Joseph swung the giggling girl in another wide circle.

"More!" Caitlin cried, the air full of her joy.

Nugget stamped her foot. "No! It's my turn."

He set Caitlin down and looked at the little girls. "You've both had turns, and now my arms are tired. Take a break and play with your dolls."

They ran toward the stumps where they'd set the dolls for a nap, and Joseph took a seat on another old stump. He hadn't remembered youngsters being so tiring. Of course his sisters were older, though Bess only by three years. Still, it had been a long time since he'd heard such laughter. Or maybe it only felt that way.

"Joseph!" Frank walked toward him, but Annabelle was nowhere in sight.

Joseph stood. "Is everything all right with Annabelle?" He wanted to kick himself for his impertinence. It wasn't his place to be concerned for her. "I'm sorry, Frank, I had no right."

"You care about my daughter. You have every right." Frank frowned, then looked over at the girls playing before turning his attention back to Joseph.

But this wasn't attention Joseph wanted. He didn't

have the right. Not when he wouldn't be there for someone who clearly needed more stability than Joseph could provide.

"I've tried to be a friend to Annabelle."

Frank nodded slowly. "What are your intentions toward my daughter?"

Joseph sighed. "Friendship is all I have to offer. Back home, I have five sisters and a brother to raise." The giggling girls drew his attention. "And then there's Nugget."

A complication he hadn't dealt with in terms of sharing with his family and figuring out how they were going to incorporate this sweet little girl into their lives. There was no question about his love for Nugget. But telling his siblings, and getting them to accept her...

"Does she know that?" Concern filled Frank's eyes.

He hadn't said so in so many words, but he knew where he stood in terms of Annabelle.

"When we were stuck on the mountain, I proposed in case there were any repercussions to her reputation. She made it clear her answer was no, even if her reputation suffered."

Only Frank stared at him like he was crazy. "Any woman with pride is going to say no under those circumstances." He looked at Joseph hard. "But the way you take up for her, it's got to make her wonder if your feelings aren't deeper."

They were. But feelings didn't make for a decent marriage. He couldn't be the kind of husband she or any other woman deserved.

"I'm sure she understands."

But as the words came out of his mouth, he wondered if this was what Annabelle felt sometimes. Wanting to give the right answer, but not sure if he himself believed it.

Joseph shook his head. "I'll be sure she's clear on my plans."

The preacher looked at him with the same kind of look Joseph often gave Annabelle. He didn't believe him for a second. "It's been my experience that love doesn't always follow people's plans."

Love? That's not what he and Annabelle had.

But Frank didn't give him a chance to refute that statement. Gertie was striding toward them, clearly intent on whatever purpose that brought her.

"Is everything all right?" Frank's attention to Gertie clearly indicated that their conversation was over, as well.

Joseph started in the direction where Gertie had come from.

"Everything's fine." Gertie held a hand out. "I was coming to let you know the living arrangements up here. Annabelle's going to watch Nugget while you search for your pa's silver."

"I'd thought to have Nugget with me." Joseph glanced in the direction of the two girls playing. His sister seemed to be thriving in this environment, but with everything, he didn't want her far from him.

"It would make more sense if Nugget stayed here." Gertie smiled, then glanced in the direction of the girls playing in the distance. "The mountains are no place for a child. With the trouble you faced at the cabin, it's even more dangerous. You'll be able to avoid the bandits easier if you don't have a child to protect. And, well, I could use the company for Caitlin. She's been lost without Susannah, and this is the longest I've seen a smile on her face since."

The longing on the older woman's face would have

been enough to get him to say yes, even if he'd been in-clined to say no.

As much as it pained him to admit it, Gertie was right. He wouldn't be able to protect his sister and find his pa's treasure.

"Annabelle won't mind?"

Frank and Gertie exchanged an uneasy look. Of course Annabelle minded. She'd made it clear that she'd rather be anywhere but here.

"She understands the importance of keeping Nugget safe," Frank finally said.

Not the same as not minding, but Joseph was hardly in a position to argue Annabelle's cause.

Her father was already concerned about the possibility of Annabelle falling in love with him. Even if Annabelle thought nothing of it, he had to be careful of people's talk. And of taking up for her out of simple human decency, that's what it was. But her father didn't seem to understand.

"It's settled then." Gertie gave him a wide smile.

What kind of life would it be with people around them who cared about one another? Annabelle had no idea how fortunate she was.

"Come on, girls," Gertie called in a booming voice, and they came running.

He hadn't seen such a big smile on Nugget's face before. It had to have been a hard life, living the way she had. He hadn't asked a lot about what had gone on in that situation. He hadn't really wanted to. It was too painful to hear about the woman who had stolen his pa's affections.

They walked back to the main area, back to the noise and chaos of the mining camp. They stopped at a tent a couple of yards from Gertie's cabin.

"This is where you'll be sleeping," she said with authority. "My boys sleep here in the summer. It's plenty warm when the weather's nice. They're already up working with Collin. The wages are good, and it's enough until Collin makes his own strike."

"And then he'll work that mine?"

"My, no." Gertie smiled in the same indulgent way she looked at the girls. "Pretty much all of the mines here are owned by the big companies. It's too expensive to buy the equipment needed to get the silver. That's the real dream here. To find a big enough strike that someone will buy it and you can go retire somewhere. I've got a sister in Denver, and it sure would be nice to be closer to her."

He hadn't thought of it that way. Of what would happen if he struck silver. "So why would my pa be hiding the fact that he found silver if he was going to sell it to the corporation?"

Gertie shrugged. "Either it wasn't quite enough to interest the corporations, or he was digging deeper to find a higher price." She looked deep in thought for a moment, and then looked at him. "Or the land he was prospecting wasn't his own."

She gave a quick nod and half smile as she looked over at Nugget. "No disrespect to your pa intended. It happens, though."

"Would it explain the people after Nugget?"

Gertie shrugged. "Perhaps. We can talk about that once we get settled."

Gertie pointed to the cabin across the small fire pit area. "That's where Nugget will be sleeping. She'll be sharing the loft with Annabelle, Polly and Caitlin."

Nugget's face lit up. "You mean it? I get to stay here with Caitlin?"

Both girls squealed with delight, not waiting for a response, but running into the cabin.

"I'd rather have Nugget in my tent. To protect her."

Gertie shook her head. "I'm afraid that wouldn't look proper. I know she's your sister and all, but being that she came from a woman of—" she mouthed the words *ill repute* "—folks wouldn't be comfortable with her in a tent full of men."

Laughter erupted from inside the cabin. "Besides, you won't deny the girls the pleasure of each other's company, will you? It'll be so good for Caitlin."

The happiness emanating from the girls was almost enough to convince him. But Gertie didn't seem to understand how dangerous the situation was.

"But will they be safe?"

Though Gertie looked offended at the question, he had to ask. She hadn't been at the cabin when those men tried taking Nugget.

"Annabelle and Polly will be up there, too. There's no better shot than Annabelle. And Polly, well, this miner tried taking advantage of her at the creek one day, and let me tell you. She done such a number on him that he left town."

Gertie's warm laugh shook her belly. "No, you won't find a safer place for Nugget than with Annabelle and Polly."

He peered inside the tent he'd be sharing with Gertie's sons. "It's awfully cramped. Are you sure I'm not imposing?"

He stood and looked back at Gertie, who'd crossed her arms across her chest.

"You've been giving me all these reasons why you can't, or why this is a bad idea, but let me tell you. You won't find a better offer or a safer place. You'll be well taken care of, but if you can't accept that, then maybe you want to take your chances on your own. I guarantee you will be looking over your shoulder every night. Get much past our encampment, and you'll find plenty willing to slit your throat over a day's wages. Folks find out you've got information on a mine, well…they'll do that and plenty worse if they think it'll get them out of this place."

Her words shamed him. She was only trying to be nice. He'd just been thinking about the wonderful hospitality, and here he was spitting on it.

"I'm truly sorry for any offense. You have to understand, we're not used to this kind of treatment. Back home, our own family and church is barely lifting a hand to help us. Where I come from—"

"This isn't where you come from," Gertie said. "Why do you think we're all here? Every person in this place has come looking to build a better life. I know there are some who think that living in a cabin and taking in wash is no life, but one of these days, we'll be able to afford a house. Maybe it won't be one of those big mansions, but it will be our house."

Wouldn't that be nice? A home where he and all of his siblings could be together without Aunt Ina breathing down their necks, barking orders and threatening them all the time.

If anyone could sell him on the dream of mining, it was Gertie. But then, he didn't need her words to convince him. He already had a mission of his own. Six sisters and a brother, all of whom who needed him. As much as he'd like to find a dream of his own to follow, that wasn't possible right now.

"Thank you, Gertie. I really do appreciate all you've done for us."

"Mama, we're hungry." Caitlin ran to them and tugged at her skirts.

"There's an extra biscuit or two in the cabin." She smiled at her daughter and patted her on the head as she raced off. "We don't do a proper noon meal here, on account of everyone being up at the mine. But I fix them all a good lunch to take with them. Supper's at dusk, and you'll want to be prompt with the way my boys eat."

She looked at him. "I know you won't be going up to the mine, but I'll still pack your lunch all the same. Mind you get home by dusk. As safe as we've made it, it's still not a good idea to go wandering about by yourself."

Her words reminded him of the bandits and the danger they faced. Yes, this was the best option. Frank reappeared. "I've got some visiting to do. Why don't you come with me so I can give you the lay of the land?"

Joseph nodded. They'd wasted so much time already. Though it had done his heart good to see Nugget so happy, it'd do him even better to have her safely settled.

As they walked back to the horses, Joseph asked quietly, "Any word on the men who were after Nugget?"

Frank shrugged. "Slade isn't back yet. I'd put Gertie and Annabelle up against any man if it meant keeping a child safe."

Though he knew firsthand how capable Annabelle was of keeping Nugget safe, it didn't cause him to worry any less. Not with the attempt against Nugget, and the niggling feeling in the back of his mind about his father's death. If someone was going to this length to find his father's silver, his father's death was looking less and less like an accident. Which meant the danger they faced was far greater than they were imagining.

Chapter Thirteen

Annabelle approached the creek where Polly was working on the wash. Lumps of rock lodged in her throat, preventing her from speaking. Not that she had any idea of what to say. What separated them called for a whole lot more than a simple, "I'm sorry."

"Hello, Polly."

Polly didn't look up from the shirt she was scrubbing. "Annabelle."

"I'm gonna be here for a while, I guess, so I thought maybe I could help you with your chores."

Brushing her arm against her forehead, Polly looked up. "Don't make no nevermind to me."

No, there was no easy fix for this. "I'm sorry about what happened, you know, when—" Annabelle swallowed. "I shouldn't have said those things to you. You were just trying to help."

"You accused me of lying about Henry to deliberately hurt you."

The words reverberated in Annabelle's head. The sight of her best friend, her face whiter than the snow she'd been standing in, filled Annabelle's vision.

Annabelle grabbed a shirt and started working. "I

said a lot of things I didn't mean. I couldn't imagine that Henry would simply leave without me. Not when he knew I'd just lost Peter and Susannah and Mother was so sick."

Pouring out her heart seemed almost easier when she had her hands occupied. She turned her attention to a spot that wouldn't come out. "I was wrong to accuse you of being anything but a friend. I'm sorry."

"You're going to tear a hole in it." Polly's voice interrupted her thoughts, and she stared down at the shirt.

"I can't get this spot out," she said, holding it up for inspection.

"It'll do." Polly took the shirt out of her hands and stalked over to where she had the other clean shirts drying.

Annabelle sighed and brushed the stray curls off her face. An apology would never be enough to mend the damage she'd done.

Polly turned and stared at her. "You barely knew Henry. Sure, he was handsome and charming and helped you deliver things to your father's parishioners. But we'd known each other our whole lives. And you'd call me a liar before you'd believe that your precious Henry would betray you."

Annabelle deserved every bit of the ire directed at her. Probably even more than that. "I was wrong," she said again, but Polly had returned to her work.

"What next?" she called over her shoulder at Polly.

"Go find my ma and tell her to put you to work elsewhere. You're slowing me down. I'll never get all this done with you around." Polly gestured to the pile of laundry.

"I'm sorry. If there's anything I can do…" She looked

for any sign of understanding in her former friend, but Polly merely frowned at her.

"Just go."

The camp was quiet as Annabelle returned to Gertie's cabin. Everyone was probably up working in the mines. With such good weather, they were probably trying to get as much extra work done as they could.

"Hey, pretty lady." An obviously drunken miner stumbled out of a tent. Disheveled, and smelling more like liquor than the mines, he reached for her with hands knotted with age. An old-timer, most likely. But who could tell with the way this place prematurely aged people.

She turned to go between the tents, but another miner stepped from behind the tent she was trying to go around. Younger, the sandy-haired man also reeked of drink.

"What's your hurry?"

Her father hadn't given her a gun to replace the one that had been in her saddlebag. Which would be a problem living in the camp. She'd gotten proficient at scaring men off with a quick wave of the pistol.

"I need to get back to my friend's cabin. She's expecting me."

The men moved closer, sandwiching her in. "We can't have no delay, now can we?"

Even with considerable distance between them, she could smell the younger man's foul breath. She looked for an escape route.

"Aw, pretty birdie wants to fly the coop," the man in front of her said with the kind of leer that spelled trouble.

This was precisely why young ladies did not venture beyond certain boundaries unescorted.

Her momentary lapse in looking for an escape gave

the man behind her the opportunity to bump into her, pushing her closer to his friend. He might have looked like an old-timer, but he was quick.

"We don't mean no harm," he whispered, his foul odor stinging her nostrils. "Just tell us where the silver is."

Naturally. That's all anyone in this crazy place wanted.

"I don't know anything about any silver," she said stiffly, realizing that a hard object was pressed into her back. A gun.

She tried to take a deep breath to calm herself, but the gun pressed deeper into her back.

"What'd you find at the cabin?" the man rasped into her ear and pushed her forward into his friend.

"Nothing. It was just a cabin." She tried to keep her voice steady, calm. These were no ordinary ruffians, but dangerous men who clearly knew much more about her activities than mere happenstance.

The man in front of her grinned an ugly toothless grin as he rubbed his stubbled chin. "And silver is just a rock."

As his eyes narrowed, she recognized him as one of the men who frequented her father's Wednesday night dinners.

"I know you." She stared at him harder, trying to remember if she knew his name. There were just so many, coming and going, and with trying to stay unattached...

"Our family has done you great kindness. Please repay that kindness and let me go."

Her words only made the man's sneer deepen. Perhaps it had been the wrong thing, to ask for repayment for what they'd done.

"We'll give you kindness, sweet lady." The man behind her rubbed up against her in a vulgar motion that sent her stomach rolling. "You tell us where the silver is, and we won't share you with our friends."

Annabelle gritted her teeth. "I told you, I don't know about any silver. I was merely showing Joseph where his father's cabin was so that he could claim his father's personal effects."

Toothless gave her a murderous look. "We seen him in the mercantile yesterday buying mining supplies with the good preacher. So no more lies. Where's the silver?"

She glared at him and tried to shake free of his friend, but the man pressed the gun harder into her back.

"If he had really found any silver, do you think that cabin would have been as desolate as we found it? Don't you think he would have spent some of it on something nice for his daughter? You know miners. There's no silver."

Her words seemed to catch the miner who held the gun to her back off-guard because the pressure loosened and he hesitated.

"You think she's telling the truth?" The waver in his voice was all she needed.

In a quick motion, Annabelle stomped back, using the heel of her boot to dig into the man's leg, then darted past Toothless. As she rounded the corner past his arms, her heel broke, but she kept running, hoping Toothless would be more concerned about his friend's yowls.

"I'm going to get you, she-cat."

Annabelle ran, dashing between cabins, hoping that somehow the weaving would keep him from catching her. A short distance, and she'd be at Gertie's.

"Gertie!" she yelled as loudly as she could.

"Your friend ain't gonna help you, so save yerself the trouble."

"Help!" Annabelle hoped the word would get someone in the area to come to her aid. She rounded the corner, feeling her ankle in the broken boot give way.

Oh, how she'd wanted these fashionable boots. But what good were they doing her with a bandit after her? At least she'd worn the sensible dress Maddie had forced upon her.

"Please," Annabelle yelled again. "Someone help me!"

A man stepped out of the cabin nearest her.

"What seems to be the problem?" Though his face was grizzled, his voice was kind.

"There's a man…" She gestured behind her at Toothless, who'd slowed up. "He and his friend had a gun. They were trying to hurt me."

Her savior stepped past her. "That you, Bart?"

Bart. Now she had a name for her father and the sheriff.

"Just a misunderstanding." Bart gave a grin that made her stomach turn, then headed in the opposite direction.

The man nodded and looked over at Annabelle. "You're all right now. Bart don't mean no one no harm."

Oh, yes, he did. But she didn't need to belabor that point with this stranger.

"Thank you, sir." She offered a small smile as she nodded and turned toward the direction of Gertie's cabin.

No one was at Gertie's cabin, making her more grateful the unknown man had come to her rescue.

She sat on one of the logs and examined the damage to her boot. The heel had been torn clean off. Her foot… For the first time since the initial pain of twisting it, she realized that it throbbed. And was swelling rapidly.

"Gertie?" She called the woman's name but received silence in return.

Annabelle leaned back and closed her eyes. Maybe if she took a few deep breaths it wouldn't hurt so bad.

The crunch of shoes on gravel jolted her out of her tiny rest. If the men had been following her, they probably realized she was completely alone.

"Please. I've already told you I don't know where the silver is. So just leave me be."

Maybe she truly was a coward, but she couldn't bear to open her eyes and face the victorious sneers of evil men who were going to triumph because Annabelle hadn't truly embodied the Christlike behavior she had been supposed to model.

"What happened?" Slade's soft voice jolted her, and she looked up, but not directly at him.

"Some men accosted me."

He had no reason to take up her cause, so the less she said the better.

"About the silver?" He knelt before her and touched her broken boot. "How bad is it?"

Pain shot through her. "Ow!" She jerked out of his grasp.

"Yes, about the silver. That ridiculous metal that has blinded everyone to decency."

His face contorted as though he'd been wounded more than her ankle hurt.

"I'm sorry, I didn't mean—"

"Yes, you did," he said quietly. "You've been seething in hate for months now. But I'm going to fix your ankle anyway."

Tears rolled down her face.

He took her foot, not at all gently, and attempted to

unlace her boot. Even Slade was ignoring what she had to say based on the prejudice she'd expressed.

She should have listened to his side of the story. "What happened that night?"

Something glittered in Slade's eyes when he looked up at her. If she hadn't been so stubborn, they'd have had this talk long ago.

"When I got to Doc Stein's house, he was passed out drunk. So I went to the hospital to see if they could spare someone. But they were busy with the influx of their own patients. I was told to bring everyone there."

Slade shook his head slowly, fumbling with the lace. "I'm going to have to cut this off. I know you prize these boots, but there's no other way."

"It's all right. They're just boots. And they're ruined anyway." Annabelle shrugged, then looked at him.

Really looked at him. Pain filled his face, and she realized that all this time, all the hurt she'd been feeling over her family's deaths, Slade had been feeling, too.

Everyone was hurting. But all Annabelle had been able to see was her own pain.

"I want to hear the rest. About the silver."

He pulled a knife out of his boot as he nodded slowly. "On my way back, I headed to the livery to get a wagon to take everyone to the hospital. I took a shortcut through State Street and got caught in the middle of a gunfight between two men arguing over a poker game. One got away, but the other..."

Pain filled his face, and for a moment, Annabelle forgot that she'd vowed to hate Slade forever. He'd been her brother's best friend, and until she'd decided to blame him for Peter's death, a good man.

"I did the best I could for him, but..."

Slade's hand stilled on her foot. "He pressed a bag

of silver in my hand and asked that I send it home to his wife. It was the last thing he said before he died."

He had been doing a kindness for a stranger. She'd hated him for his selfishness when all he'd been doing was a good deed. Annabelle hadn't thought it possible to feel more shame over her actions, but it was so strong she thought she might burst of it.

"I didn't—"

"Don't." He looked up at her with watery eyes. "Somehow I thought it would make a difference if I stayed with him until the sheriff came. I was worried about a dead man, when I should have been getting Peter to the doctor. I never imagined he would go so quickly. Your pa has told me over and over that it probably still wouldn't have saved him, but I can't help but wonder if I'd done it any differently…"

All this time, she'd been casting stones, when poor Slade had been casting them at himself. He hadn't needed her to make him feel bad when he was already doing a fine enough job of it himself.

"You did what you could," she told him quietly. "And I apologize for saying otherwise."

Slade nodded slowly. "What you saw that night was me giving the silver and information about the dead man to your pa so he could track down the family. Frank was going crazy with grief and I thought that giving him something to do would help. I never realized how much I would hurt you."

Her chest ached, and the weight of her actions pressed on her shoulders heavier than any of the boulders in the area. "I should have heard you out."

"Well, now you have." His lips twisted in a sort of grimace, and he finished taking off her boot. As he turned his focus to her injured ankle, she realized the injustice she'd done him. Her family had adopted Slade into their own because he'd had no one. Peter had been a brother to him.

Annabelle should have been comforting him, and they should have worked through all of this together.

"I'm sorry it took so long for us to talk," she said, knowing that being sorry didn't make it any better. "I hope someday you'll be able to forgive me."

The look he gave her was enough to slay her. "Already have."

If his words were intended to make her feel better, he had failed completely. Because now, she felt so much worse for having had the conversation.

Before she could think of anything to say to give him some comfort and heal the rift between them, he changed the subject.

"Your father says those men were after Bad Billy's silver. Was the little girl able to tell you anything about it?"

Annabelle shook her head. As Slade pushed on a particularly painful spot on her foot, tears sprang to her eyes.

Slade stopped his ministrations to her ankle. "I don't think it's broken, but you've definitely injured yourself. I'll see if Gertie has anything we can wrap it with."

He stood, then looked down at her. "When I get back, we'll talk more about the men who were after you. Now that you don't hate me, maybe we can fix this together."

Though she should have been gratified to know that there were rifts in her life she could fix, the nagging pain in her heart hadn't diminished. She wondered if it ever would.

Chapter Fourteen

Exhaustion had set in before the mining camp was in view. Joseph glanced at Frank, who looked even more weary. The older man hadn't been able to stop worrying about Annabelle.

Even Joseph wasn't sure about the best course of action for her. Especially the more he mulled over Frank's words to him about his behavior toward the beautiful girl. Closer to the camp, he realized that it wasn't so much that he was looking forward to being reunited with his sister and finding the silver, but that he'd get to see the smile that continued to haunt his mind.

Before they were within eyesight of Gertie's cabin, a ball of energy hurled herself at him.

"Joseph! You're back!"

Despite the fatigue, he dismounted, then picked Nugget up and whirled her in a big hug. "I think you've grown since this morning."

Nugget giggled. "Papa used to say that, too."

Her words didn't sting the way the comparisons to his pa used to. Time, and Nugget's love, had begun to heal that wound. Not that he was willing to fully forgive him, but at least he could accept his sister's love for the man.

He set Nugget down, then held her hand as he led his horse to the cabin. "Did you have a good day?"

"Yes, but Annabelle got hurt so now Caitlin and I have to stay close." Her lip jutted out in a tiny pout.

Frank stepped forward. "What's this about Annabelle getting hurt?"

"She hurt her foot, and Mr. Slade put a bandage on it." Nugget skipped along without realizing the import of her words.

But both Joseph and Frank picked up their speed. With the way Annabelle had shot daggers at Slade earlier, chances were any interaction between them had resulted in bloodshed.

But Annabelle sat by the fire, Slade next to her, chatting almost amiably.

"Annabelle?" Frank handed the reins to Joseph and dashed toward his daughter. "What happened? Are you all right?"

A wan smile he didn't recognize crossed her face. "I hurt my ankle. Slade says I'll be fine." She glanced at Slade and gave him a look Joseph didn't understand.

Joseph could hardly believe the way their interaction had completely changed in less than twelve hours.

Polly huffed past them. "I'm sure she's fine. She was when she left me at the creek with all the work to finish."

Annabelle stiffened at the words, and any hint of the ease he'd seen in her earlier had disappeared. Slade scooted closer to her. Even though that should have made him feel better, it brought a new sense of unease to him. What was the relationship between Annabelle and Slade?

None of his business.

He had no right to wonder what may or may not be

going on between them. Annabelle wasn't his to claim even if he wanted to.

Her father, though, wasn't going to let it go so easily. "It's nice to see you two together again."

Together again...well, that probably said it all. His chest tightened, and even though he'd like to blame it on the altitude...

How had he developed such feelings for Annabelle so quickly? Especially when he had no right to do so.

"I have a lot of amends to make," Annabelle said quietly. "It was time I listened to Slade instead of judging him."

Even though everyone wanted to see Annabelle in a harsh light, the reality was that she was struggling through a difficult time and doing the best she could to keep it all together. Her admission was a measure of the remarkable strength she had.

If only his circumstances were different.

Slade stood. "Frank, I'd like you and Joseph to take a walk with me. We need to talk about Annabelle's injury."

He looked at Nugget pointedly, and Joseph's stomach sank. They'd left the women and children unprotected. And sure, he knew Annabelle was far better at taking care of herself than he was, but there was something about not being there that made Annabelle's injury feel like a grievous sin.

Once they were out of earshot of the tent, Slade stopped.

"Annabelle was accosted by two thugs. She said she recognized them as men who frequented Frank's mission. One of the men in camp referred to him as Bart."

Frank shook his head. "Not Bart Wallace?"

"Annabelle's description seemed to match. And from

what she said about the other guy, I think it's Pokey Simpkins with him." Slade looked around, then continued.

"I went to talk to them, but they're gone. I imagine they've met up with whoever they're working with. They're not bright enough to be working alone. Plus, Annabelle says they don't look like the guy who tried to take Nugget."

Though Slade's words gave Joseph reason to be concerned, there was also more to give him hope. "So they believe there's silver?"

Slade nodded, but put a finger to his lips. "From what I was able to find out about the claims in the area, including where I found some equipment, it all belonged to your father. I saw signs of a lot of digging and burying."

"So he or someone else was hunting for silver." Joseph had to believe that this meant he could resolve things with his pa's estate sooner rather than later and then he could get home to his family.

Frank also looked around before speaking. "But if all they were doing is prospecting, they wouldn't have bothered covering it up. Usually folks just leave the holes."

"Exactly," Slade said, then motioned for them to keep walking. "Someone found something somewhere, but is trying to keep it a secret. There are dozens of holes, and there's no reason why everything should be covered like that. He's gone to great pains to make sure no one else finds his silver."

Silver. More reason to believe in the security of his family's future.

"What do I do next?" Joseph looked to both men, who clearly had more experience in such matters, for guidance.

Slade looked at him. "I think you'd be wise to not

go it alone. Not without knowing who Bart and Pokey are working with."

Annabelle wasn't safe. She'd gotten away from her attackers today, but what happened when someone else came for her? Or Nugget?

"They're not going to stop until they get the silver, are they?"

Slade shook his head. "I can't see why they would. Greed does things to a man."

No wonder Annabelle was so against mining. Joseph didn't need to be rich. All he asked was to be able to provide a home and a way to make a living to support his brother and sisters.

He looked over at Frank, hoping to hear the man's wisdom on the subject. Frank looked utterly exhausted.

"What do you think, Frank?"

The older man frowned. "I can't understand why whoever is behind this is going to so much trouble. And to endanger my daughter after everything we've done for them..."

Frank ran his hand down his face. "I don't know. Some days I wonder if Annabelle is right and we're wasting our time. But I believe the Lord has called me to be here working in these people's lives."

The life returned to his face, and for a moment, Joseph envied Frank the sureness of his calling from the Lord.

Frank straightened, as though God had again confirmed the calling. "I think you'd be wrong to give up. Your father clearly found something, and I truly believe he intended to provide for his family. I know a few trustworthy men who'd be willing to provide assistance if you'd be willing to share some of what you find."

"Of course," Joseph readily agreed. "I don't ask for

much. I'd never hoped to find a treasure. Just enough to get a place where I can raise my brother and sisters without wondering where their next meal is going to come from or how I'm going to get new shoes for the little ones."

If only Annabelle could understand that. She'd spoken of the greed of the miners, but what about the ones like Gertie's family, who wanted nothing more than to provide for their children?

"I'll talk to Collin and his boys, then." Frank looked over at Slade. "You'd be willing to help Joseph, wouldn't you?"

"Naturally." Slade gave an easy grin. "Now that Annabelle's speaking to me again, I'd like to learn a little more about the man who's stolen her heart."

"I haven't stolen anything," Joseph insisted. "Besides, aren't the two of you—"

Slade and Frank started laughing. "Annabelle?" Slade finally sputtered. "She's like a sister to me. I lost my own kin a long time ago, and when the Lassiters took me in, I was part of a family again."

Now it was Joseph's turn to be embarrassed. And worried. With the way his mind had been playing tricks on him over Annabelle all day, this latest turn made it nearly impossible for him to admit he didn't have feelings for her. The only trouble was that it changed nothing in his life.

When he found the silver, he had a responsibility to uphold.

"Well, that's all Annabelle can be to me, too," he told both men, the words like a foul medicine on his tongue. "She's a wonderful girl, but it's just not meant to be."

Frank's voice was soft. "You could bring your family here."

He looked over at Frank. "What made you think of that?"

"Just thinking. You've told me that's your priority, and that you intended to take them from Ohio anyway. Why not bring them here? There's plenty of things needed in Leadville, good jobs, so if you wanted to pursue my daughter, there's nothing stopping you."

Frank's earnestness almost made him want to believe. But there were so many unknowns. Too many things he had to work out and plan for. He couldn't allow himself the luxury of even thinking about falling in love until after he had his family's future settled.

"That's a fine idea, and perhaps we will decide to stay. But there's much more to consider. Courting Annabelle is not one of them."

"Maybe you should talk to Annabelle about that first," Frank stated.

"And maybe you should let my business be my business. I've already told you that I'll be careful with your daughter's heart, but that's all I'm going to do in Annabelle's direction. It's all I can do."

"But what about your heart?" Frank's quiet question was one he'd already made up his mind on.

"My heart is with my family. My responsibility is to them first."

Joseph cleared the lump forming in his throat. "Let's get back to more important business. Like our next move in finding my father's silver."

With this talk of love and hearts and things best left alone, it was more reason time was of the essence. They were engaged in a dangerous game with everything at stake. No room for any of the impossibilities Frank wanted to discuss.

Slade pulled a map out of his pocket. "Based on what

I could see, Bad Billy seemed to have a lot of claims near the Eastern side of Mosquito Pass and around his cabin. The area near the cabin is where things looked dug up and buried, but as far as I can tell, there's no evidence there's actually any silver there." He pointed to a corner of the crinkled paper. "But there's this one, all alone, in the center of claims owned by Slim Deckert."

Frank rubbed his chin. "Slim probably didn't like the idea that Billy purchased a claim in the center of his claims."

"Billy didn't buy it," Slade stated matter-of-factly. "He won it in a poker game against Slim."

Poker. Joseph shouldn't be surprised that his pa would engage in such activity, given that he'd fathered a child by a soiled dove. But surely there had to be an end to the sinful legacy left by his father.

"I remember that game," Frank said. "Slim was fighting mad over the deal and tried accusing Billy of cheating. But Lon was there, and he'd said it was a fair game."

Slade nodded. "It's the same mine where Billy died."

"Or was killed," Frank said somberly.

Now, more than ever, Joseph was convinced that his pa had been murdered. And with the attempted kidnapping of Nugget and the attack on Annabelle, whoever was after the silver was willing to get it at any cost.

Chapter Fifteen

Polly's dismissal and subsequent lie about what happened at the creek stung. Annabelle had said unkind things to Polly. And yes, she deserved to be punished for her thoughtlessness. But that didn't mean it was right for Polly to be so nasty to her at the creek and then lie to everyone about it.

"How's your foot?" Gertie asked, the familiar kindness in her voice not nearly as painful as her foot.

"It's fine, thanks." Annabelle tried to stand, but Gertie shook her head and clucked at her.

"You sit right back down and put this compress on it. Polly may think you're faking it, but a foot doesn't swell up to twice the size of the other on its own."

Gertie handed her the compress, and Annabelle tried not to wince. Still, it was some comfort to know that Polly's poison hadn't completely taken hold.

"I'm sorry for the inconvenience. I truly appreciate your kindness," Annabelle said, not knowing what else to say.

Gertie brushed her hands on her apron, then frowned. "I need to get supper started. I'd ask you to mind the girls, but I suppose you can't go chasing after them."

Yes, a lot had changed in her relationship with Gertie. As much as she'd thought it wouldn't matter, given all of the hurt Annabelle felt, she'd come to realize that it actually did, quite a lot.

"I could help with supper," Annabelle offered. "I assist Maddie all the time."

"Can you peel potatoes?"

"Of course." Annabelle smiled. "And as far as minding the little ones, why, they can help."

Just then, the little girls came bounding over, huge smiles on their faces. "Annabelle! Guess what we found?"

Nugget held out a sticky handful of tangled wildflowers.

"Lovely." Annabelle smiled at the little girl. When her foot got better, they'd have to go flower picking again.

"We brought these for you to feel better," Caitlin said shyly.

Annabelle closed her eyes for a moment, giving herself time to collect her thoughts. Yes, her heart hurt, but she had to remember that poor Caitlin had lost someone, too.

"Thank you so much, Caitlin." She made a big show of smelling the flowers, even though they were just a bunch of weeds. Still, as she gave an appreciative, "Mmm...beautiful," the smiles she was rewarded with made it worthwhile.

"Now that I've got my flowers, you two wash up and you can help prepare supper."

"All right," Nugget said with a smile. "Come on, Caitlin. If we're real good, and there's biscuits, Annabelle might let us help roll them out. Annabelle makes the best biscuits."

The compliment warmed Annabelle's heart, and for a moment, she wished she hadn't been so wrapped up in her own life that she'd failed to do such with her sister. Of course, their mother had, which was where Annabelle had gotten the idea to do it with Nugget.

"You're good with them," Gertie said quietly. "Your mother would be proud."

She looked up at the older woman. "At least I've done something right. I know she wouldn't be proud of how I've been shutting everyone out. I hope you know I'm trying to do better."

Slade's story earlier in the day had made her realize that Gertie, too, probably harbored unspoken grief over her family's losses.

"I know you are," Gertie said quietly. "I just hope you learn to do it for your sake, not for hers."

She turned, then handed Annabelle a sack of potatoes. "Your father was too generous. I invited a few other families for dinner tonight, so you can fix them all. We'll fry them up with the venison the boys brought back yesterday and it'll be a wonderful meal."

Gertie turned her back before Annabelle could respond, and she knew that tonight's dinner with all the other families would be equally uncomfortable. She'd try to put on a brave face, and hope that no one said anything that tore at the tiny pieces of her heart she was trying desperately to hold together.

The sound of gravel crunching beneath someone's boot drew Annabelle's attention. She looked up to see Joseph approaching.

"How's the foot?" Joseph bent down as if he was going to tweak her nose or something, but then straightened, like he'd thought better of it.

"I'll be fine, thanks."

The girls returned, fortunate, since she could tell by the light in Joseph's eyes that he was probably going to say something to dispute her claim.

"Joseph! I'm gonna help Annabelle fix supper!" Nugget's clear voice made it impossible to feel too sorry for herself. Though she'd done a lot of things wrong over the past couple of days, at least this was clearly one area in which she'd done all right.

Concern littered his face. "Are you sure you should be doing anything with your injured foot?"

"I'm just peeling potatoes," she told him with a smile. "I can do that sitting."

"I'll help." Joseph sat next to her in the dirt. Did he have any idea how charming that grin was? Why couldn't he be doing something useful with his life like being a banker or a teacher or a blacksmith or, well, just about anything other than a miner? As soon as he found silver, Joseph would leave, taking Nugget, and where would that leave her?

She turned away before he could see that her cheeks were feeling a bit warm. Surely she was as red as fire.

And really! She shouldn't have been thinking such thoughts about Joseph anyway. About any man. Here, of all places. Where she'd met Henry and carelessly given her heart away knowing so little about him. She'd not make that mistake again.

Stronger in her convictions, Annabelle turned back to Joseph. "Haven't you ever heard that too many cooks spoil the broth?" She dug in the bag of potatoes and began peeling the first one. "Nugget, have you ever peeled a potato?"

The little girl shook her head, and Caitlin stared at her wide-eyed. "Mama says knives aren't for little girls."

Unfortunately, that was just the right amount of inducement Joseph needed. "You girls fetch us some water and I'll help Miss Annabelle."

Miss Annabelle. Her cheeks heated again, which was absolutely silly, given the close quarters in which she'd found herself with him over the past day or so. She was used to much more familiarity from him, and yet, moving to more formal address felt… Something prickled in her heart, stinging and leaving her more alone than ever. Why had she thought that opening her heart to a friend would be a good idea?

The knife slipped in her hand, nearly nicking her skin. Why did she always have to be so clumsy around him?

Her father entered the campsite, and he looked at Joseph, then at her, almost as though he was signaling Joseph in some way. Joseph gave a quick nod.

Joseph cleared his throat. "Miss Annabelle, if I may, I'd like to escort you to the creek for some water."

Did he grow daft all of a sudden? They'd just sent the— Annabelle glanced at her father, who nodded. Of course. Her father had something he wanted to have Joseph talk to her about. Right now, her heart couldn't take any kind of talk. Especially not one encouraged by her father.

Annabelle lifted her swollen foot. "While I do appreciate your kind offer, you might recall that I'm unable to put any weight on my foot."

Polite enough to satisfy even the stodgiest of matrons. She was very tempted to stick her tongue out at both Joseph and her father for being such meddling oafs, but that would only prove just how childish she was. Annabelle sighed.

Fortunately, Joseph looked just as relieved as she felt at the prospect of not having to go to the creek together—code for having a little chat, she was now certain.

"I'd forgotten. Please accept my apologies."

"Certainly." She smiled in the direction of her father. Annabelle dropped a peeled potato in the pot.

"You thoughtless wretch!" Polly grabbed the pot off the ground and glared at Annabelle. "Have you any idea how wasteful you're being? Look how much potato you've taken off with the peel!"

The insides that had finally begun to feel more comfortable in this place knotted up. "I meant no harm," Annabelle stammered. "This is how Maddie told me to do it."

"There are a lot of hungry bellies to fill, and you've just wasted the food that goes into them."

Annabelle looked at the pot of potatoes she'd carefully peeled the way Maddie had shown her. "I've only done a few. I'll be more careful with the others."

Then, because she couldn't bear to look at her father or anyone else witnessing more of her humiliation, she looked at the ground. "As for filling hungry bellies, someone else can have my share of the potatoes. It's the least I can do."

"The least you can do is—"

"Polly!" Gertie banged on one of the pots. "Just because you're cross with Annabelle doesn't give you the right to treat her like that."

She marched over to where Polly stood over her with the pot. "You know how to fix potatoes the way Maddie does?"

Annabelle nodded. "But I can fix them the way you want. Just tell me what to do," she said as quickly as she could.

Please, please, please, please let everyone see how

hard I'm trying to be a better person. It was just potatoes, after all. Surely that wasn't something to be declared sinful.

"I haven't had Maddie's potatoes in ages." A smile
filled Gertie's face. "So if you know how to fix them,
I'll be looking forward to eating them."

Gertie glanced at Polly with a look that dared her to
defy her, but that's just what Polly did. "So you're taking her side, are you? Fine. But don't expect me to go
without because of her. Bad enough she made more work
for me with the laundry. Then she goes off and has to
play princess with the hurt foot. Well, you can count me
out. I'm through putting up with her."

Polly stomped off, leaving Annabelle feeling like a
bug that had been squashed for no other reason than ex-
isting. Pure meanness, that's what Polly's words were.

Her stomach churned and turned sour in a different
way. This is what she'd done to Polly. She'd said horrible things out of anger and hurt, and it had squashed
something in Polly's heart.

"I'm sorry," she mumbled again, knowing that no
amount of times she said it would ever change what had
caused this mess to begin with.

Joseph placed his hand over hers. "It's all right. She's
hurting, too. I'm sure she didn't mean to offend you."

At least the old Joseph was back. Even under the
weight of her father's stare, she couldn't ask Joseph to
remove his hand. Someone cared for her. Someone understood how awful this whole situation was, and how
she'd never meant for any of it to happen.

"Yes, she did," Annabelle said softly. "And I know I
deserved it, I just…"

Her throat felt raw and ached like she was coming
down with something. But it wasn't that. That she knew,

even without a doctor. "I guess I see why they say an eye for an eye makes the whole world blind. I was hurting, so I let the harsh words take over, which led to Polly hurting, and then she needed to be mean to me."

Annabelle removed her hand from Joseph's and picked up another potato and began peeling. "I suppose it'll eventually wear itself out."

Her father stood and motioned to Gertie, who followed him out of sight of the tents. Probably more discussion over how to solve the problem of Annabelle.

Joseph picked up a potato. "Why is Polly so upset with you?"

"Because." Annabelle sighed. There was so much to the story that Joseph didn't understand. That no one understood. Because the one person to whom she'd bared her soul was gone.

"I was in love once. With a miner. I thought Henry a good man, and he helped with my family's ministry. But then the sickness hit over the winter, and Henry wanted to leave. He wanted to avoid getting sick, and besides, there was gold in Alaska."

She set another potato in the pot, trying to focus on the task at hand so her heart didn't ache the way it always did when she remembered how selfish Henry had been. "I was needed at home to care for my family. He promised to wait. But then Polly came to see me. Told me he'd left without saying goodbye. I called her a liar."

Her knife got caught in the potato, and Joseph took it from her. "Let me do that. You just focus on the story."

"There is no more." She sucked in a deep breath as she turned to look over the fire. It should have been warm, only all she felt was cold inside. "I asked why she would deliberately hurt me with such lies when she knew how I was hurting already. I'd already watched as they'd taken Susannah's and Peter's bodies out to the ice-house to be kept until the ground was thawed enough to bury them. I couldn't imagine why Henry would abandon me at such a time, so Polly must've been lying."

The fire popped, and Annabelle jumped, bringing her attention back to Joseph. "Turns out, Polly was telling the truth. I believed in a scoundrel over my dearest friend."

"Your dearest friend should have understood."

Annabelle reached for another potato and began peeling again. "Maybe. But I hurt her, and I shouldn't have."

"Even if Polly was hurt by your words," Joseph said quietly, "she had no right to speak to you like that. Or even to tell lies about you."

She looked up at him. Why did he have to be so wrong for her? "Thank you." She finished the last potato and brushed off her skirt. "I wish…"

No, she couldn't say what she wished. She wished too many things that would never come true.

"Well, I suppose it doesn't matter." She turned her head, wishing she could stand and get away from the closeness of this man who confused her so.

"It does matter. And I…" Joseph looked in the direction her father had gone, then back at her. "Annabelle, your father has asked me to get something straight with you. As a gentleman, I need to be sure that I don't dishonor you in any way."

Not another proposal. Annabelle's heart fluttered in the pit of her stomach. If he asked, she'd almost say yes. Except the retelling of her story reminded her just how little she knew of Joseph. She'd known Henry far longer, had known him to be honorable, and been betrayed.

"Your father is concerned that you might have…feelings…for me." His shoulders rose and fell as he glanced again in the direction her father had taken Gertie. "I assured him that we were merely friends, but he felt it necessary to clarify my intentions."

If a person could die of mortification, she'd do so right at this very moment. How could her father be so... so... Annabelle sighed. She did have feelings for Joseph. But they weren't the sort a person ever acted upon.

Joseph cleared his throat. "You know my situation. I have a brother and sisters to care for back home. I intend to move them west somewhere, but I can't promise anything to anyone. All I know is that my duty lies with them. I can't be a proper husband to any woman knowing that I have seven others to provide for."

He looked at her with such tenderness, it made her heart want to break. "If I were to take a wife, I would want her to be every bit as bold and strong as you. But I can't. It's impossible for me to marry. Not when I have the children to raise. It's an impossible burden to put on anyone."

He had said as much before. Yet this time, it made her heart ache in an unfamiliar way. "Of course your family must come first," she said, hoping it sounded sympathetic to his cause. It wasn't as though she wanted him for herself.

Joseph's slow nod only made her feel worse. "Good. So then we have an understanding. Your father will be much relieved to know that your heart isn't entangled."

She forced a smile to her face, not caring if he saw through it or not. Over Joseph's shoulder, she could see her father and Gertie returning. For all they saw, it was a perfectly amiable conversation that wasn't creating strange feelings in her stomach. She was fine. Just fine. Or at least she would be once these feelings left. Because they all knew that based on both his words and hers, anything between them was an impossibility.

The old Annabelle had returned. Joseph watched as she greeted her father with a smile and a too-friendly tone. On the surface, the conversation had gone well, but he knew better than to trust her glib answers. But what else could he do? Carrying on the conversation meant digging in to the places of each other's hearts that neither was willing to risk. He simply couldn't afford to, and whatever Annabelle's motivations, it didn't matter.

Frank stared at him with a keen eye, questioning. Joseph gave a small nod to indicate that they'd had the conversation.

"All is well?" Frank addressed the question to Annabelle, but looked at Joseph.

"Yes, Father," she told him in a perfectly proper tone. "Joseph and I are clear that neither of us have intentions toward the other."

Frank looked almost shocked, taking a step back. Gertie's soft gasp all but accused Annabelle of being impertinent. Then again, the whole situation bordered on impertinence. Things had been fine between him and Annabelle until her father had decided to protect his daughter's honor.

Joseph rubbed his temples. He couldn't fault Frank. If he'd thought anyone trifling with any of his sisters' affections, he'd have insisted upon the same conversation.

Annabelle indicated the pot beside her. "I have the potatoes ready. If someone could put them on the fire, I would be much obliged."

The rest of the evening passed with the same sullen silence he'd had from Annabelle when they first met. No one could accuse her of being rude, and some would probably even say that she was pleasant. But she wasn't Annabelle.

Why should he care? He wasn't supposed to have these feelings. Joseph rose from his spot by the fire. "I'm going to retire for the evening."

None of the other men had come in, so Joseph lit a lamp and began looking through the books he'd brought from his pa's cabin. The first book appeared to have strange markings and notes in the margins. Almost as though he'd used it as a sort of diary, only it wasn't straight prose. Certain words were circled, but even put together, they made no sense.

Annabelle might claim there was no treasure, but his pa wouldn't have gone to all of this trouble to throw people off track if there hadn't been. He'd covered it up too carefully. And that wasn't the sort of man his pa was.

Plus with the attacks on Annabelle and Nugget... someone was after something.

Perhaps the silver wasn't worth pursuing. Not at the risk of... Joseph sighed and closed the book. What alternative did he have? How else would he provide for his family?

He picked up his pa's Bible and began searching through it. Entire passages had been underlined, not just the random words of his other book. It should have brought comfort to Joseph to know that his pa had read God's Word. How could he then justify his relationship with another woman when he had a wife waiting for him at home? His pa's first priority should have been his family, yet he'd created this whole new life without them. He could have accepted that his pa had fallen in love. But what was love when you had a family to provide for? Certainly the Bible didn't condone such a life.

Joseph wasn't going to be like his pa, forsaking family for love.

He tried reading the pages, but they seemed tainted, coming from his pa's Bible. *Lord, I know these feelings about my pa are wrong. Please help me forgive.*

Those words seemed easier to think than to live out. The words in the Bible jumbled in such a way that he could barely read them.

Maybe the Psalms would give him some peace. King David had struggled with his enemies, so perhaps his words would comfort. As he flipped to the right section of his Bible, Joseph noticed that his pa had again circled random words. None of it made sense.

Until…

As he looked back and forth between the pages of circled words, he began to see a pattern. *The. Key. To. The. Silver.*

Dear Lord, he had found it. His pa had been circling words in his books to indicate where his silver had been hidden. Joseph pulled out his journal and began copying words. Not all of them made sense, and not all of them were as easily connected as the words he'd found. His pa had left a map to his treasure, only he'd done it in a sneaky way so that others couldn't figure it out. *Please Lord, let me be able to decipher the code.*

He looked around the tent. With so many people after his pa's silver, it wasn't safe to leave the books lying around. He'd already put Annabelle and Nugget in danger, and he couldn't risk Gertie's family, as well. Tomorrow he'd find a safe place.

The tent flapped open, and Slade entered.

"I didn't know this was your tent."

Slade eyed him, then shrugged. "I stay here when I'm

at camp. Collin's boys stayed up the mountain tonight, so it's just the two of us."

Even though he had no problem with the other man and would be working with him to find his pa's silver, something about the way Slade looked at him didn't sit right.

"I'm just finishing my Bible reading, so if you'll give me a minute to put the books away, I can turn the lamp out."

Slade gave another shrug. "Doesn't make any difference to me. I've learned to sleep where I can."

He laid out his bedroll and made motions of getting ready for bed, but Joseph could feel the other man watching him.

Joseph turned down the lamp and settled in to sleep.

"What's your plan for tomorrow?" Slade's voice broke into the darkness.

"I'm at your mercy. I think going to the site we were talking about earlier today makes a lot of sense."

Slade grunted. "Be ready to ride at first light."

The man's snores soon filled the tent, and Joseph wished he could have the same ease. But every time he closed his eyes, he remembered the look in Annabelle's eyes as she talked about the heartbreak she'd endured. He understood that pain. If it weren't for their already awkward situation, they could have comforted each other. But they'd crossed too many lines, and Joseph couldn't afford to get any more emotionally involved with Annabelle.

He tucked the blanket tighter around him. He wasn't supposed to care. Didn't care. Fine, did. Now he was getting to be as bad as Annabelle. Only in this instance, the worst of his lies were the ones he told himself. No, they weren't lies. Just the uncomfortable results of the reality he found himself in. Here, in the dark of night, in the presence of the Lord, he could admit that he might be falling for Annabelle.

Please, Lord, if it's not too much to ask, could You also help me get over my feelings for Annabelle? They're entirely inappropriate, and I want to behave honorably toward her.

Chapter Sixteen

When Annabelle woke, her foot wasn't throbbing as badly. The swelling had gone down. At least she'd be able to do some work today and not be a burden. She shifted the two little girls sleeping almost on top of her, curled together like kittens, noting that Polly was nowhere to be seen. She sighed and struggled to put on her boots. Thankfully Gertie had lent her a more practical pair of shoes. If Polly was already up and working, Annabelle would be scolded for remaining abed.

Her ankle was tender as she stepped on it, but she'd manage. The fire hadn't yet been stirred up. Annabelle grabbed a poker and began stirring the ashes, exposing the red-hot coals. She then added a few pieces of the wood. The fire sprang to life almost immediately.

Remembering where Gertie kept the coffeepot, she pulled it out and began taking the steps to prepare the coffee.

The calm, quiet air felt more peaceful than what Annabelle had ever felt inside the mining camp. Mixed in with the smoky fire, she caught a hint of the pine from the remaining trees. They would soon be taken for the mining operations, she was sure. For now, though, she could watch the soft pink stripes of dawn crest the mountain, highlighting the majestic pines around them. Absolutely amazing.

In such a moment, it was almost easy to believe in God. No, that was not right. She had never stopped believing. God was still there. Still painting the sky as He directed the sun over the mountain like He did every morning. Her mother used to quote the Bible at these times—"This is the day the Lord has made, let us rejoice in it."

Annabelle's heart gave a flutter. In this moment, in the perfectly wonderful sunrise, her heart could rejoice at the magnificence of the Lord's creation.

It didn't mean that anything changed in their relationship, and certainly offered no proof of any affection the Lord might hold for her. But still she could enjoy the work of His hands.

She brushed off her skirts and looked for a bucket to get some water from the creek. As she stood, she realized that in that memory of her mother, the pang in her heart wasn't the crippling grief it had been all these months.

"Good morning!" Gertie's greeting made her jump. "I see you've already begun making the breakfast preparations."

"Just the fire. I was going to start the coffee, but I realized that there's no water, so I need to go to the creek."

Gertie held up a bucket. "No need. But we are low on wood. If your ankle is feeling up to it, you could gather some."

"Of course." Annabelle gave a small smile. "It doesn't appear to be troubling me overmuch."

She started for the woodpile, grateful that Gertie had

given her something to do other than remain idle. As she
got closer, her ankle began to throb. She'd tough it out.

"Annabelle!"

She spied Joseph coming from the other direction
and sighed. Everyone else would accept her "I'm fine,"
but Joseph would probably see through it.

"Good morning." She didn't bother trying to smile,
since with him it was a wasted effort.

"What are you doing? Your foot—"

"Is feeling much better, thanks. Gertie needed more
wood."

He let out a long sigh, the kind that meant she had yet
again managed to exasperate him. Well, that was fine by
her, since he'd made his feelings for her clear last night.
It didn't matter to her one bit what he thought of her.

"Why don't I help?"

"If you like." She shrugged. "Aren't you supposed to
be heading out to look at your father's other properties?"

"Slade was gone when I woke."

"I'm sure he'll be back soon. Someone probably
needed his help, and being Slade, he went to do it."

He looked at her solemnly. Studying her. "You know
a lot about the goings-on here."

They had reached the woodpile, and Annabelle began
picking up the wood they'd need for the fire. "This used
to be like a second home to me. But anymore—"

"You don't want to get involved," he said quietly.

She straightened, then stared hard at him. "Why
would I? Leadville might be a fast-growing city sure to
rival Denver, but it is still a dangerous place. People get
sick, people die, outlaws come, or they tire of trying to
strike it rich and head home. Or worse, they do strike
it rich. But you know what they do then? They leave.
Even the Tabors, with their magnificent opera house, do

you think they spend their days in this place? No. They have their mansion in Denver, just like everyone else."

The back of her throat had a slight tickle, like everything she'd been going through wasn't enough.

"You want my honesty, Joseph? Here's honest. You've offered me friendship. But where will that leave me? If you find your father's silver, you will head home to your family. One more person I care about gone. Trust me, remaining unattached is the only way I can survive. I've lost too much."

She turned to head back to the camp, her ankle giving slightly as she stepped on it. Well, she'd endure it. Just as she'd endure Joseph's silence every painful step of the way home.

Because in the end, he knew she was right. Her father was worried she might form a romantic attachment to the man, but given that she could barely afford for her heart to like him as a friend, falling in love was simply not an option.

Clearly, Joseph knew it, too.

Annabelle paused near a darkened tent and even darker fire to rest for a moment.

"Excuse me." A woman poked her head out of the tent. "Could you spare some wood?"

Her throbbing ankle screamed no, but the wail of a baby from inside the tent made her heart insist.

"Of course." She made one trip, she could do another.

Annabelle set the wood in the woman's fire pit and tried to stir up some of the coals, but she could already tell there was no heat left in them.

"Why don't I bring you a coal from our fire?"

The woman rewarded her with a soft smile. "Thank you. I'm afraid I haven't gotten the hang of mining camp life."

"It's no trouble at all. I'll return shortly." At least without the weight of the wood in her arms, the pressure on her foot wasn't so bad.

When they were out of earshot, Joseph said, "You're a better person than you think, Annabelle Lassiter."

"Not really. I'm just doing my duty. The woman needs help. You can't turn a blind eye to a woman needing help."

"Many would," Joseph said quietly.

Not a Lassiter. But this wasn't an argument she needed to have with him. Not in the interest of keeping their distance. Joseph did things to her heart that she didn't like. Made her feel things that she didn't want to feel, least of all for a man like him.

They returned to the cabin, where Gertie had already started breakfast.

"I'm sorry it took so long," Annabelle said by way of partial apology and as an introduction to the situation with the woman she'd just met.

Polly glared at her. "You can't even get wood."

Annabelle tried counting to ten, and she tried to hold her temper. But honestly...how much was she supposed to take? Her father would tell her to turn the other cheek, but what did that look like when someone else was constantly belittling you?

"Actually," she said with as much calm as she could muster, "I met a woman on the way back who asked if she could have some wood. She's new here, and she had a baby crying in the tent. I gave my load to her, and I'm bringing her some hot coals to get her fire going again."

Polly's indrawn breath wasn't nearly as satisfying as it should be. She didn't want to get in the jabs against her former friend, the way Polly was keen on doing to her. All she wanted was peace to reign again.

Annabelle's words sprang Gertie into action. "Oh, that poor dear. I wonder if that's Isaac Johanson's wife. I meant to call on her yesterday, but with everything…" She cast an apologetic look at Annabelle.

"It's all right. I'm sure you can visit with her later. But right now, I'd like to get some coals to her. It's chilly out still."

Gertie rewarded her with a smile. "Yes, I think that's good." She handed Annabelle a bucket with some coals in it.

"If you'll give me just a moment, I'll send you with some leftover biscuits. It isn't much, but with a jug of coffee, it'll take the edge off. You'll invite her to have breakfast with us, won't you?"

Annabelle tried to nod, but Gertie kept talking and piling things into a basket. "Give her one of these blankets. I like to keep them on hand for the new little ones."

Gertie bustled past her and for a moment, Annabelle forgot that her world had changed so completely. It was like the old days, when Gertie and her mother had conspired together to make sure everyone had what they needed. Just last Christmas, they had come together to make sure every child in the camp had received a gift.

Annabelle's heart constricted. It had been their last major project before her mother had gotten ill. She took a deep breath and swallowed her unshed tears. Her mother would have loved this.

A sleepy-eyed Nugget came down the stairs. "Where did you go? I was lonesome without you."

For all of Annabelle's promises to keep her heart to herself, loving this sweet child was irresistible. Her heart did another flip. Joseph's reminder of his impermanence in her life was something that she'd do well to continue remembering. When Joseph left, so would Nugget.

But when the little girl jumped into her arms, Annabelle couldn't stop herself from hugging her back. "Nonsense, silly girl. You had Caitlin to keep you company."

"But she's not you." Nugget sighed into her hair.

Annabelle swallowed. Someday this would be easier.

"Well," Annabelle said as she released Nugget, "you'd best get washed up because Gertie is getting breakfast ready. I have an errand to run, but then I'll be back."

Gertie handed her the wrapped biscuits. "Don't take no for an answer, because I won't hear of it."

"Yes, Gertie." Annabelle pretended not to notice Polly's scowl as she headed back to the woman's tent.

Joseph grabbed the basket out of her hands. "I'll take that. Your limp is getting worse, and you don't need to aggravate it by carrying such a load."

"Annabelle?" Gertie stopped and looked at her. "I thought you said your foot was better."

The snort from Polly was enough to make her ignore the throbbing in her foot. "It is. Just a twinge now and again. Nothing to keep me from giving a warm welcome to a woman who needs it."

She didn't care if her smile was fake or not. For the first time since her mother had died, she had a purpose, and the hurt wasn't as great. Even the pain in her foot was tolerable.

"I'll look after her," Joseph said. Which seemed to seal the deal as Gertie nodded, and Polly's scowl deepened.

Once they were out of earshot of the cabin, Joseph spoke. "You need to go easy on Polly."

Annabelle stopped and stared at him. "Me? I don't understand."

The way he pressed his lips together told her that she

obviously had missed something. Probably that whole forgiving seventy times seven thing.

"I overheard her at the river fighting with some guy named Tom. Apparently, she heard him mentioning to some of the other guys that you looked quite the picture the other day in town. She thinks you encouraged his attentions and are trying to steal him from her."

"Why, that's the most ridiculous thing I've ever heard." Surely Polly knew her well enough to know that she would never do such a thing. "Polly knows that I would never be interested in one of her beaus."

Then again, Polly had once thought that Annabelle would never think her a liar. So much had changed with a few careless words.

"I know," Joseph said quietly. "But Polly believes otherwise, and that's probably the source of her attitude."

The sincere look in his eyes made it hard to remember all the things she needed to focus on. Like the fact that he was the last person on earth who could be a friend to her.

"I'll talk to her." One more hard thing to do, but it seemed like everything in her life was a hard thing. Because she couldn't bring herself to continue the conversation with Joseph into the next logical step, which would be to let him know that they had to do something about Nugget's continuing attachment.

Yet it seemed like the more she tried pulling away from Joseph and his family, the closer they all seemed to get.

Chapter Seventeen

Annabelle had never looked so beautiful as when she held the tiny baby while its mother ate. Again, he couldn't help but think she would make an excellent mother. Her care for Nugget had shown that, but now, with such a tiny infant in her arms, it was a beautiful sight.

Why did it have to be so hard?

He tore his eyes off the captivating woman and watched the other woman gobble the biscuits. It had clearly been a long time since she'd had a substantial meal.

"Where are you from, Meg?" he asked the young mother after she'd eaten the last of her food.

"Kansas." She gave a wry grin. "Isaac wasn't meant to be a farmer, poor man. He tried, he really did."

Joseph had heard many similar stories since being here. So many people wanting a better life. Of course, he had been a good farmer, that wasn't the problem. But when the bank owned it and demanded higher payments than any reasonable man could afford and still keep food on the table…

He glanced back at Annabelle, who'd handed the baby

back to its mother. She wouldn't understand what it was like to do without. Nor would she understand the willingness to do just about anything to make sure loved ones had food to eat.

"What made you come here?" He turned his attention back on Meg.

A dark look crossed Meg's face. "His brother had written, talking about all the money there was to be made. Isaac sold everything we had and sent some of the money ahead for his brother to get us a place. Only..." Meg sighed and cradled her baby tighter.

"When we got here, we found out his brother had gambled it all and then some. There were no houses to be let, and even if there were, we didn't have enough money. One night, some men attacked Isaac, and said that if he didn't come up with the rest of the money his brother owed, they'd harm me and the baby. So he gave them the last of our money. Now we're here, and Isaac is working at the mine in hopes he'll make enough to support us."

How he hated the look on Annabelle's face. It was as if all this served to prove her theories on the evils of mining true.

He shot a glare at Annabelle, then returned his attention to Meg. "Did you talk to the sheriff?"

"For as much good as it'll do us." Meg shook her head. "He said he'd look into it, but he said not to hold out much hope."

Annabelle took the woman's hand. "At least you're all safe. As far as catching those horrible men, you should talk to my father. He's a minister in town, and he knows just about everyone. Sometimes he can find out things the law can't."

Even though Meg shook her head, a tiny light shone

in her eyes. Joseph couldn't help but notice that she squeezed Annabelle's hand back, clinging to it like a lifeline.

"All I want is enough money to get us back home. I know Isaac wasn't cut out for farming, but mining isn't for him, either. Perhaps if we went back to my parents, they'd let us stay with them for a while until Isaac can find other work."

"We'll do what we can to help," said Annabelle, a little too cheerful to have fully grasped the situation.

Annabelle stood, then looked around the campsite. "Would it be too forward of me to ask what supplies you have? We keep a number of things for people in your situation, and—"

"We won't be taking charity."

"I wouldn't dream of offering you charity," Annabelle said in a gentle voice that spoke of having done this dozens of times. As much as she fought it, she was a natural at caring for others. If only she'd open her heart to see that. "These are the leftover supplies from people who've done just as you're saying you'd like to do. When they leave, they have no use for these things, so they give them to us and ask us to give them to the next family."

Not only was Meg not appearing convinced, but she'd stiffened even further.

"Truly, Meg. It's what we do here. When someone's done using an item, they leave it for the next person who comes along. No sense in it going to waste."

Meg softened slightly, and Joseph had to give Annabelle credit for trying. When she wasn't thinking about the pain of her losses, she had such an incredible heart for others.

"I…" Meg's face indicated a debate between practicality and wanting to protect her pride. Joseph knew all about that. Had faced the same debate upon encountering the Lassiter family.

"I know." Joseph stepped in and gave a smile as he peeked down at the baby. "It was hard for me to accept their help at first, as well, but I've found that they aren't just about giving handouts, but are true friends."

Some of the wariness left Meg's face. "They helped you?"

"Are helping. I came looking for my pa, and found that I had a sister." He relayed his tale and as he shared his family's need, Meg continued to soften. True, he did not share the most private details, such as how bad things were for his family back home, but at least she would understand that Annabelle meant to be her friend.

Which clearly Annabelle did, because as he relayed his tale, she'd once again taken the baby into her arms and was playing with it quietly.

"Emma is the sweetest thing," Annabelle said, wrapping the baby snugly in her own shawl. "I can't believe how chilly it's gotten."

Annabelle's smile at the young mother melted his heart. If he was to keep his promises to both her and his pa, he needed to find a way to maintain his distance.

Joseph looked up and noticed clouds rolling in over the mountains. The sky was already darkening, which meant a storm would hit before afternoon.

He tried not to groan at what would be an inevitable delay in his mission.

"I'm not used to this weather," Meg said. "Back home, summers were so hot. I thought Isaac's brother was funning us when he told us to bring our winter things. But one of the women in town said that they've had snow in June here. June! Can you imagine!"

Annabelle nodded. "I remember it well myself. It wasn't much snow, of course, and it melted right away, but it was still quite the surprise."

Why did her smile have to be so engaging? Even though she was talking to Meg, and not him, he felt just as drawn in by the woman as Meg clearly was. Her face was animated, and her smile crinkled her eyes.

Joseph turned away, unable to continue watching Annabelle. He couldn't afford to be given one more reason to like her.

As he turned, he noticed Slade riding in. Though they would be unable to visit the sites until after the storm passed, this would give them a chance to discuss their plan.

Annabelle must have noticed his change in attention, and she followed his gaze, then stood. "Slade." She looked at Meg. "We must talk to him about what happened to your husband. Perhaps he can be of service where the sheriff was not."

She didn't wait for Meg's answer, but held the baby tighter to her as she moved in Slade's direction and waved.

"Slade!"

He dismounted and came toward them, handing his reins to a boy before arriving at the camp. "Good morning, Annabelle. Joseph." He nodded in his direction before approaching the ladies.

"Slade, this is my new friend, Meg. Her husband was attacked by some ruffians, and I'm hoping you can help find these horrible men."

Annabelle relayed the story with such passion that any doubt he'd ever had about her character and willingness to engage with others was wiped away. She had been listening, with all her heart, and was acting upon it.

Stop it, Joseph. She wasn't his to be thinking this way about. He knew better. Had warned himself multiple times to avoid doing so.

He turned his attention to Meg, who was engaging in the conversation with Annabelle and Slade.

No, that wasn't good. Because her engagement only reminded him of how Annabelle's warmth had drawn her out. Even as the baby gave a slight cry and Annabelle handed her back to her ma, he couldn't help but think of how wonderful Annabelle was with a baby.

He gave a small cough. "Since you have it all in hand here, I think I should go check on Nugget."

Without waiting for an answer, he retreated to their own camp, where he could find at least a moment's peace from his thoughts of Annabelle.

Annabelle watched Joseph retreat, feeling the chill in the air more acutely in his absence. She'd given up her shawl for the baby, and now her arms were starting to prickle against the coming storm.

"I'll make some inquiries," Slade said, as he, too, watched Joseph leave. "Now if you'll excuse me, I need to catch up to Joseph to tell him our plans."

"Of course." She gave him a smile, the kind she hoped Joseph would be proud of. "I appreciate you taking the time."

He nodded, then left, leaving her alone with Meg and the baby.

"Thank you," Meg said when they were alone. "I am so glad the Lord brought you to us. He's clearly watching over our family."

Annabelle held out her arms for the baby. "Do let me hold Emma again. She's such a dear. I'll take you to breakfast with Gertie, who will want to hold her, then I'll never get to hold her again. She does love babies so."

That warm memory, and the sweet baby placed in her arms, put a tiny crack in Annabelle's heart. Gertie did love the little ones. How could Annabelle have shut her out for so long?

They walked to Gertie's, Meg chattering about life in Kansas. Annabelle had no idea how hard farm work was. It certainly sounded just as difficult and desolate a life as these miners faced. Getting up with the sun to work in the fields all day, laboring for a crop that could be wiped out by drought, fire, animals, disease and a host of other problems.

How was mining any different?

Annabelle shook her head. Farmers weren't risking their lives and putting families in danger. They didn't spend their earnings on whiskey, women and gambling.

Joseph didn't, either, a small voice told her.

Nonsense, she told herself right back. There were plenty of reasons to dismiss Joseph.

He was leaving.

Which was why she would put him completely out of her mind.

Fortunately, it was easy enough to do when they arrived at Gertie's because Joseph wasn't there. Nugget was, and she immediately launched herself at Annabelle.

"Annabelle! You were gone ever so long!"

She smiled and wrapped her free arm around the little girl. "I was visiting my new friend, Meg. And this is her baby, Emma. Isn't she a dear little thing?"

Gertie swooped upon them. "I love babies. Let me have a look."

Just like that, the baby was taken from her arms, and Annabelle gave Meg an "I told you so" look.

Meg smiled shyly, but was immediately engaged in Gertie's enthusiastic banter as she placed a dish of food in front of the woman. Though Annabelle was pleased to see her so well taken care of, it was almost a shame to give up her job. For a few moments, it had felt like she belonged again. Back before everything in her life had become so hard.

For Nugget, though, it was a welcome change. The little girl hadn't let go of her hand. Again, Annabelle's conscience panged at the thought of this little girl leaving her. Nugget had lost so much already. Was it fair to make her lose someone else?

"What have you been doing while I was gone?"

Nugget scowled. "We had to go wash dishes with Polly. Only she got mad at us and chased us away."

That didn't sound like the Polly she'd once been friends with. Had Annabelle's attitude soured her old friend so much? Then Joseph's words came back to her. Polly was jealous. Over nothing.

"How about I go talk to her?" Annabelle ruffled the top of the little girl's head, then withdrew her hand. "And when I get back, we're going to do something with that hair of yours."

A comment that earned her another scowl, but that was fine. She didn't want to push Nugget away exactly, but if a few hair brushings was all it took to diminish Annabelle's popularity, she'd take it.

"I'm going to the creek to talk to Polly," Annabelle said over her shoulder at Gertie and Meg. "I'll be back shortly."

She avoided the path that she'd taken yesterday where she'd run into those men. Her ankle was now throbbing again. But she couldn't put off this errand. Polly's attitude was affecting everyone else.

Her trip to the creek was quieter than it had been the last time, and she easily found Polly, clean dishes in one pile, and already beginning the wash for the day.

"Hi, Polly."

The other girl didn't turn and look at her. "Go away. I don't need you slowing me down again. You tell Ma—"

"What? Something that you'll contradict later?"

Polly spun, her face red. "So what? You're going to tell on me now?"

Annabelle took a deep breath. "No. I'm sorry. I shouldn't have snapped at you." This making up was harder business than the idea had originally sounded.

"Look." She took another step in Polly's direction. "I know I said some awful things. I deeply regret them. But what I regret even more is that I've lost a good friend. So if we can talk about whatever else is bothering you, I'd like to clear the air. Even if you don't want to be friends again, at least we could be—"

"Nothing." Polly's stare was full of pure hate. "You are nothing to me, and never will be. You think you're better than everyone else, and you don't give a whit for anyone other than you."

The backs of Annabelle's eyes and throat stung. She could own a certain amount of selfishness, but surely Polly knew that there was more to her than that.

And if Joseph hadn't spoken to her about Polly earlier, she might have walked away. But this wasn't about Annabelle's behavior, not really.

"Joseph said he heard you and Tom fighting this morning. Something about you thinking he and I were engaged in a flirtation?"

Annabelle stared at Polly, ready for her to spew more venom in her direction. But Polly didn't say anything, not even as Annabelle could see the steam practically rising out of Polly's head. When she blew, it wasn't going to be pretty. But better here than with the little girls again.

"I have never encouraged Tom. I've always seen him as your beau, and I've always believed that the two of you were going to be married someday. I would never interfere with that. Regardless of what you think of me, I want you to be happy. And if he's—"

Polly shook her head furiously. "Just this past fall, you were telling me about how I could do better. I never imagined you were giving me such friendly advice because you wanted him for yourself."

Annabelle's heart hurt at the memory. She had told Polly that she could do better. Because frankly, Tom was on the lazy side. If Polly married him, she'd end up just like her mother, working hard to take care of a family while her husband squandered it all on whiskey and cards.

But that wasn't something she could say to her now. Not with their friendship so damaged.

"I was wrong to judge," Annabelle said instead. "I didn't know his heart, and I should have listened to you. I'm sorry. I've truly never had designs on him."

Her stomach ached at the way Polly looked at her. She could list dozens of reasons why she didn't like Tom, but they would only be taken the wrong way.

If she were to chase after a man, it would be someone like Joseph. She closed her eyes. Why couldn't she stop thinking of the impossible?

"I am so sorry that you don't think better of me," Annabelle said, opening her eyes to look at Polly. "I know I deserve it after how judgmental I've been. But if you could find a way to at least call a truce, for the sake of the others around us, I promise I'll do what I can to make amends."

It had taken a long time for Annabelle to find friends like Gertie and Polly, but with a few thoughtless words, she'd ruined it. Worse, though, it seemed like Polly now thought her capable of even more foul deeds than she would ever contemplate.

"You can never fix this." Polly spat out the words like Annabelle was a bug she'd swallowed. "Just leave. We don't want you here."

If only it were that simple. Because if she could go, she would gladly go visit her aunt, build a new life for herself in the city, and forget about the mess she'd made.

Polly returned to her work with the wash. This was not how Annabelle had envisioned the conversation going. Perhaps she'd been too ambitious thinking they would be able to forgive, and maybe even hug. But surely she could have done better than to have broken things between them even worse.

Chapter Eighteen

"I'll only be gone a few hours." Joseph tried prying Nugget from his legs, but she was having none of that. She'd seemed perfectly content remaining behind the day before with Annabelle and Caitlin, but today seemed to be a completely different story.

"You're just like Papa! Always leaving." The little girl's lip jutted out in such a perfect pout that Joseph was almost convinced to remain behind. After all, the sky looked like a storm was moving in.

Fortunately, Annabelle, as always, seemed to know the perfect solution. "None of that," she told Nugget firmly. "Joseph will be back in time for supper. You're going to be so busy playing with Caitlin that you'll hardly notice him missing. Now go get the brush from Gertie so I can fix your hair. Then we can play by the creek for a while."

Though Annabelle ruffled the little girl's ratted hair with a gentle wave and a smile, the set to her eyes brooked no argument, and Nugget released his pant leg.

"You promise you'll be home for supper?" The big eyes blinking at him would have extracted his promise even if he'd had other plans. He'd be home for supper, no matter what.

"I already did. Now listen to Annabelle, because I'm sure she has a wonderful day planned for you."

He hugged his sister, and then she scampered off like she'd gotten exactly what she wanted. Joseph shook his head. He'd never understand females.

"As always you know how to handle her." He smiled at Annabelle, who shrugged.

"Children aren't so difficult. I've always enjoyed them."

The genuine smile that filled her face reminded him of his previous thoughts about her and motherhood. "You're going to make an excellent mother someday."

He might as well have slapped her for the shock that registered on her face. Or at least that's the expression he thought he'd caught before she replaced it with a more serene but blank look.

"Perhaps someday. But I have no intention of marrying anytime soon. There's a lot of world to see and a lot of things I'd still like to do."

She'd spoken wistfully of her ambitions in the cabin. He still knew so little of her, despite feeling like he'd known her all his life.

"Like what?"

"Go back East, for one. I haven't seen my mother's family since I was small. My aunt Celeste has asked me to come visit, and my father says that once he's convinced my heart is healed, I can go."

An expression he didn't recognize skittered across her face. "I know it sounds silly, but I'd like to go to the balls like Mother described. Certainly, we have the theatre and other pleasant diversions here, but Mother says that the social scene where she grew up was delightful. After all, that's how she met my father."

And in that instant, Joseph understood. Annabelle's future wasn't here. Not the way her eyes had lit up at the thought of her mother's descriptions of the balls. He'd never been to any such thing himself—could not imagine what would draw anyone to them. But he'd seen his sisters giggle over pictures of ladies in their finery, and knowing how similar in character Annabelle was to his sister Mary, understood the draw.

A trip back East and a fancy ball—those were things Joseph could not reasonably expect to provide for Annabelle. Not with so many mouths to feed and feet to shoe.

If anything was capable of convincing Joseph that he needed to put Annabelle out of his mind, it was hearing of her dreams for her future. He cared too much for her to ask her to give up her dreams when she'd already lost so much.

Annabelle seemed to sense the change in his mood. She reached out and touched him lightly on the arm. "I'm not going to abandon you, Joseph. My father has asked me to be of assistance until Nugget is properly settled."

A sly smile stole across her face. "In truth, I've come to love that little scamp, and I don't think I could leave until your family's affairs are in order. And I do hope you'd allow me to write."

Joseph nodded, willing himself to find a way to speak. In her grief, he'd caught the unspoken story of the sacrifices she'd made. The things she'd given up for her father's ministry. Here she was, sacrificing one more thing. While he could tell by the light in her eyes that she didn't view her time with Nugget as a sacrifice, he couldn't ask her to do it any longer than she had to.

Annabelle Lassiter was an amazing woman, and she deserved to have a life of her own. *Lord*, he prayed, *help me set Annabelle free*.

Joseph already knew that he had to find the silver as quickly as possible, but knowing that one more life hung in the balance made it all the more urgent.

He bade Annabelle goodbye, then climbed onto the horse Slade had waiting. Hopefully they'd find silver today.

Slade had taken a look at the clouds moving over the mountains and declared that the storm would go around the area. He had been partially right.

They came to a narrow ridge, and looking across the valley, he could see the rain fall on Leadville. Glorious. The valley was packed with houses and other buildings. He could see why some of the townspeople still grumbled about wanting to make Leadville the state capitol. The city boasted growth that he hadn't seen the likes of anywhere near home.

"Your pa's mining claim should be just over the next ridge," Slade shouted back at him.

Once they crossed the ridge, Slade pulled out a map, then pointed at an outcropping of rocks. "That's it. This claim used to belong to Slim Deckert, but then he lost it in a card game to your pa. Slim thought it was a great joke he'd pulled over on Bad Billy, since none of his crews had found anything other than pyrite."

Joseph picked up a shiny rock. "I take it this is pyrite."

"Yep. No offense, but your pa was known for being a fool. There's sayings about suckers here in Leadville, and your pa could be described by just about every one of them."

He knew Slade was being honest, and with the anger

he had against his pa, he hadn't expected the words to sting so much. It was bad enough having the foul deed that had come to light, but it seemed like there was a never-ending string of missteps that had him wondering how such a miscreant could have fathered him.

What a tragic end. Though fitting, for all the foolishness his pa had done. Living a fool, dying a fool.

"Doesn't look like there's anything here." Slade rubbed his jaw and looked at Joseph. "Frank says you still have family back home. Why don't you sell the claim, take the money and go home? I'm sure there's some wide-eyed sucker that'll buy it. We've enough land brokers in town who'll gladly do the job for you. In fact, I can recommend a guy."

Suckers. If Slade hadn't used that word, he might have thought about the idea. But how could he live with himself, knowing that to provide for his family, he'd just done to another what had been done to them? Sold them down the river on a raft made of false dreams. No, he had to see this through.

"There's evidence that my pa found silver. He sent money regularly."

Slade snorted. "Gambling, probably. He's been kicked out of every saloon in town dozens of times. Everyone knew he didn't mean no harm, which is why they let him back in, but..." He gave Joseph a look of pity. "Everyone wins at the tables now and again. That's how they keep you coming back. Which is why it'd be best if you just went on your way."

Maybe Joseph was being a paranoid, but it seemed like Slade was in an awful big hurry to get rid of him. The man's demeanor was pleasant enough, but there was something about his words...

"What's it to you if I stay or go?"

Slade shook his head. "None of my business. Just figuring with your family and all, you'd want to be with them."

The easy answer did little to ease the prickle on the back of Joseph's neck. Still, what could he say to contradict a man who had been nothing but helpful?

"What do you make of the attacks on Annabelle and Nugget?"

Slade eyed him intently. "I'm not convinced Bad Billy found silver. But I do think he was into something. Whatever you've been digging into is making people nervous. If there's something going on, I want to stop it before anyone else gets hurt."

It wasn't the first time he'd heard hints of his pa's less than honest dealings. Which made him consider Slade's idea of going to one of the local land agents and selling his pa's claims. But how could he, in good conscience, have potential buyers be swindled? And, if something illegal was going on with his pa's claims, would it put those people in danger? As much as Annabelle thought he and everyone else ignored her warnings about chasing after silver, he wasn't going to sell someone else on a false dream.

Mary would tell him that he was overthinking the situation. Too bad she wasn't here to talk to him and give him advice. What would be best for everyone?

He looked around the site, wishing it were as simple as a sign saying Silver Here.

If his pa had been killed, why here? Was the chasm a convenient place to dump a body, or did it signify something more?

Joseph went over to where Slade was poking around some rocks. "What kind of illegal activities was my pa involved in?"

Slade picked up another rock, then looked at him. "I guess we've all made it sound like he was a pretty bad guy. Truth is, when he wasn't drinking, he was a decent fellow. Pleasant enough when you came across him in the street. But he got into scuffles in the saloons, and there were accusations of cheating."

A drunk and a cheat. But it didn't add up. "None of this makes any sense to me. If my pa wasn't a horrible person, then what could he have done that would have people trying to harm Annabelle and Nugget?"

The rocks clattered where Slade dropped them to the ground. "My theory is that some of the people he cheated at cards are trying to get their land back."

Which would mean— "So there is silver?"

"Naw." Slade shook his head. "They're dirtier than Bad Billy. They probably want to seed the mines to make it look like there's silver, sell it to some sucker to make a tidy profit. Then, the sucker runs out of money and is so desperate for a way home, they sell it back for a pittance. And then the cycle begins again. Happens all the time."

And Slade was suggesting that he do the same thing. After all, no one would buy this land except for the hope of finding gold or silver.

Maybe Joseph was a sucker, too, but he had to believe that his pa hadn't completely died in vain. There had to be silver out there somewhere. His family was counting on him. And he wasn't sure he could live with himself given the alternative.

"Let me think on it. I'm not ready to completely give up on my pa's dream."

Slade nodded slowly. "You do that. Lots of folks waste everything they have on hopes of finding gold or silver. Most of them lose everything. I'd hate to see that happen to you."

Another reminder of Annabelle and her words on the subject. She had more wisdom than anyone gave her credit for. She just didn't understand the difficulty in separating the wise decision from the only chance he had at getting enough money to save his family.

The ride home wasn't nearly as pleasant. In fact, the storm he had thought they'd so cleverly missed had come upon them with a vengeance—punishment for the stupidity of thinking they could avoid nature.

Joseph pushed his horse hard, trying to keep up with Slade, but Slade was a more skilled rider on a faster horse, and he didn't seem at all concerned about leaving Joseph behind.

Nothing about the site where Joseph's pa had died looked even remotely possible for having silver. At least according to Slade. Which meant that all the maps and even his pa's strange code had done nothing to help.

It was tempting to stop in town at one of the land offices to see if he could sell the claims. But all he could think of was the sadness on Annabelle's face about miners and their false dreams. Could he sell that to someone else? Could he live with putting another family through what his had been through?

No, he couldn't.

His horse slipped on the wet rocks. Continuing was becoming a suicide mission, but as he glanced around, he saw no safe place to take cover.

Lightning struck nearby, sending tiny ripples of electricity through him and making the horse's hair stand on end. Not deadly, but a warning of the power of nature. The horse reared, and Joseph did his best to control it as rocks slid under them, the edge of the ground giving way.

Though Joseph managed to get the horse settled, it had caused him to lose sight of Slade against the wind and rain. Another loud boom reminded Joseph that they were too high, and on a horse, he was almost the tallest thing around.

"Slade!" The shout went unanswered, and Slade was nowhere to be seen.

More ground gave way, and Joseph fumbled, trying to get out of the saddle, but his foot remained stuck in the stirrups. Both man and horse slid down the embankment. Behind them, rocks crashed, following like an avalanche, only with rain and mud and boulders.

"Come on." He signaled the horse and spurred him sideways, out of the path of the rocks, but with his stuck foot, was largely ineffective in controlling the spooked horse.

The horse reared and sidestepped as rocks whizzed past his head. Joseph ducked and pressed his body close to the horse, not sure which was the more dangerous move—remaining on the animal, or taking his chances among the rocks.

As he looked up, he heard a boom, then another shower of boulders headed his way.

The next lightning bolt lit up the sky, for all the good it did. All it showed was the direness of the situation. A wall of water rushed down the side of the hill. Frank had warned him about flash floods, but never did he imagine that the water would rush past like a raging river at spring thaw. Joseph looked for an escape. At the rate they were going, they'd be caught in the water in no time. If a boulder didn't catch them first. He spotted a break just to the right. Now if he could convince the horse to take it…

Tugging as hard as he could, he turned the horse toward the open space. It, too, spotted the chance at safety, and bolted in that direction.

Faster than he'd ever imagined a horse being able to go, the animal charged into the opening, then raced down the mountain. It was all Joseph could do to cling to the horse and pray that they would both somehow arrive at the bottom safely.

When they got to the bottom of the hill, a tree slid past them. Rocks were still coming down to the left of them, and a huge pile of boulders, rocks, trees and miscellaneous debris had gathered where he and the horse would have ended up had he not spotted the break. Another few steps, and they'd have been caught up in the flood.

Thank You, Lord.

He'd heard that storms in the mountains could be bad, but he'd never expected this. Between the rain loosening the ground at the edge of the hillside, and the lightning knocking down trees and shaking boulders loose, combined with the flash flood, it was amazing he'd survived.

He found a safe place to stop, then got off the horse. With the storm this bad, and so much lightning around, it was best to take his chances on foot. After a few paces, he could see Leadville, which from his vantage point would be a lot closer to wait out the storm in town than trying to get back to camp.

The rain worsened, pouring like a waterfall without breaks to indicate droplets. Hopefully Annabelle would keep Nugget… Joseph shook his head. Of course Annabelle was taking good care of Nugget. She loved his sister, and he couldn't have asked for a better caretaker.

His mind started to wander in the direction of thinking of Annabelle as a mother again, but he stopped. No. Joseph glanced up at the sky. Better to be struck down than to continue tormenting himself. He'd find the silver, then send Annabelle on her way to the life she'd always dreamed of.

When he finally arrived in town, he was sure not a dry spot existed on his person. The streets were rivers of mud, and Joseph couldn't remember ever seeing them so empty. Everyone had taken refuge from the storm.

He brought the horse to the livery Frank patronized, glad that Wes, the proprietor, came out to greet him.

"Got caught in the storm, did you?" Wes took the reins and led the horse into the stables.

Joseph nodded and took off his hat, shaking the water from it, knowing that it did no good.

"Want to come in and dry off?"

"Thanks." Joseph followed him into the stables, thankful that something around him was actually dry, even though the smell of wet horse and manure burned his nostrils.

"I think Betsy has some coffee on. We're about the same size, so I'll lend you some dry clothes."

"I'm obliged to you."

"None doing. Frank's a good friend, and I know he'd do the same for me."

More of the same hospitality he'd grown used to. Such a dichotomy between the people like Frank and the rest of the world. Clearly Frank's people loved as Christ loved, and gave freely. They'd been taught well. How could they be otherwise with Frank's example?

Wes led him into the neat living quarters off the stable. "It's not much, but with land prices here in town, it's the best we can do."

"It's fine." He looked around the room that Wes and his wife used for their home. Everything, including a cookstove and bed, was contained in that tiny room.

"Betsy, can you get our guest a cup of coffee while I find him some dry clothes?"

"Gracious!" Betsy hurried toward them. "Let's get you by the fire to dry off. You'll catch your death. What were you thinking, going out in that storm?"

"It caught me unawares. We were out looking at some of my pa's claims, hoping to find clues as to the location of his silver. On the way back, I got caught in a flash flood."

He didn't bother explaining about Slade, or how it was really the expert's fault they were in this mess. Especially since Betsy was shaking her head and clucking about risking one's life for silver.

"You sound just like Annabelle," he said as a way of trying to be friendly and breaking the ice.

Betsy stepped back. "Annabelle? I'm nothing like her. She's a preacher's daughter."

"Betsy…" Wes's warning came from the corner.

"It's all right." Joseph accepted the blanket Betsy handed him. "Sounds like you just need to get to know Annabelle better. She's one of the kindest people I know. She's been helping take care of my sister, and I can honestly say I don't know what I'd do without her."

Betsy stared at him for a moment, then looked over at Wes. "That's what he's been telling me, but I don't know. I can't imagine her wanting to be friends with the likes of me."

Joseph wanted to continue defending her, but the more he rose to her defense, the more it looked like his feelings were more… Well, they… He shook his head.

The woman was going to drive him crazy by the time he was done.

"Maybe you should invite her over. I'm sure she'd be honored to have you as a friend." Joseph's stomach ached. That was the worst part of the situation and him trying to be her friend. He'd be leaving soon, and things would be all the worse for Annabelle.

Betsy turned away, like she didn't want to continue arguing the point. Joseph had to start learning to mind his own business, especially where Annabelle was concerned.

Wes returned, carrying a pile of clothes. "Betsy'll turn her back while you get these on."

Joseph changed as quickly as he could. "I'm finished," he said as he buttoned the last button on the shirt.

"Based on you riding Frank's best horse, and what you've said, I presume you're Billy's boy." Wes looked at him, studying.

"Yes."

It couldn't be that bad if Wes already figured him out, but still supplied him with clean clothes anyway, right?

"Did you know my pa?"

Wes nodded slowly. "I took care of his horse. Had to sell it, though, to pay his past due on the stabling."

If his pa had silver, why couldn't he pay the stable?

"Mighty fine horse." Wes stroked his chin. "I always wondered where he got the money for it."

"Maybe he won it in a card game."

Wes shook his head. "Not Billy. He was terrible at cards. Used to say that losing was God's punishment for adding that to his multitude of sins."

It sounded almost as if Wes knew his pa. "Were you friends?"

"As much as a body could be, I suppose." Wes handed

him a cup of coffee. "Billy mostly kept his own counsel. Visited that girl he had over on State Street, but didn't spend too much time getting friendly with others."

The description didn't fit with what he'd been told about his pa. "Everyone I've talked to has spoken poorly of him."

The fire crackled in response, because Wes just stood there, as though he was carefully considering his words.

Then finally, "Well, I suppose he didn't do much to endear himself to anyone. Especially Slim Deckert. When Billy heard he'd roughed up one of the girls over at Miss Betty's, he went and beat the daylights out of him. No one understood why he'd take up for a woman like that, but Billy just muttered that he had a daughter her age, and that she had to be somebody's daughter."

Another story that didn't mesh with either his view of his pa, or the stories he'd heard. Though the name intrigued him. Slim was the guy his pa supposedly cheated to get the mine he'd just looked at.

"How did that make him unpopular?"

Wes shrugged. "There's two types of people in this town. One that wants to get rid of the women. They'd just as soon have them sent away and everything cleaned up nicely. The other type wants them so's they can use them, if you know what I mean."

The collar of the unfamiliar shirt felt tight around Joseph's neck. Yes, he knew what Wes meant. Because clearly his pa had taken advantage of the latter.

"Billy, he wasn't neither. He saw a man for who and what he was, and he didn't make no pretense otherwise. Didn't matter if a man wore fancy clothes or drove a nice rig. If the man was a snake, he called him a snake. The snakes around here didn't like that none."

Wes's eyes narrowed as he motioned to Joseph to lean

in more. "There's plenty of folks who wanted your pa dead, and not for any of the reasons you'd think."

Not a very helpful answer. "But was there silver?"

"I don't know. No one knows for sure. Only Billy, and he's dead now."

So close to answers, yet none that he sought. "Is there anything you can tell me that would be helpful? I just looked at a mine he supposedly won in a card game from Slim."

"I've heard that tale." Wes shrugged. "And even though Lon, the dealer, supports Slim's side of the story, I never bought it. Like I said, Billy was terrible at cards."

Which only made everything all the more murky. And made his pa's death all the more likely to have been murder. But it didn't give him any answers.

"If anyone knows anything, it would be the kid," Wes continued. "Billy doted on her. When her ma took ill, he cared for that little girl himself. Paid Miss Betty well to keep Lily and the child."

Money he could have sent home. While part of Joseph admired that his pa did the honorable thing with his mistress and their child, the other part stung at the thought of his mother and siblings struggling. How was he supposed to forgive a man for letting one family starve while supporting the other?

"Why'd he keep them at that place? Surely he'd put them in a house or something like that."

"For a while, they lived at his cabin. But when Lily got sick, she needed to be close to the doctor. None of the decent boardinghouses would have her, given her old profession. Besides, her friends were all at Miss Betty's."

It was strange to think that a person would be more comfortable in a house of ill repute than anywhere else. Especially with a child.

"Plus, if you ask me—" Wes lowered his voice again "—I heard talk of some men out to get Billy. I imagine he wanted to keep his family safe."

"How do you know all this? And why doesn't Frank know?"

"Billy was afraid of putting the preacher in danger. He figured he'd risked enough by giving him his papers to hold, but the preacher's safe is the safest in town, other than at the bank. And Billy had his reasons for not wanting to go to the bank."

"But that doesn't answer my question. How do you know all this?"

"Because…" He lowered his voice even further.

"Oh, for land's sakes, Wes. Just tell him already. I'm not some delicate flower you have to protect."

Betsy came and stood in their midst. "I used to work at Miss Betty's with Lily. Wes and I fell in love, but given my profession, we were afraid that if people knew, they wouldn't do business with Wes anymore. So we pretended like I was new to town, and everyone believed it. Except Billy, who recognized me from his visits to Lily."

She gave Wes a sharp glare. "Billy would sometimes bring Lily over to see me. None of the womenfolk here in town were all that friendly to me. I always imagined that they figured out who I really was, even though no one has ever said anything. It's like no matter how hard I try, I can't get the stain of my former job off me."

The longing on her face wrenched Joseph's heart in two. "You told me I should seek out Miss Annabelle. But I ask you, what do I have to offer a fine young lady like her? I'm not fit company, and if her pa knew what I used to do, he'd never allow it."

Obviously Betsy didn't know Frank all that well. "If that's so, then why does he let her take care of Nugget?"

"She's a child. She hasn't done anything wrong. Not like me."

The pain in the woman's eyes made him realize that she had far more in common with Annabelle than she thought. He looked over at Wes, then back at Betsy. "Clearly you haven't been to church enough. Because there you'd learn that all have sinned and fall short of the glory of God. Anyone who would judge you is just as guilty of sin as you are."

"I knew I liked you," Wes said with a grin. "I can see why Frank is so keen on you. You're a good man. I hope you find your pa's silver. If anyone deserves it, you do."

Unfortunately, he was learning that finding silver had nothing to do with deserving it. Just like the misfortunes that befell people. Frank and Annabelle didn't deserve the tragedy they'd experienced, but it had come anyway. So, too, had the hardships come to Joseph and his.

But somehow, some way, Joseph was going to make it right.

Betsy handed him a bowl of soup. "Eat this. After being in that storm, it'll do you good. Keep you from catching cold."

Between sips of soup, Joseph further relayed the events on the mountain. Even as the soup warmed him, his bones ached with the chill of being so close to death. Again, he couldn't help but thank God for keeping him safe. Surely, by the worried expressions on his new friends' faces, God's hand had been on him the entire time.

"Wait a second." Wes stared at him. "You're telling me that right before the big rockslide, you heard a boom?"

Joseph nodded. "Yes. Lightning must've struck and loosened the rocks."

"I don't think so. It would do that to a tree, maybe, but boulders? A slide that big had to have come from something like dynamite. Your story sounds a lot like what miners have described as being caught in when they've set the dynamite wrong."

The concern on Wes's face brought the chill back to Joseph. "It did sound different from the lightning strikes, now that you mention it."

Wouldn't Slade have known the difference? "So why didn't Slade come back to see if I was all right?"

He'd told himself it was because the situation was so dangerous, but wouldn't a man of God, the right-hand man of the preacher who'd assigned him to take care of Joseph, have checked?

Betsy's eyes narrowed. "I'll tell you why. Because Slade's dirty. The preacher doesn't see it, because he always sees the best in everyone. I'm telling you, Slade is the worst of them all."

Wes nodded, his lips drawn in a thin line. "You can tell a lot about a man by how he takes care of his horse. Slade's ruined many a good animal. I don't like to speak ill of anyone, but I have to agree. If I were a betting man, I'd go all in on the notion that Slade caused that landslide."

It just didn't seem right. Not with how highly Frank regarded the other man. "Has he been in any trouble? Done anything that would make you think…?"

Wes shook his head. "Nothing that could be proven." He frowned. "Not even enough that I could go to the preacher with. It just seemed like I'd be speaking ill of someone without cause."

Unfortunately that didn't do any of them any good with Annabelle and Nugget at stake. Surely he wouldn't hurt Annabelle. Not since they'd made up.

"He wouldn't hurt Annabelle, though, would he? I mean, everyone says—"

"Don't trust him with her," Betsy said too quickly. "We learned real quick at Miss Betty's to be busy when Slade came around. He liked doing things, bad things, and the more the girl cried, the better he liked it. I'm telling you, he might put on a pleasing attitude in public, but that man likes hurting people."

Betsy didn't need to go into detail for Joseph to feel sick.

"Why would he finally show his true colors now?" Joseph looked at the two, hoping that there was some way they could be wrong. That all of this wasn't true. Because if it was, Slade was on his way back to the camp with no one there to protect Nugget and Annabelle.

Wes looked at him intently. "Because you must've been close to finding the silver. I always thought that your pa's death was suspicious. He was having an assayer come all the way up from Denver, so why would he get drunk and accidentally fall into a ravine the day before?"

Because his pa had always had a weakness for the drink. "Maybe he was celebrating prematurely."

Or maybe, based on Slade's evasive answers, he was pushed.

"Slade was trying to talk me into selling the claims to a land agent."

"Who'd he recommend?"

"He didn't say."

But with the strong hints that Slade gave, Joseph was sure he'd probably had someone in mind. He'd almost been convinced to go ahead and do it. And maybe, had Slade been patient enough to not try to kill him, Joseph would have.

Now, knowing what he knew, Joseph had no choice but to see it through.

First, though, he had to find a way to keep Annabelle and Nugget safe.

Chapter Nineteen

Gertie had decided that Annabelle's foot wasn't healed enough to help with the laundry or much of anything else. Probably not a bad thing, considering that if she stepped on it just right, tears still sprang to her eyes. So she'd brought the children to collect wildflowers. Still within sight of the camp, but far enough that Annabelle could have a moment's peace while two little girls scampered in the meadow and picked flowers.

Annabelle had found a nice rock to sun herself on, and the girls' laughter was enough to almost lull her into a nap. Not that she'd do such a thing, of course. Especially since every time she closed her eyes, Joseph's smile haunted her.

Fortunately any other flight of fantasy in regards to the man too handsome for his own good was interrupted by Gertie's dinner bell. She held out her hands to the little girls. "I believe we have enough flowers to decorate the table. Let's take these back to Gertie to see what we can come up with."

The little girls gathered their baskets and took Annabelle's hands. Except Nugget's grasp seemed a little less firm than usual.

Gertie's cabin was within eyesight. "Caitlin, could you bring the baskets to your mother? Nugget and I will be right there."

Caitlin nodded solemnly, then scampered off. Annabelle knelt in front of Nugget.

"What's wrong, sweet pea?"

She wrapped her arms around Nugget, who remained stiff and didn't return the embrace. Annabelle kissed the top of the little girl's head.

"You're going away." Nugget finally looked up at her, tears streaming down her face.

"Where did you hear that?"

Nugget sniffed. "Your pa was telling Caitlin's ma. Then I heard you telling Joseph."

Annabelle rubbed Nugget's back. She should have been happy at the victory of finally being able to leave, but all it did was make her feel as miserable as the tears running down the little girl's cheeks. "So are you, remember? Joseph is going to take you to meet your other brother and sisters. You're going to finally be a family."

Light shone in Nugget's eyes. "You're coming with us?"

"No." Annabelle shook her head. "It wouldn't be proper. But I know they're going to love you."

"What if they're mean?" Nugget asked in a tiny voice. "Who will protect me?"

Annabelle closed her eyes. *Please, Lord. You don't answer prayers for me, but could You please honor this little girl? She doesn't deserve this.*

She opened her eyes and looked at Nugget. "You'll have Joseph."

"He's not you."

How did a person respond to such a thing?

"We'll write letters. And perhaps we can find a way to visit."

From the child's expression, she could tell that Nugget wasn't too keen on either of those ideas.

"I want you with me always."

Nugget flung her arms around Annabelle and clung as though she expected someone to separate them right away. But Annabelle wouldn't be so fortunate. She already knew that. She'd have more time to fall deeper in love with the girl so that when she was finally wrenched away, her heart would be broken into tinier pieces than it already was.

The pain of losing shouldn't be as bad, having already lost so much. But it seemed like this time, it was even crueler, given her vows not to be attached and the way Nugget had crawled in anyway.

As Annabelle and Nugget headed for the cabin, the first drops of rain began to fall.

"Come on, sweet pea, we've got to hurry if we're going to stay dry."

"Look what we have here." One of the men from the previous day stepped in their path.

Annabelle grimaced as he gave her a toothless sneer. From her discussion with Slade yesterday, she surmised him to be Pokey Simpkins, which meant the other guy must be Bart Wallace. Not that knowing their names changed anything.

"Looks like our sparrow that got away," Bart said.

Annabelle turned to run in the other direction, but Tom, the very man she had been fighting with Polly over, had come behind her. "I don't think so. You and the brat are coming with us."

"Run, Nugget," Annabelle shouted, but it was too late.

Bart had her securely in his arms, and even though the little girl was kicking and screaming, it did no good.

At that moment, the sky decided to open up into an all-out downpour. Everyone within shouting distance was scurrying for cover and shouting their own instructions to their people to keep safe.

No one heard their cries for help.

Tom bound her wrists with a rope. She tried kicking at him, but he laughed when she missed, and her injured ankle gave way, landing her squarely in the mud.

"Aw, the lady got herself all dirty."

The men cackled with glee, as if it was the funniest thing they'd ever seen. Too bad Polly wasn't around to see Tom with her now. Of course, she'd probably help with whatever nasty scheme these men had in mind.

"Mebbe," Tom said. "But just like a juicy piece of fruit, a bit of dirt ain't gonna stop me from plucking it."

She might be a lady, but there was no mistaking his reference. Too much time working in her father's ministry had taught her more than she'd ever wanted to know. There had always been a meanness to his eyes that she'd never trusted. And now she knew why. She'd been right all along in her instincts about this man, but being right didn't help her now.

Pokey brought around a horse. The men hoisted her up then tied her to the saddle. Tom got up behind her and spurred the horse on.

"Nugget!" She twisted to try to see the child.

"Don't you worry your pretty little head none. She's coming. Just by different route so's we can fool any rescue party."

Lightning lit up the sky around them. "'Course with this storm, no one's going to be able to track us anyways."

He stuffed a cloth in her mouth. Old and tasting of stale...well, something old. Worse, it made her feel a little woozy....

When she woke, she was inside a cave, tied up. Nugget slept next to her, also tied. Her heart wrenched at the thought of everything this child had been through in her short life.

"About time you woke up, princess." Tom kicked her in the side. "You got me into a heap of trouble, let me tell you."

She stared at him, the gag too tight around her mouth to say anything.

"Yes, sirree..." He pulled a knife out of his boot and began playing with it. "Polly overheard me talking with the boys about our plans, and I had to do some fast thinking."

Tom leaned in close, his foul breath stinging her nose. He flicked the knife along her cheek. "You're scared, ain't ya? I loves me some scared girls. Something I have in common with the boss man."

She struggled and tried using her body to strike at him, but he moved away, laughing.

Pokey and Bart entered the cave.

"Anyone follow you?"

"Nope." Bart grinned. "They haven't sent out a search party yet. No one realizes they're missing."

"Good." A familiar voice sounded in the background. "All the more time to find out where the silver is before I have to get back."

She looked up to see Slade standing before her.

"Surprised?" His eyes gleamed in the firelight. "You were right about that night Peter died. I had to see a man about some silver. Only there was no wife I sent it to."

Slade stared at her with more hatred than she'd ever

felt in her own heart. "You have no idea what that night cost me. I'd worked so hard to gain Frank's trust, to be able to hear about all the claims and mines. Playing his errand boy so that I could get the inside track. And you know what?"

He stepped in closer, shoving Tom aside. "You had to go ruin it all with your silly tantrum about how it was all my fault your stupid brother died. Your pa asked me to stay away until you cooled down, making it harder for me to find the big one. I knew then, I'd make you pay."

His laugh shook her insides. "But look how convenient. Not only are you going to pay, but you're going to get me my silver."

Pure evil. That's what Slade's face looked like. Being right was no consolation for what stood before her. He pulled the gag down off her mouth.

"What do you want from me?"

"The kid knows where the silver is. One of the girls at Miss Betty's said she overheard the kid talking about seeing her daddy's silver."

He gave her another cold stare. "The kid trusts you. Make it tell us where to find the silver."

Nugget stirred beside her, but didn't wake

"She's just a child. She doesn't know where the silver is. She couldn't even get us to her father's cabin. When we got to the clearing, she led us in the wrong direction."

Madness. That's what this all was. Nugget could no sooner help them than she could. And the crazy look in Slade's eyes told her that he wasn't going to take no for an answer.

"Besides, you know how children are. They have wonderful imaginations. They—"

Slade's hand came across her cheek in a stinging blow. "I've wanted to do that to your smart mouth for a long time. You never did know your place. Get the kid to talk."

"There is no silver." Annabelle stared at him. Or at least in his direction. She could still see spots.

"Don't lie." He struck her again, on the other side, and as his hand made contact, she tasted blood.

"I've seen the silver. Billy used it to pay Slim for his worthless claim. Was spitting mad when he found out that Slim seeded it. Now get the kid to tell me where the real mine is."

Tears prickled her eyes. How could he endanger a child like this? "You'll need to free my hands so I can wake her up."

Slade's head jerked up and down. "Fine." He gestured to Tom.

"Cut her loose." Then he looked over at his other men. "If she tries to escape, shoot her. We don't need her. Just the kid."

If Slade had no problem with hitting her and kidnapping a child, he could do much worse to Nugget. Annabelle took a deep breath as Tom cut the ropes at her wrists.

"Nugget," she whispered when she was free. Annabelle shook the little girl softly. "Wake up, sweet pea."

"My head hurts," Nugget said as she struggled awake. "I had a bad dream."

The little girl blinked, then looked around, her eyes widening as she realized it hadn't been a dream.

"Annabelle," she cried, burrowing into Annabelle's arms.

Annabelle stroked Nugget's hair. "They want your father's silver."

Nugget whimpered and looked up at her. "I thought he was our friend."

She had, too. He'd fooled them all. The worst part was how her father was going to feel when he realized that he'd been betrayed by someone he'd loved like a son.

"I'm sorry, Nugget."

"Enough." Slade held up a hand like he was going to hit her again. "Get her to tell me where the silver is."

Annabelle squeezed her precious charge. "It's going to be all right. But you have to help us get out of here by telling Slade what he wants to know."

Nugget's eyes darted over to Slade, then she looked around at all the other men, her gaze resting on Tom.

"Papa always said you were a snake."

"Shh." Annabelle pulled Nugget closer to her. "We can talk about this later. But right now, we've got to do the right thing."

Nugget pulled away. "Papa said it was a secret."

Slade's chuckle made Annabelle's heart sink. The problem with the child's reasoning of keeping her father's secret was that she didn't understand that men like Slade didn't care about promises or secrets. He'd do whatever it took to get what he wanted.

"Please," Annabelle said, looking at the little girl. "Tell him what he needs so we can get safely back to Joseph."

Another laugh from Slade. How had she missed the pure evil in this man? How had her father?

"Joseph won't be joining us this afternoon. Or ever." His features twisted into a sneer that skittered down Annabelle's back into the darkest pit of her stomach.

"What'd you do to him?"

"Joseph?" Nugget's whimper as she slid back into the protection of Annabelle's arms made her heart hurt.

Slade smiled. "I didn't do anything to him. Wasn't

my fault he couldn't keep up in the storm. Just too bad about all the lightning."

His yellow teeth stuck out from his tobacco-stained lips. "There might have been some dynamite involved. But in a storm like that, you never can tell. It'll be weeks, maybe even months before they find the body. With all the rocks on top of him, and then the flash flood washing everything away, who knows where his body ended up."

Familiar grief welled in Annabelle's heart. Why, God? Why, when she'd finally agreed to opening up her heart, did He have to take away Joseph, too?

Sure, he was going to leave anyway, but it was so much easier to think of him as being away, where she could write him and stay in touch, than it was to think of yet one more loved one gone forever.

Nugget hadn't spoken, but the wetness against Annabelle's bodice said all that needed to be said. The little girl had lost both mother and father, and now a beloved brother had been taken, as well.

So unfair.

"Now…" Slade leaned in, so foul that she had no idea why she never saw how completely indecent he was. "Since we have that cleared up, why don't you tell me what I need to know."

He reached for one of the tendrils by Annabelle's face, winding his finger in it. "It would be a shame for you and the kid to come to the same end."

The sinking feeling in Annabelle's gut told her they probably would anyway. If Slade was going to kill them no matter what, why convince Nugget to tell them what he wanted? It didn't seem right for so much to be lost for Slade to win.

Annabelle pulled Nugget tighter to her chest. "She

just found out her brother is dead. So back off for a minute or else we'll both gladly take a bullet just to spite you out of getting the silver."

"Don't toy with me, you witch." Slade used his grip on her hair to pull her head in toward his, their faces barely an inch from touching. "I will get my silver, with or without your help. I'm sure your father will do just about anything to get his precious daughter back."

So much for her grand plan. Because he was right about her father. He loved her far too much to let her go easily. Tears filled her eyes as she realized how selfish she'd been in wanting to leave. She couldn't let her father be hurt by all of this.

"All right," Annabelle said softly. "I'll do what I can to get Nugget to cooperate, but you've got to give us room. You've waited this long for the silver, surely a few more hours won't make that much of a difference."

If there was ever anything to convince Annabelle of the sheer evil in Slade, it was the way the light shone in his eyes at her offer. He'd thought he'd won. And if there was anything that ever prodded Annabelle into action, it was this.

She was sick and tired of everything evil and rotten in this world winning. This time, if it cost her everything, including her life, Slade would not win. She just had to figure out how to make that happen.

Despite the rain not letting up, Joseph returned to the stable and began saddling one of Frank's other horses.

"You're crazy to go out back out there," Wes told him, handing him a bridle.

"What else am I supposed to do? Based on what you just told me, there's no way that avalanche was an accident."

He bent to check the cinch on the saddle. Wes grabbed his arm, forcing him to look at him. "Why do you think I'm asking you to wait?"

Joseph straightened and looked at the other man. "Someone tried to kidnap Nugget. Annabelle was accosted in the camp. And the man that her pa is trusting to keep us all safe just tried to kill me. You'll forgive me if I'm not going to hesitate in making sure they're out of harm's way."

Lord, I don't even know how I'm going to do that.

"There's no way you'll beat him to the camp."

Hopefully, Slade would be counting on the fact that Joseph was dead, and was waiting in camp for the storm to let up before doing anything. But why would he act now? They'd come no closer to finding the silver than they were when he first started looking.

Except…

The Bible.

Joseph shook his head. He hadn't told anyone what he'd found in the Bible. Hadn't had a chance. He'd have liked to have shown it to Frank or Annabelle, but for whatever reason, he hadn't felt comfortable trusting Slade.

Maybe God had been protecting him more than he knew.

Joseph looked around for the saddlebag he'd had on the other horse. He hadn't even thought about whether or not the contents had remained dry.

"Where's my saddlebag?"

Wes pointed to a rack. "I hung it to dry. But what do you need with some old clothes and a couple of rocks?"

Rocks? "What about the Bible that was in there?"

"You really are a praying man," Wes said with a grin.

"Well, rest your mind about that. It wasn't in there, so you must've left it at the camp."

Joseph's stomach turned. He'd put it in the saddlebag. Hadn't wanted to trust leaving it in camp. Slade must've switched it out on the mountain. Joseph had his back turned, looking at his pa's land. Plenty of time for him to have made a switch.

He should have been more careful. And he shouldn't have assumed that Slade wasn't paying attention to his Bible reading last night. Slade obviously knew what Joseph was looking at.

"No, that means Slade took it. Last night, I figured out that my pa had used it as a key for the location of his silver. I had it in my saddlebag until I could talk to Frank and see what he thought of the code my pa left. I couldn't figure out what all the references to the places meant."

The loss of color on Wes's face was all Joseph needed to know. He turned and grabbed another saddle. "Then I'd best come with you. If Slade thinks he has the key to where the silver is, then there's no telling what he'll do to finally get it."

Chapter Twenty

The men were poring over a Bible. How could a gang of kidnapping thieves get any more ridiculous?

Nugget had ceased crying, but she remained listless in Annabelle's arms. Her brother's murder must have sucked the last bit of life out of her.

Annabelle looked around for something to use as a weapon. If she got out of this alive, she would absolutely insist on having one of those tiny pistols to hide under her skirts. Fortunately, the men seemed to be focused more on the Bible than on them. Fine time for a Bible study. She supposed she should find comfort that something her father had taught Slade had sunk in.

If only she knew which cave they were in. The landscape would give them a clue, if she could convince them to let her outside for a moment.

"Slade," she called, trying not to disturb Nugget. "I have to use the necessary."

"So?" He slammed the book shut, and the men scattered.

"Could you please escort me out so I can take care of my needs?"

Her face was warm at the thought of discussing such a personal though fabricated matter with him.

"Nope." His grin taunted her.

"Boss," Tom whispered, "maybe you could get her to…"

She didn't catch the rest of it as the two men put their heads together and began whispering furiously back and forth.

Nugget stirred. "Don't leave me alone with them. They're bad men."

Annabelle shifted the little girl so she could whisper in her ear unobserved. "I want to look around outside so I can see if there's a way to escape."

"Don't leave me." Nugget's wail nearly pierced her eardrum.

Slade looked in their direction. "Don't worry, she's not going anywhere."

He sauntered over to them, Bible in hand. "But we might let her stop and do her business on our way to the silver."

Or maybe they could find a way to escape at that time. "If Nugget tells you where it is."

"Don't need the brat." He sneered in Nugget's direction. "There's enough clues here that we'll find the silver."

He held up the Bible, and at closer look, she realized that it was the one Joseph had taken from his father's cabin. Slade had probably killed Joseph to get it.

"Then let us go." She said the words with as much bravado as she could muster, but in reality, she knew that Slade no longer had any reason to keep either of them alive. Especially since he had to know that she'd turn him in to her father and the sheriff when they got free.

"There's a few pieces we don't understand. But between you and the little one, we'll get it faster. And I owe a guy, so I'd rather get the money quick-like, if you know what I mean."

She looked down at Nugget, whose eyes had widened. Slade, too, drew his attention to the little girl.

"Where's Nugget's secret house?"

At Nugget's indrawn breath, Annabelle knew once that location was revealed, Slade would have the silver.

So close. But she wasn't going to give up. Not until the last breath had been ripped from her. She was done with letting evil take everything from her. Done.

"By the monkey rock," Nugget said in a quiet, shaky voice.

The monkey rock. Completely not helpful in the description, since many of the rocks looked like shapes of other things. They were like clouds. People saw different shapes in all of them.

"Which is where?" He pulled Nugget out of her arms and shook her.

"Leave her alone!" Annabelle jumped up and reached for Nugget, but Slade was just as quick to keep her away.

He looked at the other men. "Get them ready to travel."

Slade kept hold of Nugget, tying her to his saddle. Tom grabbed Annabelle.

"Be a good girl and don't fight."

Not likely, considering Slade was ready to leave with Nugget. She couldn't let him take her. Hopefully on the way, she'd figure out how to get them both free. Right now, though, it wasn't worth fighting, or even wasting her breath on screams no one would hear. Best to save her energy for when she could get Nugget.

As Tom dragged her outside, he whispered, "You

even think about trying to escape, and we'll kill the brat."

The rain had stopped, leaving puddles everywhere, and the kind of mud a person could sink in. Maybe she could use it to her advantage.

Annabelle pulled a pin out of her hair and let it drop to the ground. Though tiny, the small rhinestone on the end would hopefully be a clue to anyone looking for them.

Once Tom had hoisted her onto his saddle, she managed to get another pin loose and dropped it into the grass nearby. Maddie had called those pins an unnecessary vanity, but at least they were distinctive to anyone who knew her. Slade hadn't been around enough lately to know they were hers.

They headed east, and Annabelle memorized every bit of terrain. When she got out of this, she would be sure that the sheriff searched every inch for anyone else linked to Slade's gang.

If someone spotted one of her hairpins.

As they turned out of the canyon, Annabelle recognized the landscape. Not too far from the cabin, and an easy journey to the camp.

"Can we stop for a moment?" She looked over her shoulder at Tom and gave him her most pleasant smile. "You never did let me use the necessary."

Her skin crawled as she batted her eyelashes at him, trying to appeal to him in a feminine way. If Polly was mad at her because she thought he'd been flirting, then maybe she could use it to her advantage.

Tom gave a half smile back. Shy, like her being nice to him was an unexpected treat. Annabelle tried not to gag.

"Boss!" he yelled. "We need to stop."

Gloating would only ruin her chances at this point. Though it would be easy for her to get away here, it still left the problem of getting Nugget free. She had no doubt that Slade would harm her in retaliation. Even in the fun games her family had played together, Slade was known to be a ruthless competitor.

Slade rode toward them. "What's the problem?"

"The necessary." Annabelle twisted her face into an expression that she hoped looked like she had to go really bad. Her mother would be horrified at how unladylike she was being, but if it saved her life, and that of a young child, surely it would be worth it.

He glared at her, then at Tom. "Now?"

"I'm afraid if I wait any longer, and all the jostling on the horse…"

Tom got off his horse. "Boss, if she ruins my saddle…"

"Fine." Slade pulled out his pistol. "But if you try anything, remember I've got the kid."

She swallowed, then scooted off the horse. "I understand."

No, running away was not an option. Especially given that Slade had one hand on Nugget, and the other held a gun.

"I'll just go behind those bushes." She stared at him, daring him to argue.

"What happened to your hair?"

Annabelle reached up, realizing that with all the pins she'd taken out, it was starting to look a mess. She couldn't afford for Slade to look too closely or start wondering about the missing pins.

"I told you, all the jostling is rather uncomfortable. I keep trying to push my hair back up out of my face, but it's not as though any of you are taking care to make this an easy ride."

The gleam in Slade's eyes made her realize that he was enjoying every moment of tormenting her. The more miserable she said she was, the more he enjoyed it.

"We don't cater to prissy spoiled brats here. Guess you'll have to make do."

She gave him the kind of haughty look she knew he expected from her. Though she was learning to be more than the child everyone thought her, now was not the time to prove she'd changed. The old Annabelle was exactly what Slade needed to see.

"When my father finds out—"

"We'll be halfway to Mexico with the silver." He leaned forward and ran a finger down her cheek. "And I haven't decided if I'll kill you first, or keep you around for entertainment for a while, and then sell you. Pretty golden hair like yours will fetch a mighty fine price."

Slade rolled one of her curls around his finger, then gave it a sharp yank. Had he pulled any harder, she was sure she'd have a bald spot. It took every amount of energy not to kick him in the shins.

She brushed past him and headed into the bushes. She relieved herself as quickly as she could, then took three of her hairpins and fashioned them into an *A*. Maybe that would help anyone looking for her.

Now to find a place to leave it unobserved by the bandits, but in such a way that anyone looking for her would spot the clue.

As she walked back to the horses, every bandit's eye was on her. At least they weren't underestimating her abilities to try to escape. Because she would. With Nugget.

She spied a rock, that if she could just get the hairpins on it, would hopefully put them in view of anyone coming from the direction of the camp.

"Ouch!" Annabelle pretended to stumble on her way to the horse. She scooted toward the rock, pretending to try to right herself. Then, because it was so close, Annabelle went and sat on the rock, making a show of examining the foot she'd injured the day before.

"I do hope it's not worse." She glared at Slade. "It's the same ankle I hurt yesterday. I should have listened to Gertie about keeping off it longer. Then maybe you wouldn't have been able to kidnap us. We'd be safe in the cabin right now."

Annabelle started to cry, thinking she'd have to fake the tears, but as they flowed readily, she realized what a mess everything was. Her words were supposed to have been a ploy, to distract the men from noticing her setting the pins for someone to discover them. But they were true.

Slade strode toward her, his face filled with disgust.

"Even if you'd stayed at the cabin, we'd still have gotten you. Probably easier and without a fuss. You think your pa or Gertie would have objected to me taking you two for a ride?"

His confidence made her realize just how he'd fooled them all. If Slade had come to the cabin and offered to take her for a ride, she and everyone else would have agreed.

"Then why kidnap us?" She stared at him defiantly as he hauled her to her feet.

He grinned. "Because it's more fun this way."

With great ease, Slade picked her up and threw her over his shoulder. "Wouldn't want you to hurt your foot any more, would we?"

How had she not seen what a bully Slade was?

Slade handed her to Tom, who helped hoist her back onto the saddle.

"No more delays," Slade said as he tugged again on one of her loose tendrils.

Another hairpin clattered to the ground, and she couldn't help but hope that was the first one her rescuers found. It would serve Slade right for his meanness to be the instrument of his downfall.

When Joseph and Wes arrived at Gertie's, the rain had stopped, but the place was in an uproar.

"What's going on?" he asked Gertie.

"Annabelle and Nugget are missing," she said, looking over at Frank. "They were picking flowers, then the storm hit. I just don't know where they could be."

Polly slammed a pot to the ground. "I'll tell you where they are. She's run off with Tom, despite all of her protests about not being the sort to dig her claws into someone else's man."

He couldn't believe that Polly's petty jealousy was keeping everyone from looking for Annabelle. "That isn't what happened." Joseph glared at her, then turned to Frank.

"There's a lot Wes and I need to catch you up on. But we'll have to do that as we look for Annabelle and Nugget. Slade has them, and—"

"No, he doesn't." Polly stood and squared off with him. "I saw her ride off with Tom. Nugget wasn't with them. He had his arms around her, and I can assure you, she was not upset about it."

He stepped aside and addressed Frank. "Tom must be working with Slade. When we were on the ridge, Slade tried to kill me. He stole my pa's Bible out of my saddlebag. I believe it holds the clue to the location of the silver."

The doubt on Frank's face, along with Polly's screeching in the background made it almost impossible to believe they'd get Annabelle back safely.

"It's true," Wes said, breaking in to the conversation. "I've seen Slade and Tom hanging around town together. I'm sure he's got other men who've got Nugget. We need to find them—fast."

Frank's Adam's apple bobbed as he looked from Wes to Joseph. "You're certain Slade tried to kill you?"

"Yes. As I said, I'll give the rest of the details on the way. We've got to find Annabelle and Nugget."

Which seemed almost hopeless given that Frank was still doubtful about the circumstances of his daughter's disappearance, and that without his pa's Bible, they had no idea where...

Joseph glanced around the people gathered. "My pa referenced something about Nugget's secret rock house in his Bible. Does that sound at all familiar?"

Gertie nodded. "The girls were talking about one. Caitlin!"

She ran toward the tent, where a teary-eyed little girl emerged. "Did you find Nugget?"

"No."

Joseph watched as Gertie bent down in front of her daughter. He prayed Caitlin would know where it was.

"I heard you girls talking about a secret house. Do you know where it is?"

Caitlin nodded. "Nugget said it was by her papa's cabin, at monkey rock, and that someday she'd take me there to play in her treasure room."

All this time, Nugget had probably known where the silver was.

"Thank you, Caitlin." Joseph bent and gave the little girl a hug. "I promise, we'll do everything we can to find Nugget."

Please, Lord, don't let this be a broken promise. Nugget had to be safe, she just had to be.

"I know where we're going," he told Wes, who was already headed for the horses.

Joseph looked over at Frank. "Are you coming?"

The older man nodded slowly. It was clear he still couldn't wrap his mind around Slade being behind everything, but hopefully, during the ride, with Wes to help explain what he knew of the man, it would become clearer.

Now he just needed to pray that they'd reach Annabelle and Nugget in time.

Chapter Twenty-One

When they reached the turnoff for Nugget's father's cabin, they didn't turn, but rode on.

"The cabin's that way," Annabelle said, twisting to get Tom's attention.

"We're not going to the cabin, Miss Know It All." He yanked on Annabelle's hair in imitation of Slade.

What was it with these men and her hair? At least it gave her an excuse to pull out yet another hairpin to leave as a marker. She dropped an extra one, and another closer than what she ordinarily would have in hopes that they'd pick up on her clue and keep going.

What must her father be thinking right now? Had they gotten word of Joseph's death? Did he know Slade was the culprit, or would her father be wondering who could have taken her?

Did they even know they were gone?

Annabelle pushed those thoughts out of her head. She wasn't going to give up. She simply couldn't. Too many bad things had happened already, and she wasn't going to let this have the same end.

They reached an outcropping of rocks, which must've

been the other side of where Joseph's father had built his cabin.

"There!" One of Slade's men pointed in the direction of a rock formation.

Tom dismounted, then yanked her off the horse. "Walk."

She did as she was bade, eager to catch up with Slade and to check on Nugget.

When they got to the base of the formation, Slade turned toward Annabelle. "Get the kid to tell me where the silver is."

Annabelle started toward Nugget, who raced into her arms. "That man is mean."

"I know." Annabelle hugged her tight. "Is the silver here?" she whispered.

Nugget nodded. "Papa said I shouldn't tell anyone."

How could she convince a child to betray her father's confidence? Worse, how could she get the information about the silver to Slade in such a way that he'd let them live, at least long enough for them to escape?

"You know that the mean man is going to hurt us if you don't tell him?"

Tears ran down Nugget's face. A child so young should not be responsible for all the things she'd had to face.

With a look braver than her age, Nugget wiped an arm across her face, took Annabelle's hand, then tugged her in the direction of Slade.

"In that cave," Nugget said, pointing at a small fissure in the rock.

Slade went to the spot Nugget indicated, staring into it. He tried squeezing into the space, but his body was too big.

"How'd he get the silver out? Is there another entrance?" He returned his attention to Nugget.

She shook her head, then said quietly, "I got the silver for him."

If there was anyone Annabelle wanted to hurt more than Slade and his men, it was Nugget's father for putting a child in this position. How could he?

Slade, though, had no such thoughts, as a wicked grin crossed his face. "Then get it for me."

Nugget glanced in Annabelle's direction. "Annabelle has to come with me. There's enough room. Mama used to come so's the bats wouldn't get me."

Bats. Annabelle swallowed. Well, if she had to choose between bats and bullets, she supposed bats were the best option.

"You wouldn't be trying to pull anything, would you?" Slade got right in Nugget's face, but the little girl remained unmoved.

"She's a child," Annabelle said. "What exactly do you think she's going to pull?"

Slade turned to his men. "Where's the dynamite? Let's just blast it out."

The men whispered amongst themselves, then Bart came forward. "Slim used it all on Joseph. There isn't any more."

For a moment, Annabelle was sure Slade was going to shoot him on the spot. Then Slade looked over at the one she presumed to be Slim.

"Then Slim had best get in to town and get us some more."

Slade returned his attention to Nugget and Annabelle. "I guess it's time for you to prove there's really silver in there. Go in and get me some silver."

Nugget scrambled into the cave, and Annabelle followed, barely able to squeeze into the tight space.

"Nugget?"

Annabelle could hear a soft scrape, then a light shone in the distance.

"Crawl on your belly to my light."

She did as the tiny girl ordered, finding herself in a large cavern.

"Papa told me to come here if anyone ever tried to get me to tell them where the silver is."

Nugget shone the lantern around to indicate an empty cavern that had shiny flecks of some sort of mineral adorning the wall. Unfortunately, it wasn't gold or silver. That much Annabelle knew. "Mama called it my secret house."

Annabelle closed her eyes. They were safe for now, but once Slade realized they were not coming out, he'd just get dynamite and blast them out.

"But how do we get out?"

Nugget shrugged. "Papa always came."

"But your papa is dead. Is there any other way out?"

Annabelle took the lantern and looked around for some sign that the cavern had another exit. Every fissure in the cavern appeared tighter than the one they'd just entered. Nugget went to one of the spaces and pulled out a blanket.

"I want my mama," she said, plopping down on the hard ground and wrapping the blanket around her.

Annabelle joined her and pulled the little girl into her lap. "I know. I want my mama, too."

Because her mother would know exactly what to do. She always did. At some point, Slade was going to get impatient for the silver. And if he found dynamite, and the rocks exploded around them, they surely wouldn't survive.

Lord, please. Help me find a way to get us out safely. We can't have come this far for nothing. My faith is so lacking, but the Bible says that if you have faith as small as a mustard seed... Surely I have that much in me. Otherwise, I wouldn't be calling on You now.

Annabelle wasn't sure what else to say, so she cuddled Nugget closer to her and tried peering around in the limited light. If Nugget had faith that her papa would come get her, there had to be another way in if the way they'd entered was too small for a man.

"Nugget? Will you tell me where the silver is?"

The little girl sighed. "You won't tell the bad men, will you?"

"I won't tell them." *Please God, let me not break this promise.*

But Nugget seemed to know Annabelle was weak. "Yes, you will."

So Annabelle continued her search, shining the light and running her hand along the surface of the cave walls. She stumbled over a pile of rocks.

Could this be it?

She started digging among the rocks, moving them aside in hopes that they would lead to a passageway. Each rock seemed heavier than the last, but it didn't make a dent in the pile.

"It's not there," Nugget said, moving to stand beside her.

Great. Annabelle let out a long breath. She'd been working to get them out of the cave, and Nugget was still trying to protect her father's silver.

"Then where?" She tried keeping the exasperation out of her voice, but she was running out of options.

Nugget looked at her with big, watery green eyes. "I promised my papa."

"Then at least tell me how he got in."

Shadows crossed Nugget's face, and she'd liked to have thought that it was because Nugget was carefully considering the idea. That meant there had to be another way.

"Papa came in from the big rock." Nugget pointed, and when Annabelle swung the lantern, her heart sank. The big rock was bigger than the two of them put together.

"Some other bad men came for Papa once, and he told me to stay in here until it was safe." She walked to the spot where she'd found the blanket, then pulled out a canteen. "The food's gone, but Papa left us water and this lantern." Nugget held up the lantern that illuminated the cave.

This was not what she was looking for. But maybe, if she got Nugget to tell more of the story, she'd find out something that could help them. "How long were you in here?"

"Ages." Nugget let out a long, dramatic sigh. "But then Papa pushed the big rock out of the way and he saved me."

"Annabelle!" The echo through the cave reminded her that they didn't have ages. They had only as much time as the men had to bring dynamite in from town. Which, if they rode hard, only gave them a couple hours.

She turned toward the opening from which they'd come. "We're still looking. It's all a bunch of rocks."

"You best find me some silver."

If only Annabelle and God had been on good enough terms that He would listen to her prayers. But maybe...

Lord, please help us. Help me find a way to save us.

To save Nugget. You saw fit to save me when all of these good people died in spite of all my prayers. Why did You have to take Joseph, too? And now to leave me in this situation where only You can save us? This time, if You have to take someone, let it be me instead of a little girl who hasn't done anything wrong.

Because that, of all things, was her greatest fear. That somehow, God would once again take someone she loved and leave her behind to regret.

Annabelle took Nugget in her arms. "They're not going to be patient much longer. Please, if there is silver, tell me where to find it."

The little girl looked up at her with tears in her eyes. "You don't believe me?"

But this…breaking a child's heart, was probably the worst of all her sins. Faith was supposed to be about believing in things unseen. These men had never seen the silver. Joseph had never seen the silver. But they were all willing to fight for it. How much so should her faith be?

She couldn't even believe in silver when she was supposed to believe in God.

"I just…" Annabelle hated the way her heart churned. "I've seen no evidence…no…"

A voice inside the back of her head asked her if she hadn't seen evidence, or if she hadn't seen the evidence she'd wanted to see.

Annabelle took a deep breath. "I'm sorry, Nugget. If you say there's silver, then I believe." She had to choose to believe.

Annabelle looked Nugget in the eye. "I know your father said to wait here for him, but what did he say to do if he didn't come?"

The uncertainty in the child's eyes didn't give her any comfort. But Annabelle had to do something. Oth-

erwise, sitting here, thinking about the men after her…
Men who'd killed Nugget's father. And Joseph… No,
she couldn't think about him. Not now. Otherwise, the
pain might completely immobilize her.

Nugget's voice piped up. "Papa said for me to sing
some songs so I wouldn't miss him so much while I
waited for him to come. I could sing one my mama
taught me."

The earnestness in the small child's voice gave Annabelle the strength she needed to keep fighting. "That
sounds like a great idea."

As Nugget began singing "Rock of Ages," Annabelle looked around for something to use as a lever. If
the rock moved one way to get Nugget out before, surely
she could find a way to make it work again.

Joseph slowed his horse just before the turnoff for the
cabin. Maybe his pa had left more clues there. Something to tell him where to find the secret rock house or
Monkey Rock.

Lord, please. Help me find Annabelle and Nugget.

Something glinted off a rock in the sunlight and
caught his eye. He stopped and looked closer. The letter *A*, made out of Annabelle's hairpins.

"Frank!" He twisted in his saddle and waved at the
other man. "I've found something."

Without waiting for Frank's answer, Joseph jumped
off the horse and picked up the pins. He searched the
area around where she'd left the clue. She'd been here,
but which direction did they go?

Frank joined him where he stood and examined the
pins. "I've always appreciated that she didn't worry herself into a tizzy the way so many ladies do. I just wish…"
He shook his head.

Joseph put his arm on the other man's shoulder. "Don't wish. We're going to find her and Nugget, and we'll bring them home safely. Then you can tell her all the things you wish you could have told her."

Like that fact that he was kidding himself to think he could only be her friend. No other woman would have the kind of gumption Annabelle did. And in the face of being kidnapped, she still found a way to fight. She'd given his sister her heart and loved her in spite of all the reasons a respectable woman wouldn't be so kind to Nugget. Even though she had to face her own grief to do so.

If anyone could hold her own against Slade and his gang, Annabelle could.

Joseph held up the pins. "Annabelle left us some clues. Do any of you see anything that looks like a monkey rock?"

The men scanned the area, and Joseph's stomach sank at the realization that none of the rocks in the area looked like a monkey.

"I found another pin!"

Frank's shout gave Joseph more hope. Annabelle had left them a trail. Surely as they followed her clues, they'd find a monkey rock.

They were headed east, by the looks of things. He turned toward the other men. "What's east of here? Anything that would be like a monkey?"

Wes's face turned white. "I know where they are. It's not monkey rock, it's long key rock, and it looks like a long key."

He watched as the other man shook his head slowly. "I can't believe the silver was there the whole time. He even tried to get me to buy the claim off him, said he needed to send money home. Said he didn't want just anyone to have it."

Hearing of his pa's honor, or what looked to be it, caused Joseph's gut to churn in an unfamiliar way. No matter how much he thought he knew about his pa, it seemed like there was always something more to be learned. Just as he'd been unable to fit Annabelle into a box, so too, had he failed to do so with his pa.

Joseph went to his horse, prepared to travel to Long Key Rock, but as he headed in the direction of the pins, Wes stopped him. "That's the way they went, but I know a back way. They won't be expecting us from that direction, so maybe we can get a jump on them."

Wes turned toward the men who'd ridden from camp with them. "Someone get the sheriff."

They followed Wes through a tight canyon, so tight that they could barely fit their horses through. If Joseph had been in charge of navigating the passage, he would have been tempted to turn back. It seemed to be nearly impassable as his horse slipped on some rocks.

"Careful!" Wes called behind them. "We're almost there."

A large boulder blocked their path. Wes jumped off his horse. "We'll lead the horses through here. Funny, I don't remember this boulder being here before."

They managed to squeeze past the boulder, and from there, Wes's description of being almost there didn't seem to be so far off. The canyon opened up, and to their right stood a large rock formation. Ahead, nothing but sheer cliffs and the edge of the mountains. From his vantage point, facing the villains directly seemed almost the smarter choice.

"We can tie up the horses here." Wes gestured at a

tree with well-worn ground. "Looks like this is probably where someone else did."

That someone being his pa? Or someone else? Joseph examined the rock formation that Wes said was the rear of the rock where they'd likely taken Annabelle and Nugget. He clambered up the pile of debris. Piles of rock had been dumped here and there, almost as if someone was searching for silver but hadn't found it yet. Someone had been prospecting here.

The other two men joined him, scrambling up the rock, looking for a way to sneak around the front. A fissure in the rock appeared to be almost large enough for a man to squeeze through. If his pa had hidden silver in here, he'd made it nearly impossible for anyone to get to it. But maybe that was the challenge. The way he'd kept it safe all this time.

And why two people were in grave danger.

Joseph peered into the rock opening. Could there be a way through here to where Annabelle and Nugget were being held?

A sound, almost like someone calling Annabelle's name, reached his ears. Joseph squeezed in deeper. Could they have escaped?

"Annabelle...." The word echoed to his ears.

They were there. Had to be.

He squeezed back out of the cave and motioned to Wes and Frank. "I can hear someone calling to Annabelle through here."

Without waiting for their answer, Joseph returned to where he'd positioned himself.

"I've got a lantern." Wes's voice sounded behind him, and light filled the tight space.

Joseph pressed against the wall, realizing there wasn't

enough room for two men to walk comfortably in the space, which dead-ended only a few feet ahead of him.

"Annnnnnnaaaaabellllllleeee…." The voice came again. "Bring out my silver, or we're going to use dynamite."

Dynamite. The hair on the back of his neck stood up as the air grew distinctly colder.

In a cavern like this, who knew how stable the rocks around them were. Dynamite could get them all killed.

A child's voice singing "Rock of Ages" echoed through the cavern. Nugget.

"Give me the lantern." He reached back to Wes, who handed him the light.

Joseph held it up, shining it against each side of the rock around them. Surely there was some passageway to lead them to the girls.

Light seeped through the crack of the boulder that Nugget had said her father pushed aside to get her out. Was it one of Slade's men? Or someone come to save them?

"Rock of Ages, cleft for me. Let me hide myself in thee."

Though Nugget's childish voice spoke of Christ, Annabelle looked around for a hiding place in the rock they were already hiding in. Was there a deeper place for them to find themselves in?

A small voice inside her told her to have a little faith. And she was reminded that she needed to simply believe.

"Annnnnaaabellleee…." Slade's voice came from the other end, though sounding closer than his previous threats had been. "Bring out my silver, or I'm going to use dynamite."

Surely he wouldn't be threatening dynamite if he was sending someone else in through the other side.

"Nugget." Annabelle got the little girl's attention, and indicated to the rock. "I see light coming from there."

The little girl jumped up. "Papa!"

She ran to the boulder and clawed at the crack. "Papa, we're here. The bad men are trying to steal our silver."

"Nugget!"

Joseph. Tears clogged her throat at the sweet sound of a voice she'd never imagined she'd hear again. Annabelle closed her eyes and breathed a simultaneous prayer of relief and prayer for his safety. Against these evil men, Joseph would be no match.

Still, he was alive. All the regret over his death could be erased. She could love him, and let him love her in return.

If they got out alive.

She spoke low and urgently, not wishing for their voices to echo back to Slade. "We're both here, and we're safe. But I don't know for how much longer. Slade is threatening to use dynamite if we don't bring out silver for him."

"Papa moved the rock out of the way to get me out of here," Nugget added.

"Who else is there?" Slade's voice called out. He yelled something to his men, probably to either look for the other entrance or ready the dynamite. Neither would end well for them.

Annabelle knelt in front of Nugget. "Can we send some silver their way? If we tempt them with something, it will give Joseph more time to get us out of here."

Nugget looked in the direction they'd come from, then back at the boulder. "But Papa said…"

"If there's a lot of silver, it won't matter if we give

them some. Besides, it'll give the sheriff a way to find them."

The little girl examined her like an older, wiser, person would. Weighing the risks and benefits of her plan. But mostly, she looked like she wanted to cry.

Nugget nodded slowly, then walked over to another rock. "Behind there."

It looked like any other rock in the place. Part of the many piles of rocks that seemed to lead nowhere. But she trusted Nugget. Annabelle pushed against the rock, but it didn't budge.

"Help me."

Nugget joined her, pushing with all the might the little girl had. Her face reddened with the exertion, but nothing seemed to move.

From the direction of the other boulder, Annabelle could hear sounds of scraping at rock, but no movement.

"Annnnaaabellle…." Slade's voice threatened.

"I'm trying," she called back. "Truly. I just need to move this rock."

She pushed harder, using all of her strength. Nugget grunted as she helped Annabelle push against the rock, which began to move slightly.

Finding silver would give them more time for Joseph to get through the other entrance.

"Dynamite can move the rock."

His voice sounded closer, like he'd managed to find a way through the tiny passageway.

Nugget seemed to realize that, too, as she cast a worried look in Annabelle's direction.

"Come on." She motioned to Nugget, and pointed at the other boulder.

They moved to the other boulder. "Slade is coming," Annabelle said in a harsh whisper.

"Push!" Annabelle said loud enough for Slade, or whoever he might be sending after the silver, to hear.

They gave a couple of shoves at the rock, just as Slade entered the larger cavern.

Annabelle's heart stuck in her throat, and she willed it to go back to normal. To cling to the hope that Joseph would find a way to get them out.

Slade's clothes were torn and covered in dust from using a pick to get to them. Dirty, messy work, and he clearly wasn't happy about having to do the work himself. And, she noted, he'd had to leave his gun behind. Maybe they stood a chance after all.

He tossed the pick at them as he held up the lantern. "What kind of trick is this? There's no silver here."

Annabelle shook her head. "Nugget says it is. She said her father came for her from behind this rock, so it must be here."

Slade looked even more imposing than ever. "That so?" He shone his lantern around the rock. "Yes, we'll need some dynamite."

Hopefully Joseph had heard.

Nugget tugged on Annabelle's skirt. Annabelle looked down at the little girl, who looked terrified at the prospect. "Papa said—"

"I don't care what that no-account papa of yours said," Slade roared as he spun in their direction. "All's he had to do was give me some silver and we'd have been square. But that lyin', cheatin'—"

"Enough!" Annabelle gave him a stern look. "There's no call to use such language."

Then, she looked down at Nugget. "Or dynamite. Clearly, with these tunnels, this is an established mine. We need to dig out the access to the silver, and when we have a better sense of the layout, then you can dynamite where appropriate. If you randomly blast things, you're going to make an awful mess, and I'm sure it'll be that much harder for you to get your silver."

Slade leaned in at her, his eyes gleaming with enough avarice to make her wonder how anyone could have seen anything other than what a cold, hard man he was. His laughter rang through the cavern, surely carrying through to the other tunnels where the others could hear. They were in grave danger.

Slade kicked the pick. "Start digging."

Annabelle took the pick and started swinging it, aiming for the gap in the rock where she knew Joseph would be, but far enough away that she wouldn't strike him with debris. She hoped.

"Help. Please," she said the words as quietly as she could, but Slade immediately jumped up.

"Who you talking to? Who's there?"

Annabelle spun. "I suppose your praying was just for show, so you have no idea what it looks like to truly pray."

Her own words shamed her. How long had she merely given lip service to her faith? Making people think she believed when she had none? Even now, her faith was weak, so weak she could hardly defend it. But here, in the cleft of the rock, she had to believe that she was in the protection of a greater rock.

"Your God's not going to help you. He didn't help your family. Didn't help mine. You think you've uncovered some elixir to make Him listen?"

She closed her eyes, trying to drown out the shame of his words. But just as the familiar darkness threatened to overtake her, another truth sprang to the back of her mind. And her mother's voice came to her, clearer than anything else she'd heard in a long time.

It said in Isaiah, "For My thoughts are not your thoughts, neither are your ways My ways," declares the Lord. "As the heavens are higher than the earth, so are My ways higher than your ways and My thoughts than your thoughts."

It didn't matter what her thoughts were, or how she perceived the situation. The Lord's purpose was far greater than she could see. She just had to believe.

"You hated me," Slade's voice taunted. "Because I didn't get the doctor in time to save your brother. You thought I was too busy going after silver."

Annabelle's eyes flew open, and she looked at him. "I put my faith in the wrong man."

"That you did." He gave the kind of laugh Annabelle imagined only came from a truly wicked being.

And, with the most callous of looks she'd ever seen, he grinned. "Sorry."

Rage boiled inside Annabelle at the unfairness of it all. How long she'd suffered for her supposedly rash judgment of this man, which, as it turned out, had been right all along. But then she remembered a passage from Genesis, when Joseph's brothers feared that he would take retribution for what they had done to him. "You intended to harm me, but God intended it for good, to accomplish what is now being done, the saving of many lives."

Whether Annabelle had been right or wrong, the Lord knew, and not only would He take full accounting of all that had gone on, everything, including all of this, would be used for the Lord's purpose.

Oh, how she'd resented her father trying to comfort her with placating words of how the Lord's will would be done. But now she understood. The Lord saw, and He knew.

Annabelle had a choice. To act in accordance with what the Lord had commanded her, or to act on her pain.

A flash on the other side of the rock caught Annabelle's attention, and she noticed that Joseph had almost worked his way through.

"May the Lord have mercy on your soul," she whispered, setting the pick down with a loud clank, and going to where Nugget sat, whimpering.

"What's that?" Slade looked past her, toward the spot where Annabelle had been digging.

Moments later, his face mottled with rage, he spun. "You've been stalling so's they can —"

"Annabelle, get Nugget out of the blast area so we can blow this rock." Joseph's voice rang through the cave.

She didn't need another invitation. Annabelle grabbed Nugget by the hand and yanked her in the direction of the other tunnel. Though Slade's men waited at the other end, at least it would offer them some protection from the blast until Joseph could get to them.

Slade shoved at her back. "Make way, you stupid—"

An explosion rocked the cavern. Rocks and debris flew everywhere, filling the area with so much dust Annabelle could hardly breathe. She covered her mouth with a sleeve as she pulled her handkerchief out of her pocket to cover Nugget's. At least it would afford the child some protection.

The heavy weight of Slade's body pressed her to the ground, and she shifted to keep most of the weight of the two adults off a squirming Nugget.

"Are you all right?" Annabelle choked the words out, thankful that at least she knew Nugget was alive. Slade, on the other hand, remained a dead weight on top of her.

Nugget coughed, and Annabelle thought she might have heard the little girl say yes.

"Don't try to talk. The dust's too thick."

"Hey, boss!" A man's voice called from the other end of the tunnel. "You ready for us to get the silver?"

Though the heavy man on top of her was most uncomfortable, at least he wasn't able to answer and warn them that rescuers were on the way.

"There's a lot of dust," Annabelle called back. "Best wait a while."

She could hear murmuring, probably the men discussing why she'd answered instead of Slade. And no quick retort came to her to explain. Instead, she felt the weight being moved off her, giving her room to shift toward a dim light.

Two familiar eyes glowed back at her.

Joseph!

Without thinking, she wrapped her arms around him, feeling the warmth of a body she'd believed dead.

"Shh…it's all right. Where's Nugget?"

Of course. Annabelle should have realized that his sister would be a priority in his mind. She shouldn't have… Her face heated. Had she truly put her arms around this man? No matter what she might have vowed otherwise, she'd had no business doing so.

As Annabelle moved out of the way, she heard yells and gunshots coming from the end of the tunnel where Slade's men had been waiting. "The sheriff?" She looked for confirmation from Joseph, who nodded.

"Your pa is waiting on the other side."

He picked up Nugget, then led Annabelle through the cavern, where dust still settled.

"Keep your mouth covered. You don't want to breathe in all the dust." He pressed a handkerchief into her hand, which she gratefully took. It was a sight better than her sleeve.

She followed him out into the sunlight. A setting sun, but sun nonetheless.

"Father!" She ran into his arms, and he hugged her tight to him, tighter than she could ever remember being held.

When he finally pulled away, he picked at her hair. "Why, Annabelle, I do believe you've got silver dust in your hair."

He ran his fingers along the strands, then held his hands up to look. "Joseph! Wes! Look here! There really is silver in that mountain!"

The men gathered round, exclaiming over the silver in Annabelle's hair, and as they examined her further, even among the folds of her dress. Nugget merely lifted her head from her brother's shoulder and gave a shrug as if to say, "I told you so."

On the way back to the camp, she shared what she'd discovered with her father, whose face grew more ashen as he realized the depths of the perfidy of a man he'd loved like his own son.

But they passed camp, taking the trail instead toward town.

"Aren't we stopping at the mining camp?"

Her father shook his head. "There's men to be put in jail. Plus, you could use a bath and to sleep in your own bed."

Annabelle closed her eyes for a brief moment. A bath and her own bed sounded just about perfect. Only… "What about Gertie? I'm sure she must be worried sick."

Even when Annabelle chose to shut the other woman out, Gertie had loved her. It was time Annabelle let her.

He pulled his horse to a stop in front of her. "We sent a rider to let them know what happened. Getting you safely home is the priority now."

"Do you think we could go up and see her soon? I know she won't be satisfied until she hugs me herself."

The look on her father's face was the final piece of healing she needed. "I'm sure she'd like that."

But then the wrinkles on her father's forehead deepened more than she'd ever seen. "I'm sorry, Annabelle. I was blind to a lot of things, like your pain. You were hurting, and instead of talking to you, I assumed I knew what was best. I forced you to help in a ministry that you didn't believe in."

Annabelle swallowed, wishing she could say something to ease the pain in her father's voice. "It's a good ministry, Father."

"But it's not your ministry. Can you forgive me for being so blind? I feel it's my fault for placing you in danger by forcing you—"

"No." Annabelle wished they weren't both on horseback so she could reach for him and offer him some comfort. "If I hadn't been here, Slade would have taken Nugget, and there would have been no one to protect her. But I was here. And it all worked out, all of our mistakes, for the saving of lives."

Her father brushed his hand across his eyes. "You are something else, Annabelle. Your mother would be so proud. Just as I am."

She'd never imagined her father would ever say such a thing of her. In that moment, all of the pain she'd endured through this ordeal was completely worth it.

Joseph slowed his horse alongside them. "Is anything wrong?"

"No," her father said. "I was just telling Annabelle how proud I was of her. And, if she still wishes, I'll be putting her on the next train East to visit her aunt Celeste."

Annabelle's heart leaped. Finally! After all this time. But Nugget's tiny gasp made her stop. How could she leave Nugget?

Her father had been right. Having been forced to confront the pain and push past it, her heart didn't hurt so much anymore. The people she loved were safe, and she wanted to cling to them rather than push them away.

"Father, I…"

Her throat seemed to swell, and it wasn't from all the dust she'd breathed in. Everything she'd ever dreamed of was being offered to her with no price, and yet, it felt wrong somehow.

"I shouldn't have been so selfish in keeping you here."

Her father's voice was gruff, but she wasn't looking at him. Rather, she couldn't keep her eyes off the lone tear trickling down Nugget's cheek.

Her place was with Nugget. But how could she insist? Joseph had said nary a word to her since her rescue, and he'd already made it clear that his future was about taking care of his family, and…

There was no room for Annabelle in Joseph's life. Though she was ready to accept his love, he had none to give.

"Thank you, Father," she said quietly, no longer feeling joy in her newfound victory.

Then she looked over at Nugget. "Remember what I said. We'll write. And if Joseph is agreeable, then I can visit, or you can visit me. It'll be all right. You'll see."

But her stomach churned. None of it felt right. Joseph would have what he wanted. His silver, his family, and Nugget. And though Annabelle was also finally getting what she wanted, she didn't want to leave anymore. But she had no right. Not to Joseph, and not to Nugget, as much as she'd grown to love them both.

It should be enough for her that Joseph finally had the means to provide for his family. Annabelle's prayers had been answered.

Chapter Twenty-Two

They rode to the Lassiters' house, where everyone was promptly dispatched to take baths and get into clean clothes.

After Joseph had a bath and his soiled clothing was taken to see if any silver dust could be found in its folds, he wandered to the back porch, where he sat while everyone else made merry in the house, with an emptiness he couldn't quite describe.

Everything should be perfect. Slade's men were in jail, and now that Slade had finally come to, he would soon be joining them.

Nugget was safe. Joseph had the silver he needed to provide for his family. In fact, he'd spent a good deal of the time on the ride home talking with Collin MacDonald, who'd given him solid information on the next steps to opening his mine and making it profitable. From what Collin said, if the vein opened by the explosion was as deep as it appeared, they could be looking at one of the largest fortunes to be gained in Leadville history.

They'd been back at the house for less than an hour when all the local mining barons or their representatives began coming to call. Everyone was willing to buy him out at a handsome price. Haunted by Slade's words about all the people wanting to take advantage of others, and seeing firsthand what greed would do to people, Joseph decided that he couldn't risk anyone else being taken advantage of. He'd see his father's mining dream through.

With recommendations from Frank and Collin, Joseph had already begun to put a team in place to open his father's mines. Collin's sons had remained behind to guard the newly opened silver vein until he could put together a security team.

In his wildest imaginations, he'd never thought his father's dream could so richly come true.

Joseph wanted to throw back his head and laugh at the irony of how everything had worked out. His only regret was that his father hadn't lived long enough to see it. Yes, regret. While he didn't approve of all his father's choices, he'd come to realize that his father lived a complicated life. Even his father's bad choice of taking a mistress had a bright side. Joseph couldn't imagine life without his precious sister.

It was, as Annabelle said, all for the benefit of saving many lives.

Joseph was going to miss her and their partnership. He knew if he asked, she'd stay.

But even now, with the promise of real wealth in their future, he couldn't ask her to give up her dreams.

As if to confirm his belief, he heard Maddie in the kitchen. "We'll have to go shopping to buy you new dresses for the trip. I'm sure Celeste will want to have new ones made when you get there, but we don't want you going in rags."

"That sounds lovely."

Without being able to see Annabelle's face, he

couldn't read her attitude, but the clatter of something falling to the floor was unmistakable. Annabelle didn't want to go.

"Oh, you! You go on and sit on the porch or something. You're too excited to be of any use to me."

Annabelle murmured a reply, then the door opened and closed behind her as she joined him on the porch.

"Exciting times, eh?" Joseph smiled at her as she sat beside him.

"Your family will be so happy."

Annabelle gave him the kind of fake smile that made him want to dig deeper. But he'd given up that right. Maybe someday, when she'd had her taste of the world, she'd come back to Leadville, and maybe they'd both be free to pursue the what-if questions they'd been unable to face.

"They will. I've already begun the arrangements to bring them here. My sister Mary will be able to take care of Nugget."

Joseph wasn't leaving. "You're staying?"

"I've just said that."

The dark hid whatever expression might have flashed across Annabelle's face. But he knew it wouldn't make her happy to be so easily dismissed. What else was he supposed to do? If she thought she was needed, Annabelle would stay.

And he couldn't have her sacrifice her dreams again.

"What about until then?" Annabelle's voice drifted to him, almost too soft to hear.

"Collin said Polly was undone at the knowledge of Tom's involvement in everything. It will do her good to get out of the camp for a while. She'll be down in the morning to help with Nugget."

Annabelle tried to push away the pang in her heart

at the mention of Polly's situation. Her friend had been through so much, and then to find out that the man she thought was going to marry her was so… Annabelle sighed. People were never what they seemed.

She stole a glance at Joseph. He'd barely spoken to her since her rescue, and even now, things were so different from how they used to be.

Everything had worked out perfectly. Joseph was staying in Leadville. Annabelle was leaving on her dream trip.

So why did she want to cry?

The stair beside her creaked. "Nugget wanted to say good-night to Annabelle before Frank takes you to the hotel."

"The hotel?" Annabelle looked up at Maddie and spied a miserable-looking Nugget on her shoulder, then brought her gaze back to Joseph. "Why would you and Nugget stay at a hotel, when there's plenty of room here?"

"I don't need to impose any longer." His voice was quiet. Firm.

"But I thought—"

"It's for the best. We've got arrangements to make, and I don't want to be in the way." His tone was nothing like that of the Joseph she'd come to care for over the past few days. In just the space of a few hours, he'd turned into a man she hardly recognized.

One of the things she hated about silver was how it changed people. It turned decent men like Slade into greedy monsters. Hardworking men like Gertie's husband into gamblers and drunkards. And friends into people too good to share your roof anymore.

"Come give me a hug, then, Nugget." Annabelle tried to keep her voice steady, so that the little girl at least wouldn't know how desperately her heart was breaking right now.

Nugget slipped out of Maddie's arms and into Annabelle's embrace. "I want to stay with you."

She did, too. But when she glanced up at Joseph, he gave her a stern look and a shake of his head that told her she dared not agree with the child she dearly loved.

"Joseph will take good care of you." Annabelle held the little girl tight against her, breathing in the sweet scent she'd forgotten how much she loved. The air was so still, she could hear Nugget's heartbeat, mixed with the choked breaths of a little girl trying not to cry.

"It's going to be okay," Annabelle said, trying to be as cheerful as she could with her heart breaking.

Joseph wasn't just hurting her with his decision to pull away, but the little girl he'd so fiercely claimed to be protecting.

Maddie cleared her throat. "I need to see if a few of these other things fit Nugget before you go. The child's got to have at least a change of clothes, though I'm sure you'll be wanting to buy her new ones."

Joseph gave a small jerk of his head, and Nugget followed Maddie in, leaving Annabelle alone with him again.

"You're sure you can't stay here? Nugget and I—"

"She's already too attached. And with you leaving, I don't want to make it worse."

His jaw was hard, unflinching. And if it wasn't for the tiny spot of tenderness in his dark eyes, she'd think she wasn't even looking at Joseph.

"I promised her we'd stay in touch."

He shook his head. "You'll forget all about her once you get settled with your aunt. I hear she's already planning a fancy party in your honor."

"I would never forget. She's worried that when she meets the rest of your family, she'll face the same rejection she's met from others because of her birth. I could help ease some of that."

Joseph looked like she'd stuck a knife into his gut. "They're good people. They'll accept her. She needs to learn to rely on her family." The "not you," wasn't spoken, but Annabelle heard it loud and clear. This wasn't the Joseph challenging Annabelle tone she'd gotten used to. This was something darker, like that of a changed man.

She'd never expected that finding silver would change Joseph. But surely there was hope.

"I could stay," Annabelle offered. "I needn't leave right away. I can help get Nugget settled with your family, and—"

"No."

His easy dismissal and refusal to even hear her out stung worse than anything Slade had ever done to her.

"But if she's eased into the situation, and has people she knows around her, it won't be so bad when I—"

"You've done enough."

Who was this man, and where was Joseph? "Can we just talk about this? I mean, we—"

"There is no we, Annabelle. I've always made it clear that my family has to come first. Go visit your aunt. Live your life."

Before she could try to argue further, the door opened again, and Maddie ushered Nugget out with a bundle of clothes. "You come back and visit me anytime, you hear?"

Nugget nodded solemnly but made no move toward Joseph.

"Come on, Nugget, it's time to go." He held out his hand, and in the time it took for the sob welling inside Annabelle to finally find its way out, they were gone.

Chapter Twenty-Three

Annabelle hadn't seen Joseph in the days leading up to her departure. She'd even dallied over her shopping in hopes that she'd spot him or Nugget in one of the stores. But she hadn't been so fortunate. When she boarded the train to Denver, she did so with every ounce of her body wanting to throw herself to the ground, kicking, screaming and protesting that she didn't want to go.

But of course, she wouldn't. Not when she'd fought so long and hard to make this trip. Not when she'd finally earned her father's respect and belief in her dreams.

Not when Joseph was so cold.

Her father had somehow managed to procure her a seat in front of a family traveling with a little girl who might have been about Nugget's age. Though she was sure it wasn't intentional, there was something almost cruel about it. Especially when her chosen traveling companions were Lucy Simms and her mother. Mrs. Simms, apparently, had a fondness for children.

The little girl kept twisting in her seat and looking at Mrs. Simms wistfully. Which, of course, Mrs. Simms encouraged with her questions for the child.

Eight hours of this just might kill her.

It wasn't just the loss of Nugget she'd felt so keenly, but that of Joseph. Every time she thought of Nugget, she couldn't help but think of Joseph. And while she'd strengthened her relationship with her father, and their conversations were no longer as stilted, he didn't talk to her the way Joseph did. He didn't see her the way Joseph did.

How had finding his father's silver blinded him so?

Since rescuing her and Nugget from the mine, Joseph had barely talked to her.

So why did the thought of leaving him break her heart?

"I don't know what I'm going to do with the lot of you." His sister Mary smacked Joseph on the back of the head with a newspaper as she joined him at breakfast.

The table was full and set for everyone to join them, but so far, at half past the time they were due, Mary was the first to arrive.

"What's that supposed to mean?" He stared into his coffee already knowing her answer. He'd made a mess of things, thinking that this transition for his family would be easy.

Mary reached past him for one of the hotel's fine biscuits. "The girls are still pretending that the little one doesn't exist, and Daniel eggs them on. Then there's the two of you. The little girl, who won't say a word, and you, who's got the personality of a wet rag in a rainstorm."

He looked up at her. "A wet rag in a rainstorm? That's the best you can do?"

"You know what I mean." Mary took a sip of her tea and stared at him. "It's like the life has been completely sucked out of you. Sometimes I think we were better off—"

"Don't say it." Joseph glared at her. "After everything we've all been through, everything I've done to get us all together."

He'd failed, that's what. The air in the dining room had suddenly grown a lot warmer. Possibly from Mary breathing down his neck. As he adjusted his collar, a bundle of energy and tears ran into his arms.

"I hate them. Papa said they'd love me, but they're horrible and mean, and I want Annabelle."

The only person Nugget would speak to was him. And mostly it was to ask if she could see Annabelle, or if Annabelle had written. Her train wasn't scheduled to leave for another hour yet, and already his baby sister wanted her to write.

He looked up at Mary, a silent plea for help.

"Nanette, you need to sit in your own seat."

Nugget looked up and glared at her older sister. "It's Nugget."

"Nanette is a good name, and it's listed in the family Bible as your given name, so you'll learn to answer to it."

Joseph rubbed the bridge of his nose. Ever since Mary found that entry in their pa's Bible, she'd insisted on calling Nugget Nanette, which had only made things worse. Annabelle would have found a way to smooth things over.

But he couldn't impose on her, not when it meant delaying her own dreams. No, he'd find a way to do it without her. After all he'd put her through, nearly getting her killed in the process, he owed her the freedom of her own life.

"Annabelle thought Nugget was a fine name," Nugget said, sticking her finger in the jam.

Mary turned her attention back to Joseph. "I would have at least liked to have met Annabelle. I can't imagine why she couldn't have had the decency to respond to my invitation to supper. She could have given me some idea as to how to manage Nanette. Instead, I've got to deal with her and five mutinous siblings who are all furious that you'd do this to them."

Joseph finally looked at his sister. "I didn't deliver the invitation."

"I beg your pardon?" The glare he got was no worse than he deserved. But he couldn't have borne it any other way.

"I didn't deliver it. She was busy with preparations for her trip."

"And she couldn't have delayed it by a few weeks, or even a few days?"

Mary's tone was enough to set the fire back in him. "It wasn't her choice. It was mine. I made her go."

Every morning, he questioned that decision. Wondered if he'd just taken her up on her offer of helping ease the transition with Nugget, if maybe his entire family wouldn't be ready to kill him right about now. If maybe they could write, and she'd…she'd what? Be willing to give up everything she'd dreamed of to raise his siblings? No. He couldn't do that to Annabelle.

Joseph reached for the pot to pour himself another cup of coffee, but Mary took it from him. "Now why would you do a stupid thing like that? It's as plain as anyone can see that you're in love with her. Mooning about, but dodging anytime you catch a glimpse of her so she doesn't notice you."

"I'm not the man for her," he said quietly. "She's wanted this trip for a long time, and I'm not going to stand in her way."

Mary shook her head, her face filled with disgust. "You didn't even tell her how you felt, did you?"

"There's no point." He refused to meet her eyes. "I know how she feels about mining. Annabelle doesn't want this life, and even if I were to convince her to stay for a while, she'd resent not getting to live her dreams."

"Is this because you asked her, or because you assumed and made the decision for her?"

He hadn't asked Annabelle. In fact, he'd pretty much pushed her out and forced her to go on that trip even when she'd tried to offer to delay it for him.

"You don't understand." He addressed Mary while hugging Nugget to him and smoothing her hair. "My responsibility lies with all of you. And Annabelle—"

"Could help you with that responsibility if you'd give her the chance. Why are all men so pigheaded as to think that they need to make the decisions for us?"

Joseph had never known Mary to be a bitter woman. But the anger spewed at him wasn't just about his treatment of Annabelle, but of something else.

"What's really going on? How is this situation with Annabelle suddenly about all men?"

Mary dabbed her lips with her napkin, then tossed it on the table. "Because it is. And because from everything I've seen and heard, you've found yourself a good woman to love and rather than going after it, you're hiding behind the excuse of providing for a family that's got everything it needs. You are just like Pa."

Her barb hit him firmly in the part of his heart that was still struggling to forgive a man who didn't deserve it. The table shook as Mary pushed back in her seat and stood. Even Nugget raised her head from his shoulder and looked up at her.

"Worst of all, you're hurting an innocent little girl because of your pride. Maybe Aunt Ina did take the switch to the younger ones more often than I'd like. But at least she never broke anyone's heart with her cruelty."

Mary stormed out of the restaurant, leaving Joseph alone with a teary-eyed little girl and a table full of food with no one to eat it.

No one had ever accused Joseph of being cruel before. Nor had anyone compared him to their pa. He'd only thought to spare Annabelle the trouble of being forced to decide between the duty of caring for a child who needed her and the dream she'd been putting aside for too long. But had he asked his pa about his reasons for his actions, would he have said something different than what Joseph had assumed?

Had his pa tried to get their ma to move the family west? Had he fought his feelings for Nugget's ma? Wes painted his pa as an honorable man who rubbed people the wrong way for not taking the side they wanted him to.

Joseph had done a lot of judging, and misjudging, as he'd been quick to accuse Annabelle of. But this last judgment was one he needed to let go of. Joseph needed to forgive his pa, and in forgiving, needed to let go of his own expectations of people and let them make their own decisions.

He looked down at Nugget, a child too young to understand the pain of his thoughts. "You never even got to say goodbye, did you?"

Nugget shook her head, messy half-curled hair that spoke of the others' neglect bouncing in every direction. Mary was trying, he'd give her that, but he could see the strain in her eyes when she looked at Nugget or had to do anything for their sister's care.

"Are they terribly mean to you?"

In front of Joseph, they put on a good front, but he'd seen past it. He'd just been helpless to do anything about it. With getting everything ready for their arrival, and trying to procure a house for the family, and putting things in order with the mine...

Nugget's slow nod tore at him.

Those things should have been secondary. And in his pride, he'd ignored the fact that Annabelle would have been able to help him. He hadn't even given her the consideration to discuss it.

"I'm sorry, Nugget." He pressed the little girl to his chest. "How about we try to catch that train to say goodbye?"

Nugget jumped off his lap and ran for the door.

Harrison Avenue was overly congested, already filled with wagons and people and more activity than he'd imagined normal for a day like today.

The train whistle blew when they were two blocks from the station.

Surely Annabelle was onboard by now.

Nugget's pace slowed. "It's too late."

"Sometimes they get delayed. We'll still try."

His spirits sagged when they arrived at the platform just as the train was pulling out.

He calculated how much money he had on him. Based on getting his own family here, Annabelle would most likely have to spend a day or two in Denver to catch whichever train would take her east. So if he bought a ticket for the next train, they could get to Denver and then...

Surely they'd have a few hours to talk.

Nugget let go of his hand.

"Sweetheart, I'm sorry." He turned so he could bend down and talk to her, but she was gone.

"Nugget?" Joseph spun, looking around the station for the little girl. Though the train had departed, people still milled about, catching up on their business, and carting luggage to and fro.

"Nugget!"

He walked in the direction of the departing train. Had she run after it? Joseph picked up his pace, scouring the area for any sign of her. A porter laden with baggage bumped into him, blocking his path.

"Watch it!" the guy yelled as Joseph darted around him.

And then he stopped short.

There was Annabelle, kneeling in front of Nugget, her back to him. He took a deep breath, trying to compose himself as he approached.

"I cannot imagine what has gotten into your hair. You must've been tossing and turning all night to undo your curls and have only half your head fixed."

Annabelle put her hand in Nugget's hair, mussing it slightly before declaring, "Well, there's nothing that can be done, I suppose. We'll braid it, and you'll still be cute as a button. What do you think of that?"

Nugget didn't say anything, but looked up at him, causing Annabelle to turn her head slightly until she noticed him. "Oh!"

Annabelle stood, then took Nugget's hand before facing him. "It seems like you've let her run absolutely wild since I've seen you last."

Her words rushed past him. "What are you... You're supposed to be..."

She looked at him long and hard. "I never could tolerate a bully. And frankly, your behavior toward me in regards to my leaving is nothing short of being bullied. Nugget needs me, and I'm not going to shirk my responsibility toward her just because you act like a bear about it."

Joseph closed his eyes. So that was it. More of Annabelle doing her duty. The worst of it was, he almost wanted to let her. But he couldn't. Didn't she understand that as much as everyone wanted to make him the bad guy, this was killing him?

"She's not your responsibility." He opened his eyes and looked at her. "You need to live your life, Annabelle. Follow your dreams."

"Of course she's my responsibility. I love Nugget, and I…" Annabelle looked away for a moment, then back at him. "Well, you don't leave the ones you love. Not when they need you and you need them."

The lump in his throat made it hard for Joseph to swallow, let alone speak. Annabelle had already done this for her father. And now for Nugget? It was too much.

But what was he supposed to do, to say? The selfish side of him wanted to keep her here, to be close to him, to help Nugget, to help Mary figure out how to keep peace, to…to do dozens of things, all of which had everything to do with him and his needs and none to do with hers.

"Please, Annabelle," he finally said. "I'll buy you a ticket for the next train. This is what you've always wanted, and I—"

"You have no idea what I've always wanted." She stamped her foot in such an insolent way that he wanted to kiss her. But that was beside the point.

"Yes, I admit that when we first met, I wanted nothing more than to leave this place and stay with my aunt, and discover the world outside. But I've grown since then. I've changed. And I can't believe that you'd think that the woman standing before you is still that silly girl who thought of nothing more than wearing the latest fashions."

Her words shamed him. Mostly because he'd tried so hard not to fall in love with that silly girl, but as he watched her grow into the woman standing before him, he'd realized that there was nothing about her, including her silliness, that he didn't love. He hadn't given her the courtesy of an explanation, and now it was time to make good on changing his earlier regrets.

"All right, Annabelle." Joseph took a deep breath. "What do you want?"

The triumphant grin she gave him nearly slayed him. Did she have any idea what that grin did to a man? Of course she did.

Joseph shook his head, trying to rid himself of all inappropriate thoughts, especially the urge to kiss her senseless.

"I want to stay here and see to it that Nugget is properly settled in with the rest of her family. I want to go back to the camp and spend more time with Gertie, and maybe get Polly to start talking to me again. I want you to talk to me like you used to, and for us to be friends again."

Friends. Joseph wanted to kiss Annabelle senseless, and she wanted to talk about their friendship.

"I'm sorry, Annabelle. That's not possible. I can't be friends with you."

"Oh." Her face fell, and those pretty little dimples that punctuated every point she made disappeared. "I don't know what I did to offend you, but maybe I could—"

"You misunderstand."

He hated the thought of baring his heart like this, of putting himself out for Miss Annabelle Lassiter to reject, but he also couldn't bear the thought of her feeling guilty over ruining yet another relationship.

"I can't settle for friendship with you. Not anymore. I see you differently. Not as a friend, not as a sister, but in such a way that is entirely inappropriate for…"

Were her cheeks turning pink? And, in the difficulty of him explaining a rather embarrassing and untenable position, a saucy grin twitched at the edges of her lips.

Annabelle was actually enjoying this.

Worse, when he looked over at Nugget, the little imp had started giggling.

But perhaps worst of all, others had stopped what they were doing and were completely, without any shame, eavesdropping on the conversation.

Joseph straightened. "Well…I think that about covers it." He held out his hand. "Nugget, come on. We need to…"

Escape was the first thought that came to mind. But Nugget stood there, shaking her head.

"You are never going to get her to marry you like that. You have to get romantical and tell Annabelle that you love her, then take her in your arms, and—"

"Nugget!" Both he and Annabelle said it in unison.

And when Annabelle knelt to the little girl, her face still red, Joseph understood.

"I told you why I sent you away," he said quietly. "You thought it was because my regard had changed. The truth of the matter is that I wanted you to stay, desperately. Not for Nugget's sake, though that's a bonus, but for mine."

Annabelle finally looked up at him, murmured softly to Nugget, then stood.

"I thought that the noble thing to do when you love someone is to give up what you want for what they want," Joseph continued. "But I didn't find out what you wanted, only made assumptions based on what you'd told me. I love you, Annabelle. And I wanted your dreams for you more than I wanted mine. I'm sorry that it caused you pain."

"Of course it caused me pain. Because I love you, too, and I didn't know that you loved me back. So it's all forgiven. I'm here now, and here is where I will stay."

They stood there in silence for a brief moment, interrupted by a tiny voice that asked, "Are you going to kiss her now?"

So he did.

Epilogue

One year later

Annabelle stood on the porch, watching for the children to arrive home. At half past three, they should have been there nearly a quarter of an hour ago. She smoothed the apron over her rounded belly and debated about taking it off. There was still so much baking to be done for tonight's church supper. Maddie was having a tougher time keeping up with the miners' needs, so Annabelle had agreed to do some of the cooking at her home.

The men were due at any time to help carry everything to the church. Now that Annabelle's condition was more advanced, both Joseph and her father said she shouldn't be lifting heavy things. Which meant relying on others helping her for a change. But as she glanced back down the street, worries about whether or not the children had met with foul play took over.

There were, Annabelle told herself, five of them. Surely together, they were safe enough walking home from school. At least that's what Joseph always argued. Evelyn, Helen, Daniel, Bess and Nugget could take care of themselves. A handful, but most of the time, Mary and Rose were such a big help that Annabelle hardly noticed.

However, on days like today, when Annabelle scurried down the street toward the school, she wondered how she thought she could manage all these children, help with her father's ministry and care for a baby besides. But if something happened to the children—

Annabelle's heart constricted, and she turned the corner. Nugget came running toward her, screeching, "Mama!"

She embraced the little girl, and continued in the direction from which Nugget had come.

Daniel was engaged in a fistfight with another boy, and the girls were egging him on as other children circled the fighting boys, cheering.

"Daniel Edward Stone!" Annabelle pushed through the crowd. "I insist you stop this minute!"

"Not until he apologizes for what he said about my sister!"

Before he could get another punch in, her father and Joseph arrived and pulled the two boys apart.

Nugget huddled at Annabelle's side. "Mama, please don't be mad at Daniel."

The little girl had taken to calling her Mama shortly before her wedding to Joseph. Even though certain people, like the unfortunate boy whom her father was sternly lecturing, didn't seem to want to forget where Nugget came from, most of the time, no one remembered Nugget wasn't her daughter. And, as Annabelle tightened her arm around the little girl, she wasn't sure she could remember a time when Nugget wasn't hers.

"You know fighting is wrong," Joseph told Daniel sternly.

"So's what he said about my sister."

Though Annabelle knew she needed to remain quiet and let Joseph do the parenting, part of her wanted to cheer for the fact that the boy who once refused to even look at Nugget, let alone call her sister, was now fighting for the little girl's honor.

"The other boy started it," chorused Evelyn, Helen and Bess.

Annabelle looked down at Nugget. "That so?"

Nugget shrugged. Apparently, she wasn't going to risk her newfound solidarity with her siblings.

Joseph escorted Daniel to where they were waiting, and Annabelle noticed her father walking the other boy down the street. Probably to talk to his parents.

The other three girls trudged behind, their heads low, as though they thought the other boy had Daniel's beating coming. Annabelle sighed. Raising Joseph's siblings was not for the faint of heart. But watching them heal from the pain of their rough past and come to love one another was worth it.

Joseph came along Annabelle's other side and slipped his hand in hers. "Never a dull moment, is it?"

"Of course not." Until she'd found herself with a houseful again, she hadn't realized just how much she'd missed having the warm bodies, the laughter and even the fights to add color to her life. Some days, she still missed her siblings, especially Susannah, and most days, she desperately missed her mother. For only a mother could advise her on how to handle this rambunctious crew.

A carriage was parked in front of their house.

"Caitlin!" Nugget pulled away from Annabelle's hand and dashed in the direction of the carriage, her siblings following suit.

Annabelle looked over at Joseph. "I didn't know

Gertie was coming down today. I thought they were waiting until Saturday."

"I thought you'd like having her sooner." A knowing look filled his face. "You've been overly tired lately, and she told me to send for her if you needed help."

No, Annabelle didn't have a mother to advise her on such things. But she had Gertie, who loved her like one. Even though Gertie would never replace her mother, and there were times when having Gertie around increased the ache of her mother's absence, mostly, Annabelle didn't know what she'd do without the other woman.

"Daniel, what have you done to your eye?" Gertie's exclamation told Annabelle that Gertie probably had plenty of experience dealing with her own sons' fights. Later, the other woman could help her figure out how to handle this latest development.

Annabelle turned to Joseph and kissed him softly. "Thank you. You always seem to know just what I need."

He kissed her back, then grinned. "Or maybe I want to get a little time alone with you myself. Won't be much longer until we've also got a baby to manage, so I figured I'd best take advantage while I still can."

This time, Annabelle didn't stop herself from throwing her arms around him. Well, as best as she could fit, anyway. She was, after all, expecting a baby. And even though some ladies in town said it simply wasn't done when one was in such a delicate condition, she kissed her husband until they were both breathless. Let everyone say what they will. Annabelle Lassiter Stone had opened her heart to love, and now that she'd found it, she wasn't about to let anyone tell her not to show it.

* * * * *

Dear Reader,

I am so excited to be sharing my love of Leadville with you. When my husband's family came to America at the turn of the century, Leadville was where they settled. While we no longer have living relatives in Leadville, we have a family home there we regularly visit, and spending time immersed in Leadville history is something we've always enjoyed.

When I decided to write a historical, I knew it would have to be set in this beloved town. The story itself came when I read an old newspaper from the 1880s that featured an ad for a debate between two pastors on whether or not miners were beyond redemption. It intrigued me to know that in those days, certain classes of people were viewed as too low for salvation. Hence, Pastor Lassiter and his mission was born. It is the perfect place for a man like Joseph to find help, and for a woman like Annabelle, on the verge of losing hope, to find it again.

I hope this story encourages you, and no matter where you are situated in life, you know that there is always hope.

I love connecting with my readers, so please stop by www.danicafavorite.com and say hello.

Blessings to you and yours,
Danica Favorite

Questions for Discussion

1. What was your favorite part of Annabelle and Joseph's story?

2. Joseph struggles with forgiving his father. Have you had to deal with forgiving someone who's already dead? If so, how were you able to deal with it?

3. Annabelle's grief has kept her isolated from her friends and family. How have you coped with grief?

4. How did Nugget bring healing to both Joseph and Annabelle?

5. Do you think it was reasonable of Annabelle's father to keep her in Leadville to deal with her grief before sending her out into the world?

6. Joseph struggled with being able to listen to Nugget's stories of their father, yet knowing their father's misdeeds. Was he right in allowing Nugget to maintain those happy memories?

7. Annabelle struggles with being a preacher's daughter who doesn't believe God hears her prayers. Should being a preacher's daughter have an impact on her faith? Have you ever struggled with believing God hears your prayers? How did you handle it?

8. Joseph is afraid to court Annabelle because of his responsibility in raising his younger siblings. Is it

Joseph's responsibility to put caring for them above his own desires?

9. Annabelle doesn't want to get close to Joseph because she's afraid of the pain she'll feel when he leaves. Have you ever held someone at arm's length because you thought they were leaving? How did that work out for you?

10. The Johansons, like many of the people who came to Leadville, are finding out that their dreams of becoming wealthy aren't as easy as it sounded. What dreams have you had that have been more work than anticipated? Have you been able to still pursue those dreams?

11. How do you think Slade was able to fool the Lassiters for so long? Have you been betrayed by a dear friend? Looking back, were there signs you missed? How did you get over that betrayal?

12. Why do you think Joseph's father entrusted Nugget with the mine's secrets?

REQUEST YOUR FREE BOOKS!

2 FREE INSPIRATIONAL NOVELS
PLUS 2
FREE
MYSTERY GIFTS

Love Inspired
HISTORICAL
INSPIRATIONAL HISTORICAL ROMANCE

YES! Please send me 2 FREE Love Inspired® Historical novels and my 2 FREE mystery gifts (gifts are worth about $10). After receiving them, if I don't wish to receive any more books, I can return the shipping statement marked "cancel." If I don't cancel, I will receive 4 brand-new novels every month and be billed just $4.74 per book in the U.S. or $5.24 per book in Canada. That's a saving of at least 21% off the cover price. It's quite a bargain! Shipping and handling is just 50¢ per book in the U.S. and 75¢ per book in Canada.* I understand that accepting the 2 free books and gifts places me under no obligation to buy anything. I can always return a shipment and cancel at any time. Even if I never buy another book, the two free books and gifts are mine to keep forever.

102/302 IDN F5CN

Name	(PLEASE PRINT)

Address		Apt. #

City	State/Prov.	Zip/Postal Code

Signature (if under 18, a parent or guardian must sign)

Mail to the Harlequin® Reader Service:
IN U.S.A.: P.O. Box 1867, Buffalo, NY 14240-1867
IN CANADA: P.O. Box 609, Fort Erie, Ontario L2A 5X3

Want to try two free books from another series?
Call 1-800-873-8635 or visit www.ReaderService.com.

* Terms and prices subject to change without notice. Prices do not include applicable taxes. Sales tax applicable in N.Y. Canadian residents will be charged applicable taxes. Offer not valid in Quebec. This offer is limited to one order per household. Not valid for current subscribers to Love Inspired Historical books. All orders subject to credit approval. Credit or debit balances in a customer's account(s) may be offset by any other outstanding balance owed by or to the customer. Please allow 4 to 6 weeks for delivery. Offer available while quantities last.

Your Privacy—The Harlequin® Reader Service is committed to protecting your privacy. Our Privacy Policy is available online at www.ReaderService.com or upon request from the Harlequin Reader Service.

We make a portion of our mailing list available to reputable third parties that offer products we believe may interest you. If you prefer that we not exchange your name with third parties, or if you wish to clarify or modify your communication preferences, please visit us at www.ReaderService.com/consumerchoice or write to us at Harlequin Reader Service Preference Service, P.O. Box 9062, Buffalo, NY 14269. Include your complete name and address.

LIH13R

SPECIAL EXCERPT FROM

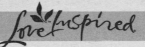

Don't miss the conclusion of the
BIG SKY CENTENNIAL *miniseries!*
Here's a sneak peek at HER MONTANA CHRISTMAS
by Arlene James:

"Robin," Ethan said, just before his face appeared in the church belfry's open trapdoor, "come on up. It's perfectly safe."

He reached down a gloved hand as she put a foot on the bottom rung of the wrought-iron ladder.

"How does this thing work?"

"It's very simple. There's a tall pole with a hook on one end. I used it to slide open the trap and then pull down the ladder. When I'm done, I'll use it to push the ladder back up and lift it over the locking mechanism, then slide the trap closed."

"I see."

"Oh, you haven't seen anything yet," he told her, grasping her hand and all but lifting her up the last few rungs to stand next to him on a narrow metal platform. In their bulky coats, they had to stand pressed shoulder to shoulder. "Take a look at this." He swung his arm wide, encompassing the town, the valley beyond and the snow-capped mountains surrounding it all.

"Wow."

"Exactly," he said. "There's a part of Psalms 98 that says, 'Let the rivers clap their hands, let the mountains sing together for joy...' Seeing the view like this, you can

LIEXP1114

almost feel it, can't you? The rivers and mountains praising their Creator."

"I never thought of rivers and mountains praising God," she admitted.

"Scripture speaks many times of nature praising God and testifying to His wonders."

"I can see why," she said reverently.

"So can I," he told her, smiling down at her with those warm brown eyes.

Her breath caught in her throat. But surely she was reading too much into that look. That wasn't appreciation she saw in his gaze. That was just her loneliness seeking connection. Wasn't it? Though she had never felt this sudden, electrical link before, as if something vital and masculine in him reached out and touched something fundamental and feminine in her. She had to be mistaken.

He was a man of God, after all.

Even if she couldn't help thinking of him as just a man.

*Will Robin and Ethan find love for Christmas,
or will her secrets stand in their way?
Find out in HER MONTANA CHRISTMAS
by Arlene James, available December 2014 wherever
Love Inspired® books and ebooks are sold.*

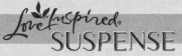
"Just tell me what happened to my daughter."

"We don't know. You were alone when we found you."

"I need to go home." Scout jumped up, head spinning,
the room spinning. The knot in her stomach growing until
it was all she could feel. "Maybe she's there."

She knew it was unreasonable, knew it couldn't be
true, but she had to look, had to be sure.

"The police have already been to your house," Boone
said gently. "She's not there."

"She could be hiding. She doesn't like strangers." Her
voice trembled. Her body trembled, every fear she'd ever
had, every nightmare, suddenly real and happening and
completely outside her control.

"Scout." He touched her shoulder, his fingers warm
through thin cotton. She didn't want warmth, though. She
wanted her child.

"Please," she begged. "I have to go home. I have to see
for myself. I have to."

He eyed her for a moment, silent. Solemn. Something
in his eyes that looked like the grief she was feeling, the
horror she was living.

Finally, Boone nodded. "Okay. I'll take you."

Just like that. Simple and easy, as if the request didn't

go against logic. As if she weren't hooked to an IV, shaking from fear and sorrow and pain.

He grabbed a blanket from the foot of the bed and wrapped it around her shoulders then took out his phone and texted someone. She didn't ask who. She was too busy trying to keep the darkness from taking her again. Too busy trying to remember the last moment she'd seen Lucy. Had she been scared? Crying?

Three days.

That was what he had said.

Three days that Lucy had been missing and Scout had been lying in a hospital bed.

Please, God, let her be okay.

She was all Scout had. The only thing that really mattered to her. She had to be okay.

A tear slipped down her cheek. She didn't have the energy to wipe it away. Didn't have the strength to even open her eyes when Boone touched her cheek.

"It's going to be okay," he said quietly, and she wanted to believe him almost as much as she wanted to open her eyes and see her daughter.

"How can it be?"

"Because you ran into the right person the night your daughter was taken," he responded, and he sounded so confident, so certain of the outcome, she looked into his face, his eyes. Saw those things she'd seen before, but something else, too—faith, passion, belief.

Will Boone help Scout find her missing
daughter in time for Christmas?
Pick up HER CHRISTMAS GUARDIAN to find out!
Available December 2014
wherever Love Inspired® books and ebooks are sold.

Big Sky Daddy
by
LINDA FORD

FOR HIS SON'S SAKE

Caleb Craig will do anything for his son, even ask his boss's enemy for help. Not only does Lilly Bell tend to his son's injured puppy, but she offers to rehabilitate little Teddy's leg. Caleb knows that getting Teddy to walk again is all that really matters, yet he wonders if maybe Lilly can heal his brooding heart, as well.

Precocious little Teddy—and his devoted father—steal Lilly's heart and make her long for a child and husband of her own. But Lilly learned long ago that trusting a man means risking heartbreak. Happiness lies within reach—if she seizes the chance for love and motherhood she never expected…

Montana Marriages

Three sisters discover a legacy of love beneath the Western sky

*Available December 2014
wherever Love Inspired books
and ebooks are sold.*

Find us on Facebook at
www.Facebook.com/LoveInspiredBooks

LIH28290

Love Inspired

An Amish Christmas Journey
by
Patricia Davids

Their Holiday Adventure

Toby Yoder promised to care for his orphaned little sister the rest of her life. After all, the tragedy that took their parents and left her injured was his fault. Now he must make a three-hundred-mile trip from the hospital to the Amish community where they'll settle down. But as they share a hired van with pretty Greta Barkman, an Amish woman with a similar harrowing past, Toby can't bear for the trip to end. Suddenly, there's joy, a rescued cat named Christmas and hope for their journey to continue together forever.

BRIDES OF
Amish Country

Finding true love in the land of the Plain People

Available December 2014
wherever Love Inspired books
and ebooks are sold.

Find us on Facebook at
www.Facebook.com/LoveInspiredBooks

LI87927